EVERYTHING I DREAMED

EVERYONE ROAD

BOOK 2

EVEY LYON

EVERHOPE ROAD

Everything I Wanted

Everything I Dreamed

Everything I Needed

ABOUT

Ending up in the same bed with my brother's best friend during an unexpected road trip to my brother's wedding was never part of the plan. Yet, when Oliver and I got stuck overnight at a hotel with one bed, temptation got the best of us, and what was meant to be a one-time thing was only the beginning. Because now he's secretly my husband.

For convenience, of course… I think.

You see, I have my eyes set on a business venture, but it's only possible with a husband by my side due to logistics. He swept in to help me, and there wasn't much protest from me. Okay, none. But we want to keep things simple and don't want my brother to lose it or our friends to grab the popcorn and watch our situation unfold. Because Oliver is the guy that I've fantasized about for years, and it turns out the feeling is mutual. Now we're stuck in a marriage that wasn't supposed to be real, and I might just run, because how could I be so lucky that Oliver and I may just be everything I dreamed?

Oliver and Hailey are a brother's-best-friend romance with an epic road trip, one bed, and a secret marriage that is low on angst. It is the second book in the small-town Everhope Road series and can be read as a standalone.

HAILEY

Blood.

There's blood.

The room is spinning, and I'm praying for a hot doctor.

A doctor does stitches, right? Or is it the nurse?

Staring down at my thumb, the nausea returns.

Why in the world did I have to have a ditsy moment today? I should be out enjoying the June sun. Instead, I'm here. In an emergency room. Because of my stupidity.

My cell phone lying next to me vibrates on the exam table's paper sheet, and the name on the phone catches my eye. It's my brother, Liam. With one hand, I jab the green button on the screen and put him on speaker.

"Hailey, what the hell? What's going on? Your voicemail has me freaking out. You sounded like you were about to throw up."

Taking a deep breath, I try to steady myself, my stomach swirling as my feet dangle from the table in a cubicle with a curtain drawn. "That's probably because I'm stuck in the emergency room in a tiny hospital in the middle of nowhere Illinois," I bite out.

"Whoa there, Everhope isn't the middle of nowhere. It has a great riverboat restaurant on the river. Lake Spark isn't far, and Chicago is a solid hour and a half away, which is why I am here to pick up the re-sized rings before I fly out to Colorado for my wedding. I mean, I know I'm your emergency contact when you're teaching, but the school didn't call, and I'm nowhere near you to come running. So, what's going on?"

I sigh while my eyes drop down to my finger where the cotton gauze is soaking through. "That's because my little mishap didn't happen at summer school. I'm waiting for someone to stitch my thumb. But you know how I am with blood."

He hums a sound. "Still doesn't explain what the hell happened."

"I was cutting a bagel." I leave it at that.

"Why? We have Foxy Rox in town, and they have great bagels. Rookie move to try store-bought bagels."

The heat stinging my face returns, and my head is a little light. "Well, desperate times. What can I say? Anyhow, the bread knife went quickly through and cut my thumb. My kitchen looks like a murder scene."

"Aren't bagels a little tough to cut, why so fast?" he wonders. He must be outside, as I hear a crosswalk signal.

Grumbling to myself, my lips quirk out, and I debate how honest to be. "That's because… I didn't realize… it was…" The words trail from my mouth. I'm preparing myself for the next thirty seconds. "A pre-sliced bagel," I squeak out.

The burst of laughter fills my ears, and I curse to myself for my stupidity.

I wait a solid thirty seconds as predicted for his chuckle to fade. "Okay, I'm never letting this go," he promises, as I suspected.

My jaw tightens. "Stop it. I'm not so happy that you are amused by my suffering. Right now, I need someone to pick me up. Kelly across the street was able to drop me off on her way to Lake Spark because I couldn't drive."

"Well, I won't be able to get back for two hours. Rush hour is about to hit and won't ease until I get on I-88. What about Esme?"

"My stellar best friend is absent in my time of need. She went down to Bluetop to the Blisswood winery with Keats. Some romantic getaway or some misery like that." I'm sarcastic but I'm happy for her, really I am.

"Okay, let me—"

The swoosh of the curtain being pulled back breaks our conversation, and I'm greeted by a doctor who causes my jaw to go slightly slack.

"Have to go, the doctor is here. I'll call you back or text me," I quickly string a sentence together to inform my brother what's going on, then hang up while I smile nervously at the man before me. He has a friendly facial expression and height that towers over me, and his eyes are sky blue too. *Also*, there is a silver ring around his finger. Married.

Maybe I'll be that one day.

A wife to a husband who I'll make laugh. And he'll treat me like a queen. He'll be so damn sexy that I'll want to pounce on him whenever I can. Kind of like…

Nope. No, Hailey.

I will not think of the man I've known for years right now. The man who causes my heart to constrict when it shouldn't or who smiles at me as though it's only for me.

Stop this. It will never happen.

"Hey there. I'm Doctor Watson." The doctor brings me out of my daze.

"Like from Sherlock Holmes?" My face squinches.

He swings a stool closer to the exam table. "Is he a doctor?"

I shrug.

"I recognize you from Lake Spark Academy. You teach there, right? I think you might actually teach my daughter Sammy next year. She's going to be in seventh grade."

"Oh, fun," I breathe out a reply as I try to tamp down my pain.

Lake Spark Academy is a private school. It's half an hour from here, but I enjoy the fact that it means I'm less likely to run into my kids on the weekend. I take that back—not kids, teenagers. I need a break from teenagers. Teen students take a little more patience. Sometimes, I regret that I didn't choose to teach preschool, but there are not many private preschools in the county.

The other week, I went to a real estate open house for a building with a great garden on Main Street. I'm not sure why I went, but when I walked through the rooms, it became obvious that I was entertaining the idea of starting my own private preschool. Pure dreams. We all have one or two.

The doctor gestures to my thumb. "Well, maybe I should be worried that her new social studies teacher has had a few questionable accidents." My face falls from his sentence. "Relax, it's a joke. I heard what happened from the nurse." His professionalism hides the slightest of humorous smiles wanting to escape. He unwraps the white bandage I've been pressing against my thumb to stop the bleeding. I refuse to glance down. "For sure, we're going to have to stitch you up."

"Figured. But these days they have those clear roll-on stitches, right?" I'm hopeful.

"No can do. Your cut is too deep." He examines my thumb. "Maybe even cut a nerve"

I gasp, and new warmth flushes through my body. "A nerve! Is that why I'm really struggling right now to feel my thumb or is it just pure pain from my stupidity?" My voice cracks as I whimper.

"All of the above. I would say four stitches and a brace on your thumb, and then in about ten days you'll have to return to have the nurse remove them."

"Fuck," I mutter to myself, and I attempt a few yoga breaths, but it fails to calm me down. "Okay."

"So let me grab some supplies, then I will stitch you up." I chuff a laugh. "Must be your excitement for the day, I guess."

He grins. "I would assume that you're implying that this emergency room doesn't see much action. Believe it or not, we've had a busy day. Tetanus shot due to a wild animal bite, someone had a burn from coffee. All the end-of-the-world things, you know."

"We're a quaint town," I quip.

"That we are. Let's do this. We'll stitch you up and get you on your merry way."

He quickly grabs a few things from the side cabinet before returning to his stool where he places his supplies on the tray next to him, and I notice the needle with liquid nearby.

"What is that?" Panic sets in.

He doesn't spare me a glance and gets to work on his tools. "Lidocaine to numb the area before I stitch." My eyes follow his movements down and then my entire body spins.

Blood. Needle. My thumb.

Then the world goes black.

———

"HAILEY."

The feeling of a cool cloth against my forehead helps my body begin to stir. I blink repeatedly as I wake groggily and try to grasp my bearings.

"There you are." A smiling older nurse greets me. She slowly helps me to lie on my side while a warm rush flows down my body. "You fainted."

Oh yeah, because I hate everything that involves sharp objects and blood. Apparently, just not bread knives.

"I think I'm beginning to feel better," I mumble.

"Here." She hands me a small cookie, those dry ones with vanilla in the middle. *Disgusting.* A crime to the cookie community, to be honest. "The sugar will help," she says, trying to convince me.

Reluctantly, I take one bite, and it's as revolting as I remember.

The doctor stares at me with a warm smile. "Welcome back to earth. We're going to have to stitch you up now. I can't leave it any longer, it's not good for your thumb."

I suck in some air through my nostrils.

The nurse rubs my arms to comfort me, while I internally wish my brother would get here, but he said he is too far. Another problem for my day.

The sound of a man's voice in the hall causes my head to tilt to the side as I try to figure out who is approaching the other side of the curtain. Familiar. Definitely familiar.

I wince from the doctor poking my thumb just as *he* opens the curtain.

Oh no.

No. Why?

In my weakest moment, too.

"Liam sent me to get you home," he explains with that subtle sly smirk that melts me every single time. Sometimes he laughs and a dimple appears. His brown hair complements his matching eyes. He shaved today, I can tell.

I'm totally screwed, and unfortunately, not by him. I may be in my late twenties but around this guy I'm as hopeless as the teens in my class. I stop just short of writing his name in the margins of my notes, drawing hearts around it.

Of all the people Liam could call to help me out, it's the one guy I shouldn't think about.

The man I most definitely do not want to see me in this frazzled state.

But my brother chose who to rescue me, and it's Oliver.

My older brother's best friend.

2

OLIVER

Of course I came running.

Liam called, and it took only a millisecond before I raced to grab my car keys. I was working at home after hours, admittedly, a great pastime of mine. But that's what I signed up for when I became a lawyer, and handling legal for the Spinners hockey team over in Lake Spark only levels up the extra workload.

But taking a break from my laptop isn't the reason why I was in my car so fast. It's because of the woman lying on the exam table, currently looking at me like a deer in headlights. It doesn't deter from the fact that her soft dark blonde hair frames her face, and her gorgeous hazel eyes glimmer no matter her mood. Fuck, I love her lips. Always with a coat of gloss which only highlights the perfect line of her mouth, not too plump. *And...*

Nope. Can't go there.

She's Liam's little sister. Out of bounds.

I can be ruthless with negotiation when it comes to my job. Out of the office, I'm a little more relaxed, except when it comes to this situation.

I follow protocol; Don't go there.

After all, I don't want to risk losing a friendship with a man I've known since high school. I didn't take notice of Hailey back then because she was the little sister a few years behind us in school, but since she returned to Everhope a few years ago, I've more than noticed.

She's beautiful, funny, and a completely inappropriate fantasy.

It's so simple. I'm supposed to be the good guy, but inside, I want to break every damn rule and let my filthy thoughts of this woman come to fruition. Hailey hasn't broken the rule, either. She a good girl like that. If only I could whisper that in her ear while undressing her.

Focus, Oliver.

"D-did Liam say what happened?" She seems wary, her bright doe eyes landing on me.

"No, only that you had to rush to the emergency room." She seems relieved. "Everything okay? What's going on?" My eyes are transfixed on this beautiful creature before my gaze shifts to the side to try and understand the situation.

"I… I… just a normal kitchen mishap. You know, knife gone rogue, most definitely nothing out of the ordinary." She swallows, and I can tell she just lied to me, especially as the doctor's mouth tugs slightly and in an entertained way.

I play along. "Okay, well, looks like we're keeping knives away from you for a while." I step farther into the area. I remember blood freaks her out. A kid in her class once scraped himself on a tree and she vomited. Liam had to pick her up from work.

Her eyes hold mine, and I hate that she's in pain. I'm fiercely protective of her, the same level as her brother.

"Almost done?" Hailey grits out to the doctor.

He cuts the suture. "Sure am. Your boyfriend can take you home."

Hailey's strained face probably matches my own. "Uh... not exactly boyfriend," I correct him, and I hate that I have to. Basically, I'm totally infatuated with this woman who is always so close but not in the way I would like.

By association, she's in my circle of friends. That's what happens when your friend invites his sister to every BBQ or that our town is small enough that random run-ins are a given. There is also the fact that she lives down the street from me.

It's a form of torture. Our level of flirtation isn't just in my head, I'm too smart to misread it. But our level of respect for one another is even higher. We would never want to taint the circle of friends or our own friendship. There are too many risks if I were to slam my mouth onto hers because her eyes narrow in on me with that playful warning that crosses her lips far too often.

The doctor swings his eyes between Hailey and me. "Ah, apologies."

Hailey clears her throat, and it's an awkward silence for a few seconds.

The doctor ignores us as he helps Hailey up to sitting. "Well, it's great that you can drive her. Make sure to keep the stitches clean until they come out," he tells her. "No tetanus shot is needed but I'll write up a prescription of antibiotics as a precaution, as it was a deep cut and you'll need to start those today, along with a lot of rest today. I'll get the discharge papers moving."

A few minutes later, a nurse gives more detailed instructions and has Hailey sign papers. When it's time to go, Hailey hesitates to hop off the table.

I'm aware it's because of me.

The thing is, we can have a good time around each other. There are also certain moments when something else lingers, and it causes us to not say much.

Right now? Evidence of that.

"Are you still feeling dizzy? Need help? Maybe we should get you something to eat," I list. The overbearing concern ripping through me returns.

It causes her to crack a gentle smile. "I'm okay. Just want to get home to my couch."

"Yeah, of course."

She stands up, and we walk out to the parking lot. I'm quick to open the passenger side door of my sports car so she can slide onto the seat.

When I start the engine, the energy feels different to our normal encounters with one another.

"So, uh, the wedding is almost here," I say in an attempt to start our conversation as we drive off.

"Yeah, Liam is excited. Colorado should be fun." Liam's fiancée, Ava, is from there, so they decided to have their wedding where her parents live.

"Lucky you for flying out." I grimace

She chortles. "Why did you volunteer to drive?"

"Because I'm a good best man and Liam needs his car for their honeymoon driving around the Rockies."

"Well, it's sweet of you. I would never be able to drive that far. I want to save humanity, and my driving will not help with that."

True. Her driving scares the hell out of the entire street.

We turn onto Everhope Road, where lush green trees line the street, with yards and mailboxes at the end of driveways that make the houses feel more like homes. Hailey is now renting out her friend Esme's old house. Esme moved next door to be with my buddy Keats. And I live down the street.

It's enough distance to subtly avoid people if need be. My brother lives even farther up, on the corner of our street. It's all a crazy coincidental map.

Parking then turning the engine off when we arrive in front of her house, I don't hesitate and quickly exit my car and circle around to help her.

Her mouth stretches into half a smile. "I'm okay, really. Just need to chill on the sofa."

I hold my hand out, and she fishes out the keys from her purse.

I'm a gentleman, so I'm going to ignore her insistence that all is well and assist her inside, stealing the opportunity to enjoy every second of touching her.

She tosses me her house key, and I catch it before my hand lands on her back, causing her breath to catch because of the second of a magnetic pull that draws her eyes up to meet my own. Our lingering gaze drops, and we mosey our way to the front door, and I unlock it. Walking in, I'm surrounded by the smell of cedar. Her home is cozy. Throw pillows and blankets in the living room. A lot of candles, too.

She drops her purse onto the floor and saunters straight to the living room where she plops down on the sofa, sighing in relief.

"Let me get you something to drink." I'm already halfway to the kitchen while she gets comfortable, not giving her any opportunity to protest.

As soon as I'm in the kitchen, I wince at the sight. It looks like a crime scene. There is blood on the floor and a drenched kitchen towel. My eyes draw a line up to the counter where there is a cut bagel and a knife nearby. "Yikes. Are you sure there isn't a dead body buried in the backyard or something?" I call out. Debating, I decide to grab her a bottle of water from the fridge before I clean this mess up.

Opening the door to the fridge, I catch sight of something from the corner of my eye. Closing the fridge with one slow push, I examine the contents of the bag of bagels on the counter.

Huh, pre-sliced.

My eyes travel between the bag and the floor. *Ah.*

With water in hand, I stroll back to the living room, and I do my best to keep a straight face. I shouldn't find this funny, but I kind of do.

I lean over the back of the sofa to hand Hailey the bottle of water. "Here you go. Where are your cleaning supplies? Something tells me paper towels won't cut it, no pun intended." I lick my lips, struggling to keep my grin in.

"You don't need to do that. It's my blood."

"It's okay. You're kind of missing a finger right now."

Her brows rise, and she huffs out a breath in agreement.

I scratch my chin, debating if I should, but I just can't help it. "I noticed the bag of bagels."

Her shoulders sink and eyes roll. "Har-har."

Teasing her always brightens my day. "A pre-sliced bagel?"

She seems embarrassed, but after a few seconds, a line draws on her mouth, a smirk. "I'm never going to hear the end of it, am I?"

"Probably not."

"I had a moment, okay? Lesson learned, and I think I hate bagels now."

I feign shock. "Bagels are on the bad list? Oh no. Part of your soul must be dead."

Hailey looks good when she's in a light mood, and lucky for me, she appreciates my humor.

Rounding the couch, I sit down on the other end. "Relax, we all have our moments."

"Have your moments ever led to perhaps never feeling your thumb again?" she challenges, and she holds up her hand.

I want to swoop up her thumb to kiss it better, but that's not a great idea. "Thumbs are overrated." She narrows her eyes at me, playing along. "Besides, it isn't that bad, just needs to be on the mend."

"I guess you're right. Least the stitches will be out for the wedding in two weeks."

"There ya go."

Our eyes lock, and we both pierce the other with the connection. It's silent in the room, but the lack of words feels loud. The air feels heavy.

Maybe we both notice because in unison we search for another focal point away from each other.

"I'm sorry I ruined your… whatever you were doing… probably work."

"You know me so well. Yes, that was the case."

She shakes her once. "Tsk-tsk, Oliver. Work-life balance is key." The way her tsks roll off her tongue could be my undoing right here, but I've grown restraint over the years.

"You're just lucky you have a lighter work week for the summer, Miss Teacher Extraordinaire."

She throws a pillow at me with her good hand. "That's because we teachers need to recover from the rest of the year."

"Fair point."

It's way too easy to shoot the breeze with Hailey. Maybe that's why Liam has never noticed. He just assumes Hailey and I are good friends.

"Speaking of recovery, I'll go clean what's left from the crucifixion of the bagel, and I can go pick you up something from the store so you can eat to keep up your strength," I offer.

She stretches her bare foot, nails painted with dark purple nail polish, out across the couch to jab my leg with her toe. I'm not sure what's better? Her touch or how even her toes are hot as fuck. "Stop it. You don't need to take care of me. I'll manage."

I attempt to keep a straight face. "But I think the grocery store is having a sale on pre-sliced bagels." She digs her toe deeper into my calf, and I yelp even though it didn't hurt. "You fainted who knows how many times at the emergency room due to blood. I'm not sure walking into the kitchen is the best of ideas. I'll do it."

The only thing I see in her gleaming eyes is pure appreciation with a hint of affection. I love it. I wonder if she realizes how much she deserves to have someone treat her like a queen. She has a heart of gold, is kind to all, and lightens every social gathering. I mean, for fuck's sake, she had us all dressed up for a 20s-themed murder mystery last year. And there was the real crime that happened—her legs in a flapper dress while she dragged me along to solve clues.

A twinge twists in my stomach because I can never be her king, and I hate the idea of her with anyone else.

She's dated guys in the past, and whenever she was single, I wasn't. Then there were the months that she was settling into her new job and I was deep into the hockey draft. Basically, the timing was never in our favor.

Plus, her brother would kill me.

And I get it.

Abruptly, I stand up. "Okay, you just chill here while I take care of the kitchen."

"Really, thank you. Maybe Liam will be here soon."

I grab the throw blanket and spread it across her body,

tucking her in because I love touching her when it's allowed, and she appears cozy and peaceful.

She touches the back of my hand that's fixing the blanket on her body, causing me to still. "You're my hero."

One squeeze of her hand and it takes all my strength not to swoop down and kiss her on impulse. She realizes her error, and her hand leaves mine in a flash.

I leave her be and clean the kitchen, every once in a while chuckling to myself about the situation. It was a whole-grain bagel. Kind of boring but fine. A few thrown-away towels, a hell of a lot of cleaning spray, rubber gloves well used, and I'm done.

"Okay, I'll head to the store," I say as I meander back into the living room, and I smile as I soak in the view of a sleeping angel.

Hailey is asleep, with her face delicate and her lips tipped faintly in a smile. She must be dreaming. Stepping forward, I selfishly take the opportunity to lean down and tuck a tendril of her hair behind her ear. She doesn't stir, and I just admire her for a few seconds.

Some people might label this as bordering on obsession territory, but I consider it as just grabbing an opportunity.

Sighing, I step away and head to the door. One more glance over my shoulder, and the corner of my mouth tugs at the picture of her. But I can't stand here forever.

Opening the door, I nearly run into Liam who has concern imprinted on his face.

"I owe you." He is quick to step through the door, brushing me aside.

"She's asleep."

He pauses on his quest to find Hailey and eases. "I mean, it's not a major injury, so that's a relief. We've all had stitches at some point, right?"

I nod in agreement. "I'm sure she will laugh about it in the future."

Liam swipes his hands through his hair. "Totally right. Thanks for picking her up. I'm so lucky that you were around. It's times like these I wish Hailey had a boyfriend to help her, but then I fear that they might be like you and focus on work and not her."

His words hit a little harder than I would like, and I'm offended. "Someone is being a little honest today." I'm almost curt in tone but hold myself back.

He grins and lightly pushes my shoulder. "You know that I'm messing with you. I'm sure you would feel the same way if she had a boyfriend. You are protective of her like a sister."

My stomach sours because that is most definitely *not* how I view her.

Scratching the back of my neck, I accept that her brother is here to care for her and my services are no longer needed. "I'll head out. She probably needs some dinner soon. Don't bug her too much about the bagel incident, I already have."

A cheeky look shades his face. "That ain't happening."

I chuckle. "Fair enough. Are you ready for the big day?"

"I am. Just a shame that a wedding entails a lot of logistics and planning. Ava is about to lose her cool. It will all be worth it, though." She travels a lot for work, so I don't know her as well as I would like, but she is sweet and completely softens Liam.

"It will be great. Cigars, whiskey, the whole shebang."

"Thanks again for driving out. I owe you one."

I wave him off. "You'd do the same."

"You can still add a plus-one for the wedding if you want."

"Nah." I shrug. "Solo is fine." Don't get me wrong, I'm by no means a saint, but none of the women that I've been with have kept my attention. Plus, there hasn't even been anyone lately.

"Don't say I didn't warn you if Ava throws one of her single bridesmaids at you." He grins.

Hailey is a bridesmaid, and she's also not bringing a plus-one, but I won't hold onto the hope that she gets steered my way. Liam would never allow it.

"I'll make a run for it. Anyhow, I'm going to head out."

"Thanks again."

I shrug it off as though it's nothing then leave the house. As I stare at Everhope Road, where neighbors are walking with dogs and kids are playing on the street, I can't help but feel that something is missing, there is a dullness inside of me.

I should go find a distraction.

For the most part, this whole situation doesn't bother me. That is until every time I come face to face with Hailey, and then I go a little haywire.

———

MY BROTHER HANDS me a coffee that he ordered at the counter of Foxy Rox. This place is great. A very relaxed vibe with delicious coffee and a few tables and sofas. The background music is Indie and mostly the under-50s find themselves here. There is a restaurant on the river boat that the older generation prefers. The bakery selection here is second to none, too.

Carter takes a sip of his own coffee as he sits across from me. He's older than me, divorced, and is the town sheriff. "You leave tomorrow for the wedding?" He was invited but can't take the time off work.

"Yeah. I'll stop overnight somewhere when I get too tired of driving."

"Don't speed." He gives me a pointed look and grins. "I would hate for a sheriff in the middle of Kansas to give you a ticket."

His jokes are so old but still make me smile. "Nah, I'll just throw on a podcast and drive through America's cornfields until I hit Colorado."

"Good. I'm happy you have a little downtime even though it's busy at work for you."

I sigh at the reminder. "Tell me about it. The draft is coming up, and after that, we have free agency. I'll be turning out hockey contracts on the double."

"Good. Me and everyone else is hoping that the Spinners take the cup next year. Need a solid team for that."

Everyone around here is a Spinners fan. Football or baseball are forgotten sports here; instead, we all back hockey.

"A few days off will reboot my engine. Anyhow, what else is new?"

"I picked up a stray dog that I had to take the shelter if you are still looking for a new companion."

I snort a laugh. "As much as I love dogs, I'm traveling too much in the coming months. Besides, sometimes I'm not home all day, so the little guy won't have many walks. As for companions, I have friends."

Carter slides his coffee to the side. "Okay, I won't press. Everything else good? You seem a little, I don't know…" He tips a shoulder up toward his ear. "Lacking energy. Are your gym sessions not delivering?"

"Nah. All good. Sometimes, I just need to shift my mind when a big wedding is added to my calendar."

"Yeah, I'm not a fan of big weddings." Of course, he would say that. His own wedding was small. "Rosie's parents never let us forget it that we chose that route. Maybe that should have been my sign."

"You grew apart and she is younger than you. It's not like you two are going to kill one another if you cross paths."

He ponders my statement for a few beats but doesn't comment, instead shifting his attention to something else. "How are Liam and Hailey? I see Hailey around. Sometimes at the grocery store."

I swirl my coffee with the spoon. She texted me a thank-you the other week, and it's been two weeks since I've seen her. "I'm sure she's fine. Liam is busy with his wedding prep."

Or I'll kill whoever may cause otherwise.

"Okay." He doesn't ask any more, instead eyeing the menu on the wall, which is ridiculous since he always orders the same thing. "I'm kind of starving. I should probably order a muffin or something. Breakfast is the most important meal of the day, right? I'll need to take it to go, I have a meeting with Dad."

We both groan from the thought. Our parents are local elite, if we are honest. Their words more than ours, even if it's true. Our dad used to work in finance in Chicago before settling down in Everhope. They have a big house along the river a few streets over from Everhope Road.

"Dad still trying to push you to run for mayor next year?" The pressure stems from his own agenda, even if Carter would be good at it. Our dad is now retired but seeing one of his sons in government and having a little control of local taxes is a bonus.

He continues to study the wall. "Hell if I know. I'm only going for entertainment. I normally zone out as soon as Mom hints that I should reconnect with Rosie." It exasperates him always. They love his ex-wife. "Okay, bran muffin and another coffee." His cell begins to vibrate as he stands, and he quickly answers on his approach to the counter.

I don't listen in, instead my eyes wandering to the wall to examine the menu, even though I know everything on there. But my eyes stop and pin on where I see Hailey walk into the café.

Shit.

I pretend not to look at her, and I'm saved when my brother touches my shoulder. "I need to run. They need me at the station."

"Don't worry, Carter, we always have a muffin on standby when you're here," Sara, the owner, calls out, and he winks at her.

But her calorific gesture brings attention to us, and Hailey's eyes swim straight to me, and the corner of her mouth slowly lifts.

"See ya," I distantly hear my brother say. I only tip my nose up to acknowledge that I heard him.

As he leaves, saying hi to Hailey in passing, Hailey slowly walks my way.

"Hey."

"There you are. Did you come for a bagel?" My cheeks tighten from a grin.

She sits herself on the chair that my brother just vacated. "Quiet, you." She points a finger at me with a warning glare. "And I need coffee. I'm flying out tonight."

"All packed?"

"Yeah, and I should even be able to keep my carry-on. I hate when they make you gate check."

Sara arrives at our table. "Can I get you something?" she asks Hailey as she wipes her hands on her apron that is covered in flour.

"Yeah, a flat white with oat milk."

"To-go or for here?"

A scratchy sound escapes from Hailey's luscious lips before her eyes sweep between me and the barista. "Uh… you know what?" Confidence seems to overtake her. "For here."

I'm relieved she said that. But also, a bit pissed.

Now I have to remind my dick to be a warrior and keep it together.

3

HAILEY

I watch Sara scurry back behind the counter before my eyes land on Oliver.

The corner of his mouth always curves a little when he sees me. It's the dimples that appear that cause me to wonder if I should call the fire department because the room suddenly feels too hot, but right now, I need to keep it together.

"Your coffee is on me. The least I can do for being my superhero the other week," I offer. He's a knight in shining armor, but that's because the man in front of me has character and cares, wearing his heart on his sleeve. I envy whoever will be lucky to be his other half for life. Alas, I'm just the one to offer coffee while I'm melting on the inside.

Instantly, he whips his palm up in protest. "That will not be happening."

My eyes roll to the side because I wouldn't expect anything less. I'm lucky that I work at an elite private school, which means my salary is a little higher than many teachers. But it's nothing compared to Oliver who makes bucketloads as a lawyer in the sports industry. It's impossible to argue with him. It's not the first time in Foxy Rox that he's been adamant that I will pay no such thing, and he probably already gave a sign to Sara that he will pay for my coffee too.

I really don't care about money. It's just a shame that it makes the world go round.

"Never argue with a lawyer," I reply and bite my bottom lip to try and suppress my wide smile that is dying to escape.

His sight drops down to my thumb. "It's gone. The stitches and brace. They didn't need to cut your thumb off."

Holding up my thumb, I examine it and smile proudly. "Only a scar. It feels a little different, but I should survive."

"Well, that's good. Ava might lose her cool if she loses a bridesmaid."

I shake my head and pick up the glass canister of sugar, even though I have no plans to pour some into my coffee later. "Trust me, she'll still find something to lose her cool about."

She's good for my brother, but she's a different kind of person when it involves wedding planning. A nervous wreck at best. It's understandable. By no means do I have a mood board of my wedding dreams tucked away in my closet, but I'd be lying if I didn't have an idea of what I might want for a wedding one day in the future.

"I haven't seen you around. I know we live on opposite ends of the street but normally you go for a jog. Not that I'm a stalker, it's just sometimes I notice routines from neighbors and friends of brothers."

His tongue swipes to the corner of his mouth. Did I sound flustered? I didn't mean to. He just always has an effect on me.

"It's been raining a lot, and I wanted to tie up some work. The usual."

I frown at him, unimpressed. "Your life sounds a little stale. You might want to liven it up a bit."

He stifles a laugh. "I might follow your advice... one day."

"You should. Oh!" I flap my hand, excited. "Apparently, the Dowes at number 21 had a wild party." I flash my eyes at him, hoping he gets the hint, but he just stares blankly at me. "As in *couples*..."

His head perks up. "Oh yeah?" I nod. "Huh... they didn't strike me as living the lifestyle. I guess I can see it now."

"Our street always has drama or gossip and I only just moved there." Thanks to Esme shacking up with Keats, her neighbor and Oliver's colleague.

"You missed the days when Keats and Esme would argue on the front lawn," he reminisces.

"Oh no, they still have a little quarrel here and there," I assure him.

Our street gossip is interrupted when Sara returns with my coffee and sets it in front of me. "I hear you checked out the building down the street," she comments to me.

The one that would be perfect for a preschool but is way out of my budget. I even asked the bank the other day.

"Let me guess, Molly mentioned when she came in?" Molly is the town's only realtor.

She smiles brightly. "Yeah, and said you were thinking something for kids, right? That's what you want to use it for?"

My head cocks to the side. "Yeah, a preschool. It's silly," I say, brushing off my idea.

Her shoulders sink. "Nah, what's silly is the price the sellers are asking, and apparently, they have a whole list of stipulations for who they will sell to."

I chuckle nervously. "Molly mentioned. Anyhow, it's a great space, but it will be for someone else."

"As long as it won't be a new café," she retorts.

I offer a weak smile as she leaves our table, and I turn my attention back to Oliver whose brows are furrowed, and he stares at me with a peculiar interest.

"What am I missing?"

Stirring my coffee, for some reason I'm near bashful. It's probably because I don't often share my wishful idea, but with Oliver, it comes easy. "It's nothing."

"Clearly not." His tone is persistent and scorchingly hot.

So much so that I dissolve into compliance. "I kind of had a crazy idea to open a preschool. As much as I love teen drama, I would rather teach kids who learn through play and every little thing is new."

"I never realized how serious you were about it. You mentioned a few times at Liam's that you wanted to teach younger kids." He sounds truly intrigued.

Now, I'm just playing with the spoon to avoid meeting his eyes that feel like they are drilling into me. "It's a silly idea. Not sure why I went to the open house."

He reaches across the table, and the moment his fingers touch my wrist, fireworks boom inside my chest.

"Probably because it could be a reality. Tell me about the place."

Get your fingers off me and maybe I can think straight.

He must read my mind, and after one caress of my wrist, he abandons our touch.

No, keep your fingers on me.

My eyes shift up to find him staring at me intently. "The building that used to be a furniture store is on the market. There is space for a classroom and an office. Also, a side room that would be ideal for crafts. There is a courtyard in the back for outside play, too."

He instantly has a warm, wide smile. "It sounds as though it could be something great."

Picking up my cup, the warmth of the coffee hits my tongue, and it hits the spot every single time.

Swallowing, I set the mug down. "Well, tell that to the bank. I mean, I'm lucky that our small town means the building is affordable compared to the suburbs of Chicago, and I have a little bit for a downpayment. Maybe not all but enough, and on no planet would I ask Liam for a loan. Besides, the owners have some out-of-this-world demands."

"Such as?"

"Apparently, they only will sell to a married couple. They mentioned businesses owned by couples always do better, so they think the building won't need to be sold again in a year or two from something failed."

His eyes squinch. "That's sort of discrimination. Then again, it's their private property as of now. They also may want to double check the statistics on married couples in business together." He winces.

I wave him off the topic. "It doesn't matter. I mean, there is also the aspect that I would need building safety checks, to register with the state, and so many admin details. Plus, it's all an impractical thought. I'm happy at Lake Spark Academy, really." *Eeek*, the enthusiasm could be worked on. I sound 75% positive, and I should be 100% happy with my job.

"You would be good at it. Handling little monsters, I mean."

He traps my gaze, and my face softens from his compliment. "Thanks. I will just have to create my own brood of little monsters one day when I settle down with someone."

Oliver's face falls, or am I imagining it? Are his eyes darkening?

What the hell? What did I say?

"Right," he states tightly, and he thrums his fingers on the table. "You need to find a Prince Charming."

I snort out a laugh. "With the current look on your face, you are as bad as Liam. Will you be participating in his interrogation when the time comes? I bet you will cross-examine whomever it may be," I joke. I find it funny, but apparently, he does not.

A chirp notification sound breaks the air, and I quickly scramble to grab my phone from my purse. The moment I see a new message on my screen, my mood deflates, and I'm joining Oliver on the not-impressed train.

"Shit. My flight is cancelled." I unlock my phone then scroll the screen. I have a text message and an email all relaying the same information.

He straightens his posture, waiting for me to explain.

"Apparently, there is a computer problem affecting the plane." Panic sets in, and I hit the link in the email to reschedule my flight.

"That's not great. You have to be out there early for family stuff, right?"

I nod my head while my eyes skim the website. "My parents are already there. Esme and Keats, too, as they took a little vacation before his groomsman duties start."

"You can reschedule for an earlier flight maybe." He checks his watch. "You could make a mid-afternoon flight."

Anxiousness now overtakes me. "They only have one flight a day unless I drive out to Chicago O'Hare. Oh, fuck." I'm seeing only one thing on the website. "Tomorrow's flight is full too." I hold my phone up so Oliver can see.

"You should probably phone Liam and Bridezilla." He recoils.

I drop my face into my hands with my elbows set on the table. This is just my luck. "I'm positive I'm cursed. Every time I fly, there is always a delay, or the flight has major turbulence."

"Let me go find some sage to burn to cleanse your energy," he jokes. Sometimes his dry sense of humor peeks out, and every time it causes me to smile wryly, even now.

Hitting Liam's name on my phone, I set the cell on the table on speaker. I need both my hands to take a chug of my coffee

"Hey, what's up?" he says as he answers after two rings.

"No flights. That's what."

"What do you mean?" His tone lifts an octave.

"My flight is canceled, and the one for tomorrow is already full."

"*Nooo.*" It trails from his mouth, and I can tell that he is shaking his head, too. "We need you at the wedding. Are you making this shit up? Is this your way of messing with me while I'm scrambling with last-minute wedding prep?"

I chortle a laugh. "Trust me, I'm not that cruel… today. Oliver is here, I ran into him at Foxy Rox. He is my witness that I'm not joking."

"Hey, Liam," Oliver speaks up.

My brother growls at the other end, frustrated while Oliver and I stare at one another with pained looks.

"Well, we need you on a plane, Hailey. I can't have a wedding without my sister. You're already going to miss family dinner, it seems."

I rub my forehead, trying to shake away irritation that I now have to deal with airlines, tickets, and probably a gazillion layovers just to reach my brother's wedding. But that's my problem, he doesn't need this issue on top of his to-do list.

"I'll figure it out," I promise.

"Hailey, I love you, and I wish I could solve this, but I'm going to need you to take this one over on the solution train."

My entire body sinks into the chair, accepting this reality. I agree with Liam but that doesn't mean it's any less daunting. I'm already gearing up for a conversation with a disgruntled airline agent on the other end of a call.

"Oliver," my brother snaps.

Oliver scoots closer to the table to listen. "Yeah, man."

"You're driving out. Take Hailey." My brother's demand is clipped.

In unison, Oliver and I zip our wide eyes to one another.

"What?" Oliver peeps out.

"Easy solution. Doesn't take a rocket scientist. Hailey will ride with you."

Oliver seems to be contemplating, but I can't read his mind, and he is giving no indication of what he might be thinking.

"Uh, I, right… I can drive with Oliver." I swallow my nerves.

But this isn't a big thing. No, siree, just a normal day when you end up driving across the country, alone in the car with the guy you might have had too many dreams about.

"Totally. I can ride her." My eyes turn into saucers from Oliver's word choice, and he instantly realizes his error. "I mean, she can ride me." He is fumbling with his words. "Uh, with me… in the car… yep, she can ride with me in the car. Problem solved."

"See, guys? A little teamwork. Now, I have to run. Ava's parents want to meet for breakfast. Let me know when you guys are safely on the road."

"Sure thing." I watch my pointer finger dab the end-call button then grab my coffee, avoiding the set of heavy eyes on me.

Silence surrounds us for a beat. Truthfully, my mind might be imagining the whole ride-him scenario, which is his fault for triggering the reminder of my fantasies.

"I'll pick you up at six tomorrow morning."

Blinking a few times, I whip my attention to see Oliver calmly sitting across from me. His stoic face isn't helping matters because I'm just not sure if he is thrilled or pissed by this change of events.

"Oh, yeah, of course. Since we're driving my brother's car, it won't look like we're stealing it if we get pulled over, right? I mean, the registration is in his name, and I have the same last name." I sound half serious and joking at the same time.

"Why would we get pulled over? We're not conducting an armed robbery, are we?"

"No, we're not. It's going to be a long day. We can stop somewhere to stay overnight." Worst idea ever, but there is no other way.

His lips roll in and maybe he is reflecting on the logistics of our road trip. "Makes sense." An unreadable pause hits us again. "It will be too early to grab coffee to-go from here," he mentions, since Foxy Rox only opens at 7.

I'm going to be stuck in a small space with him for two days. I'll smell him, feel him close, maybe argue with him over music. Shit, is this going to be a quiet car ride? No. I will not allow that to happen.

"I'll pick up snacks for the road tonight. Stock us all up. Buy a map too."

His face turns perplexed. "Pretty sure modern technology will navigate us."

My face beams. "Loosen up, a paper map is classic. Probably out of date, but you never know when technology will fail and we need a backup. Either way, we'll probably get lost at some point."

"Directions gone rogue are one of the top reasons that couples argue."

"We can't have that now, can we," I tease. I'm relieved that our banter can reappear again.

"So what snacks are you planning?"

I bring a finger to my chin. "Definitely licorice laces, granola bars, fruit, water bottles, pretzels. Maybe I should just pack a cooler?" I'm getting lost in my thoughts because this whole unexpected plan is exciting.

But it's the deep velvety chuckle of the man in front of me which is probably the real reason this feels exhilarating.

"Are we going to a deserted island? You're really stocking us up there."

I shrug. "We've gone from armed robberies to deserted islands? Seriously, though, we could get stuck in a cornfield. Speaking of which, do you think we can try and make our break stops kind of thrilling?"

Oliver inhales a sharp breath and shifts in his seat.

Right. Because he probably has a mind as dirty as mine sometimes.

But shocker, I actually wasn't thinking about *that*. "You know, a quirky road stop or lunch spot."

"Totally."

"And music? I'll set us up with a playlist."

His smile hasn't shifted an inch. "You're going to play 'Life is a Highway' as soon as you set up the music in the car, aren't you?"

My eyes blaze open with more excitement to give him his answer.

"Are you going to be this hyper on our road trip?" he adds.

Reaching across the table, I poke his arm. "You'll love it. It was going to be a boring drive and now it won't be."

His eyes travel from my hand, following the path straight up to my face. I hope he doesn't realize the dazzle in my eyes is for him.

"You're right," he rasps. "It won't be anything like I planned."

The air stills, and that flutter in my chest returns.

We're going to be together on a road trip. And it doesn't feel like anything average.

A sort of adventure that we're going to embark on together.

His lips twitch, and it feels as though my thoughts just flew straight into his mind.

I think I'm already lost, and it's not even because of an outdated map.

———

I THROW my pajamas in my suitcase while I trap my cell phone between my ear and shoulder. Even though I already packed for the trip, I need to switch up my outfit choices since my trip itinerary has changed.

"Will you stop laughing?" I plead to Esme on the other end.

"Sorry." I can hear that she is trying to calm her hysterics. "But this is the best news."

"Why? Oliver and I are going to be in tight quarters. We could drive each other nuts." I open my drawer to search for underwear.

"You two flirt like crazy. Just do it at a roadside stop. I'll never tell anyone. You might find that it finally relieves that tension around one another."

"We don't have tension," I protest with the lie of the century.

"True. You're like friends, but it's obvious that you both want to upgrade that label."

I give up and lean against my dresser. "It won't happen. Oliver is too loyal to Liam."

"But you want to, you know you do," she goads me.

"I'm not sure why I called you. You should just go back to your romance fest. Like what the hell? Two weeks ago, you went away for a night together and now you love birds have added a few extra days on your trip."

"Someone is a little icy today."

Sighing, I realize she's right. Maybe a pang of jealousy is the cause. "Anyhow, I just finished my epic playlist creation and stocked up on snacks. Maybe I should take a first-aid kit just in case or a flashlight."

"What the hell? Are you planning on a natural disaster or something?"

"I mean, we are going through tornado alley. You never know," I justify.

"I'll make it easy for you. Pack something lacy," she deadpans.

I laugh her off but then eye my bra choices and consider if I need to spice it up a bit.

No, Hailey. No X-rated detours on this trip.

"You're hilarious," I counter.

Esme lets out an exhale. "Okay, well, you will figure it out. Just don't always do what you think everyone expects."

"Yes, ma'am."

"I need to head out. Don't forget to pack your phone charger. Everyone forgets those."

"Thanks. See you in two days."

Hanging up, I ponder her jabs and advice. She's reminded me many times of the same thing, but it just hits differently this time. Don't do what everyone expects, right?

But I'm just going to do what Oliver and I always do. Have fun around one another. Good old-fashioned platonic fun. Follow the traditional rule that your brother's best friend is off-limits. I've been doing it for years, and the next few days will be no different.

My lips roll in and out while I stare at my underwear and bra options. Quickly, I snatch up a few extra lacy choices.

My subconscious, I'm sure.

And the next morning at 6am, with the sunrise just lighting up the sky, I'm waiting on the curb in front of my house and throw out my thumb as if I'm hitchhiking when Oliver drives up. He's in my brother's silver SUV.

He rolls down his window. "Need a ride?"

"Yeah. You wouldn't happen to be a gentleman who won't murder me and is willing to help a girl out?"

His natural suave grin has its own category when the early-morning sun lights his skin.

"Depends, did you pack enough snacks for a family of five?"

"Of course." I smile.

He motions with his head. "Then let me pop the trunk, and welcome to your chariot."

Oliver exits the car and rounds the back to help me load everything up. Our arms cross, bumping into one another as he attempts to lift my bag, then it's a shuffle of feet.

We're already tangled, and we aren't even five minutes into our adventure.

Hailey gives me an over-the-top stern look that I notice out of the corner of my eye. We've been driving for an hour, and early morning kept us not so talkative until we managed to get a coffee for the road. Now she's full-on energy.

And trying to feed me a muffin.

"Come on, Oliver. As our driver, you need to be focused and fueled." She continues her quest to stuff the baked good into my mouth.

"You were not joking about your snack box."

We're lucky that all the traffic is heading the opposite direction and the interstate is quiet. This should be an easy drive until our next stop.

"I would offer you something else, but this muffin has fiber and vitamins. It's banana bran, after all." She smiles mischievously and attempts to feed the muffin to me by bringing it closer to my mouth.

Like a shark, I take one snappy bite to appease her, nearly biting her fingers in the process.

"Yay, you listen."

Only to you.

The way she feeds me a few more bites would look ridiculous to most, but it works for us. Because *obviously* there is nothing wrong with your buddy's little sister feeding you a muffin in a tight space while you're reminding yourself that the backseat is not an option.

Hailey shifts in her seat when the muffin is gone and pulls out a granola bar from her bag.

"What? I could have had a power bar and you made me eat a messy muffin?"

She throws me a sly grin. "It was more fun." She reaches toward the dashboard to adjust the sound system, and when she's satisfied with the music, she pulls out a map that crinkles open, along with a travel book.

"Doing a little studying there?" I ask her as I continue to focus on the road.

"I highlighted a few possible stops, and using my phone for everything isn't good for my eyes." She sounds very serious, and it's adorable.

I can't help but smile to myself. This road trip will be anything but boring.

She takes a sip from her coffee that we picked up at a gas station twenty minutes in and sets it back in the cup holder. "When was the last time you traveled somewhere like this and not on a fancy private plane for work?" she wonders aloud.

Thinking about it a few ticks, I search my memory. "Probably a while back when my brother and I did the whole upper Great Lakes."

"That sounds cool. My most exciting trips lately are school field trips. Don't get me wrong, it should be fun. It's just, middle school kids are too busy whispering about who is into whom and the latest drama."

I cringe. "You couldn't pay me to go back to those times"

"I know, right? Yet I do it on a daily basis."

"You observe them. There is a difference."

Hailey shrugs.

"So, what is *really* stopping you from starting your whole preschool idea?"

She sputters a sound. "As you are aware, the owners have the ridiculous marriage clause. Plus, I doubt they would want to sell to someone on a teacher's salary. Even with a private school salary. I'll need money to invest in renovations and supplies. I don't want to take a loan from Liam. The bank would give me the loan only if I have a higher income on file. I'm halfway there, just not enough."

It disappoints me just as much as it does her, and it doesn't surprise me that she would want to be self-sufficient and do it all on her own.

"And if there weren't a clause and you had the money?"

"I guess, it would take a little while to really set up the place and find students. I mean, there are a group of moms who hang out at Foxy Rox for coffee sometimes and I heard them mention that they wish there was a preschool closer to Everhope. The one that was here never reopened after it was flooded a few years ago. Also, they would love if the preschool serves healthy snacks and maybe even teaches a few Spanish words so kids can become bilingual."

Lines crease my forehead. "Do you even speak Spanish?"

"Barely. I would have a native speaker come in." Watching as the faint joy on her face falls is heartbreaking. "Sorry, I'm talking your ear off for a silly idea."

"It's not silly."

"Easy for you to say. You are exactly where you want to be."

"Sure, job wise, house wise, fitness wise… apparently

road-trip wise." But life is missing someone to share it with. "The league headquarters in New York has been offering me a position on several occasions. Still, there are just a few more things in life that I could be satisfied with."

Her head whips in my direction and her lips part. Yeah, because it's us then that's where her mind has just gone.

"Let's just leave it at that." I'm not going to deny that we probably just shared the same wavelength of thought, and we need to move on to something neutral, so I switch topics. "My brother wants me to get a dog," I say while I overtake a truck.

"I *love* dogs," she coos. "Actually, I would love a Labrador and to get him qualified as a therapy dog, then one day he could be with kids and listen while they read. It really calms them, especially kids who need a little extra help with reading."

Everything warms inside of me, not because I want her but because of her kind heart. She's selfless and wants only the best for people. "One day you'll have all of that."

She sinks back into her seat and sighs. "I would love it if my dog is one of those dogs that walk down the wedding aisle carrying the rings. He would have on a little bow tie."

Right. Marriage, dogs, a future. Probably, shouldn't let my mind wander, I need to focus up ahead anyhow.

"Hey, is your brother really going to run for mayor? The rumor is spreading like wildfire on the street."

I want to rub my head due to exhaustion from the crazy scenario. "Well, he is the golden child, and I think he might actually really want to do it, but since we both enjoy defying our parents, then he might tell my parents no just to keep them on their toes."

"Golden child? That's what you think?"

I hiss a little whistle. "Oh, I know so. They are for sure

proud of me and happy I'm a lawyer… but it's the wrong kind of law. They would be a lot happier if I didn't involve sports in the equation. I should settle down, too. Family dinner normally involves them mentioning so-and-so's daughter. They probably have a whole book of options."

"But your brother is solo. Well, divorced, so he once wasn't, I guess. Rosie is cool, we hung out quite a bit and still stay in touch. She's the kind of person you could pick up with right where you left off. A shame they didn't work out, they're good for one another."

"She was younger and wanted to explore the world. Plus, we can't always have what's good for us." You underneath me, for one.

"True."

Hailey smiles. "Your mother is so sweet. Nancy always looks out of this world, no hair out of place. Insistent that I come over even though I never do."

"She's crazy about you." It only adds more oil to the fire because the reasons that Hailey should be mine seem to mount.

"What's not to like?" She splays her hands out, and I couldn't agree more. "A shame your parents can't be there for the wedding."

That is also true. Despite the sentiments they make me feel sometimes, they are good people.

"Yeah, my dad has some engagement at his old grad school where he is speaking, and my mother is going with. She already picked out an overpriced toaster to send to Liam and Ava as a gift."

Hailey shimmies in the seat to get comfortable, and she grows quiet while she begins to study her map and examines her book that already has a few post-its sticking out.

I'm still entertained every time I steal a glance at her book. "You randomly had this travel book lying around?"

"Actually, yeah. For years."

Lines form on my forehead. "And you had time to bookmark?"

"I couldn't sleep."

"And yet you have this energy."

I quickly glance to her as she throws me a wicked look. "That's just me." She winks at me.

The next three hours we go back and forth in conversation. At times, she rests a little bit and admires the cornfields. Other times, we make chit-chat.

I take a look at the clock and my arms feeling tired inform me that it's time. "We should stop for a break. Stretch a bit," I suggest.

Enthusiasm takes over her, and she is quick to grab her travel supplies and begin to search with her pointer finger. "Perfect. We're on the Old Lincoln Highway, and there are so many fun little places to stop along the road. The signs say our next stop is ten miles from here, and there is a stop where they make buttermilk soap."

"Sounds good." I wish I could slap my brain because I just imagined lathering her up with the damn soap bar.

And next thing I know, we're walking around a store with various knickknacks. Bottles of honey on one wall, woven blankets on another, a whole section of cornmeal in jars. This is all kinds of random but nobody walking outside seemed to be complaining about the slow-churned ice cream shakes with straws in their hands.

I continually tilt my head to examine items. Currently, the milk soap with a picture of a cow with a bell on it holds my attention. That is until I notice Hailey up ahead with a blissful radiant glow as she touches the wind chimes and the sound floats through the air.

Sauntering to her, I admire her peaceful state in the process.

"I love wind chimes. The wind reminds us of a shift of energy, good or bad. I like to think that it sweeps in luck," she notes as we come face to face.

Why does she have to be so beautiful right now? Her eyes bright, her cheeks high due to her smile, and a loose lock of hair nearly brushing against her brow.

My finger darts out to touch her silky hair and tuck the loose lock behind her ear. It's when she nuzzles her cheek into my palm that I realize what I did, but I'm not backing away. Partly because her gaze has chained me down with a hint of whimsy in her eyes. Neither one of us moves, and she's right. There is a shift in the air, and it doesn't scare me.

Am I stealing a moment to touch her? Is this my sign that I should say fuck it to any code of honor? Or am I making a mistake?

Her lips taunt me, but I'm in a pioneer store in the middle of who knows where with an old lady behind the cash register observes us.

All I offer Hailey is the barest of smiles, and she returns it with her own. One last caress of her cheek and my hand falls away. Clearing my throat as I step back, I focus on the chimes in front of us.

"Help me pick one," I say.

"What do you mean?"

"I don't have one at home and I should, according to you. Choose one for me."

Suddenly, she's a child in a candy store and her eyes swirl around the options. "Long or short? Where will it go?"

"Probably the back deck. Long and strong?"

She throws me a devilish grin. "Is that a question or a fact?" Her eyes bulge out, and she's back at it with our banter.

"Funny. Maybe the wind will blow toward an answer for that," I warn her as it sinks in that I have quite a drive ahead with her close to me, and my restraint is dissolving into history.

She enjoys that I give back as much as she throws at me. "Long and strong it is," she rasps.

I roll my eyes at her humor.

Straightening her back, she studies the chimes and then spots the winning one.

"Here you are. Perfect."

To me it is a simple wind chime with various extended silver bars hanging and a ball in the middle.

She's satisfied with her choice, and her eyes return to the one that she was staring at earlier.

"You like that one?"

She hums a sound. "Yeah, I would for sure have a chime if I ever open a school. Also, the chimes using bamboo. There are many options, but this one has a little moon shape in the middle."

"You should get it," I insist.

She shakes her head, dismissing the idea. "I don't want to jinx myself so that everything I want won't come true one day."

"Didn't you say that it can carry luck?"

The corner of her mouth snatches up. "I know but..."

I jump right in. "Then I'll buy it and keep it at my house until you have your preschool."

She snickers. "You may be keeping it a while."

I'm already unhooking the chime, refusing to let her say no. "I'm the driver today, so I'm making the decisions."

Hailey crosses her arms and taps her foot. "Is that so?"

"Yep." I turn my back and beeline it to the register where the jolly lady beams brightly and bounces her eyes between me and Hailey.

"Great choices. What a cute couple you are."

"We're not a…" We both say in unison, yet neither one of us manages to complete that sentence.

We realize and our eyes droop, but then I paste on a smile for the lady as I hand her my card.

A minute later, with a bag in hand, we find ourselves back at the car and standing in front of it, like two magnets trying to pull ourselves apart to venture back to our seats.

"Thank you," Hailey mentions shyly.

I hold the key fob up. "You don't need to thank me."

Our moment lingers, and I'm not sure what she is thinking. I can't appraise her for too long as she puffs in a breath and pivots on her foot back to her side of the car.

When we drive off, Hailey is quick to turn the music on, and we both seem occupied with our thoughts.

Only when we're two miles further on the interstate does she pipe up. "Apparently, there is a storm that's passing through around dinner time, we should probably find our stopping point and plan to stop around four for the night."

"That's a good idea. We'll have driven eight hours today, our halfway mark is in good ol' Nebraska," I agree.

"Are you sure you don't want me to drive a bit?"

"Nah, it's okay. Just enter your highlighted destination address in the navigation." Her face remains blank, and she seems slightly unimpressed. "Oh fine, use the map since we are going retro." I smirk as I give in, and that causes the corners of her mouth to curve up.

"There is the world's largest ball of stamps if you feel like venturing off track. Oh my God." Now she's flapping her hands like a penguin.

"Yes?" I glance at her, concerned yet bemused.

"Tomorrow, we so need to stop at the Big Foot museum in Hastings. Totally."

My brows rise. "As in the fictional ape thingy?"

She swats my arm to tease me. "I don't think he is an ape, I'm not sure. Maybe he isn't fiction at all. There was a foot-print, after all."

"Was there?" I doubt her for fun but lose at keeping a straight face.

"We shall find out." She gets comfortable again and rests her feet on the dashboard. "By the way, have you practiced your best man speech?"

I scoff a sound. "Absolutely not."

She side-eyes me. "You're going to wing it too?"

"You're the groom's sister, I'm confident you can't wing it. It needs to be heartfelt."

She waves me off. "I'll wing it." She sounds defiant and smirks to herself.

I attempt to keep my laugh under my breath when Hailey turns serious and pulls out a compass divider for her paper map, and after measuring the distance, informs me that we have an hour and a half more of driving before we settle for the night. Clouds have covered the sun, but there is no indica-tion of rain. That changes when we're about forty-five minutes from our destination; the gray clouds turn dark and the lightning strikes fiercely in the distance. Cars driving the opposite direction were clearly caught in the rain.

"I'm kind of thinking that we should stop earlier," Hailey comments.

"You're probably right."

Her phone begins to vibrate, and I notice her brother's

name flash across the screen. To be honest, we've both ignored our phones today. Not on purpose, just we had no need to. Each other's company has been a distraction, a positive one.

"Hey, Liam," Hailey answers on speaker phone.

"How is the drive? You guys on schedule?" he asks her calmly. If she says anything that might freak him out, then he might go bananas. Wedding jitters and all.

Hailey looks to me then back to her phone. "All good. We're about to stop for the night. It's been a long day and the weather is about to turn."

"Good. Storms can change quick there."

"I'm sure we're fine. Nothing looks unusual other than your car. Sorry about spilling a chocolate shake all over your cream interior."

"What?" he barks out.

She chuckles to herself. "Take a joke, will ya? All is fine. Oliver is treating your car like a precious newborn baby."

"As he should. Oliver, is she annoying the hell out of you yet? Try not to throttle her. We need her in the wedding party photos."

"True. Sisters are sisters forever," she comments. "Girlfriends of groomsmen you might need to erase out of photos in a few years."

I bark a laugh. She has a point. We'll both be in the photo but not as a couple. It's safe. We get to share photographic space without any repercussions in the future. Just Hailey and Oliver. Groom's sister and the best man. Nothing more.

Fuck me, I hope this hotel has a good cold beer.

"Yeah, Liam, she's fine. I'm keeping her under control. I debated tying her to the roof about fifty miles back but refrained. I have a reputation in law to maintain."

"I'm happy it seems to be an okay trip, and also, it works

out well since you will both get here on time despite canceled flights." I can hear by his voice that he is smiling.

"We'll see you soon." Hailey ends the call with a fond, caring look. She adores her brother, and he adores her.

Nobody would want to get in the middle of that.

She points to the upcoming exit. "We should probably pull off. Maybe there is a hotel there or at least a place for early dinner to sit out the storm."

"Yeah, that sounds good."

Pulling off the highway, we drive a mile until we enter a small town in the middle of nowhere. Other than a pickup truck turning up ahead and a diner with only a few full tables that we can see through the window, this town is kind of empty.

"This is fun. Totally unplanned, slightly concerning, but ooh, there is a bed-and-breakfast up there that actually looks really cute and normal," she observes.

Peeking over the steering wheel, I look through the windshield to examine the Victorian house on the corner with a painted sign on the lawn, surrounded by potted plants.

The place appears decent. Not a motel, instead it's quaint.

Hailey claps her hands together. "Perfect." She reads the sign. "The Wagon House." Hailey flips pages in her book until she reads over a section. "This place is actually in the guidebook. It's fine. We won't get locked in the basement by a serial killer."

I look at her strangely before I slow the car and park out front with the rain beginning to pick up. "Riveting," I say dryly.

She unbuckles her seatbelt. "Seriously, this place has good reviews and is ideal for travelers without kids. There are even nightcaps and biscuits for breakfast. Hopefully they have two rooms."

"The town doesn't look busy."

So this option sounds pretty solid to me. Plus, I'm tired too.

Turning the engine off, we both hop out of the car and walk up the stairs of the wraparound porch that has rocking chairs and a bench swing.

Before we even manage to open the perfectly painted door, a woman probably in her 60s greets us on the other side with a warm smiling face.

"Hello. May I help you two?"

Hailey smiles charmingly. "I know we didn't make a reservation, but we decided to stop early due to the storm approaching. What are the chances you have two rooms?" She pretends to pray. "We've been driving since six from Illinois."

The woman steps to the side and glances up at the sky. "You'll want to stay off the roads. We're on a tornado watch."

"All the more reason we hope you're our miracle today, ma'am." I never say ma'am, nor hurt my cheeks from an overly measured smile, but here I am.

"I'm Patricia. Come inside." She gives us a little space to walk through the door where the hallway has dark pine floors and a classic staircase.

"You can, of course, stay here. It's busy. We have newlyweds, a couple driving home to California, and a professor conducting research nearby. The guests who were supposed to show up for the other room cancelled last minute. That room is now available, but I do only have the one room."

My entire body tenses in a heartbeat.

One room.

"Oh," Hailey says, but I can't figure out if it's a simple oh, excited oh, or a disappointed oh.

I swear my dick is stirring inside my pants at the mere prospect of being stuck in a bedroom with her.

"The next town is another five miles from here. I can call ahead for you if you really need two rooms."

The sound of thunder startles Hailey as much as it does me, except I don't think it's the elements that have us on edge.

We both look at one another, debating, wondering, waiting for one of us to decide. I'm positive she is thinking the same as me, but I can't be 100% sure.

Our eyes are in a battle of who will answer Patricia.

Then we both burst out with, "Okay."

Our voices in unison seem to take her aback. I guess we both had a little vigor in our tones.

"Wonderful. I'll get you the key and prepare a snack plate for you. I serve brandy at 9pm unless the do-not-disturb sign is on the door… of course." She assesses both of us, then she turns on her heel and disappears down the hall.

"Are you fine with this?" I whisper to Hailey. Because this is a test of resilience.

"Yeah, why not? We've been in a car all day together." Her voice seems uneven.

"You're right."

Patricia returns holding up a key. "Here you are. The sheets are fresh and the pillows fluffed."

I accept the key. "Thank you. We'll grab a few things from the car then head on upstairs."

"Alrighty then. Snacks are on the way, and I will also let you know if we all need to move to the storm cellar. I think this one will just be a severe storm."

"Thank you," Hailey politely replies.

We both head to the car and quickly grab our overnight bags and leave the large suitcases in the trunk. Little balls of hail begin to fall, and we quickly jog up to the porch where the roof provides protection.

Hailey pauses and focuses on the wind chime hanging in the corner. The sound dings as the chimes swirl in a near violent rage. Yet, a subtle fondness sweeps across her face as she stares.

"Is this warning us?" I wonder, with my jaw slack.

Her eyes slide to look at me.

"The chime reminds us of the wind. You know, some Native American tribes in the plains would often call a tornado a devil wind. Some believe it is an angered spirit, while others believe that a strong storm is cleansing for a new beginning," she explains whimsically.

Her stance is soft and innocent yet sinful and persuading. We take a moment before we head inside and upstairs.

We open the door to the room, and I'm beginning to understand what the wind is trying to tell us.

Because there is only one bed.

● **5**

HAILEY

I'm shaking.

Yet nobody would be able to tell because it's inside of me.

The sound of the door gingerly closing behind me breaks my moment of soaking in the charming room, with a dresser, wood floor, and a big window with rain trickling down the glass from the sky, a dark early evening. It's cozy and sophisticated. Tiny features of a century ago.

I spin on my feet and see Oliver standing there.

In this bedroom.

With one bed.

With me.

All day my resolve has broken off piece by piece. We haven't ever had a day just he and I. I mean, sure, we would run into one another at Foxy Rox or when friends need group help. Then there was my brother's engagement murder mystery last year where we ended up on a scavenger hunt together, and I swear he would have kissed me, but every corner when we found ourselves alone, someone would interrupt us.

Today is different. I feel it in my bones.

It sticks in my head that he bought me the wind chime to hold onto. I could say it's sweet, but it feels more profound. He touched me and he has no idea. It was inside my constrained chest of emotion.

One day someone will be so damn lucky to have him.

He's biting his inner cheek because he is trying to stop a smirk. Is it because he is amused by this turn of events?

I'm not complaining, except there are nerves swirling.

Oliver clears his throat and scratches his cheek, unsure of what to say. "I'll take the floor."

Instantly, I sputter out a laugh. "I think we are two mature adults who can handle sharing a bed."

He steps forward, composed. "Okay, then I guess I'll go shower while we wait for that snack plate."

"Yeah. You deserve it. You've been driving all day. I'll get ready for bed later." A strong sound of thunder causes me to flinch from surprise, and it only heightens the thousands of floating dots inside of me.

He drops our bags in the corner of the room and begins to unzip one of the outside pockets of the bag. I just watch as he lifts his laptop out.

"Oh no you don't, mister." It's a shame he likes to work. Oliver is funny and fun to be around, but when you unmask relaxed Oliver, then it's even better. Sometimes I wonder why he hides behind work so much.

His eyes survey me. "Uh, why not?"

My hand falls to my hip while I squinch my eyes at him. "No work. Besides, you know lightning can strike a laptop? It's a thing. A rare phenomenon, but you might not want to risk it."

Oliver stays mute and for a few seconds assesses me before he ceremonially tucks the computer back into his bag.

I smile brightly at my victory. "Good choice."

"I don't have many options. If I don't listen to you then you might steal the blanket during the night or something."

My body rockets in heat again at the reminder. "Nah, I'm not that mean."

"True. You're alright if I sleep in boxers?" He throws that question out at me as though it's simple.

But it is. I don't need to act like a shy woman. This is logistics, and neither one of us needs to read anything more into it.

"Oliver." I inhale a strong breath, choosing to channel my confidence that I always possess. "It's fine. I mean, we've seen one another in swimsuits before, and it's the same amount of clothing as my bra and lace panties. It's just that society makes us think that seeing someone in their underwear is a big deal."

He drags a hand across his face with a closed-mouth smile apparent, even though something is bothering him. "You had to mention lace, huh?"

That's what has him in this state? I really like that.

And now we're alone in a room. I get to stare at a sleeping Oliver shirtless. He mentioned shirtless, right? Or do I need to crank up the AC?

A knock on the door breaks this moment, and I watch Oliver as I walk backwards until I have to turn to open the door.

Our attentive host greets me on the other side with a plate in her hand and balancing a bottle of wine and flashlight with her other arm. "I already had an extra serving on hand."

She passes me the plate full of fruit, cheese, crackers, hummus, and cut-up veggies, not to mention a few pieces of fudge that appear to be local based on the wrappers.

"That's very kind of you."

She grabs the flashlight that she had tucked under her arm and hands it to me. "This is for you two. Just in case we lose electricity. It looks to be just a storm that will clear the area in about an hour. I'll be back around 9 with brandy unless the sign is on the handle."

My eyes dart to the inside handle and I see the do-not-disturb sign.

Before anything she said registers, Oliver appears at my side and spears his eyes straight into my own. With purpose, he slides off the sign then plants it onto the front handle, not breaking eye contact, and coyness shades his face.

"Forgot to put that on," he declares. My eyes widen enough for him to appear satisfied that he caught me off guard.

"No problem. Breakfast is from 7 and late checkout is possible, too." We don't give Patricia any notice.

"Perfect. Have a good night." Oliver can't close the door fast enough.

We both step back into the middle of the room. I'm trying to digest what just happened, and when I turn, he's standing there with his hands free. But that smug and determined look remains. Without a word, he takes my plate and wine then sets it aside on the bedside table.

Who will speak first?

The room is quiet, except there are a thousand fireworks exploding in my mind. It feels as though we're challenging one another.

"Didn't realize we would be needing the sign," I comment flatly. I'm still trying to discern what is running through his mind. He doesn't need to know that I'm mentally flipping through a catalog of every filthy fantasy I've ever had for him.

Oliver prowls forward, and it raises my attention again as he closes in. "Cut the crap, Hailey."

"Excuse me?" My eyes grow big.

I shudder the moment he plants his fingers on my arm just above my elbow. There is a gust of wind that nearly knocks me down, but it's not from outside; it's purely due to his touch.

"You really needed to inform me of your lacy details?"

"That's what is bothering you?"

He flexes his jaw and then his mouth forms his signature cocky smirk that causes my entire center to tighten. My breathing grows faster, and I'm hanging on by a thread. All because of his sexy mouth that displays something different.

A dare, perhaps.

No. It's a warning.

He watches as he strokes the back of his knuckles gingerly up my arm, sending a ripple of sensitivity through my body.

"We can be responsible adults and sleep in a bed half naked as though it's a normal day. But you know the thing about that?" he asks softly.

"What?" I rasp.

"Neither of us wants to just sleep." His eyes strike up to mine. "Care to admit that too? We're both thinking the same thing." His fingers begin to curl around my arm, holding me still with no escape.

And the coy smirk slowly spreading on my lips informs him that I wouldn't want to anyhow.

"I admit it." Suddenly the words I thought I should never say become so easy. For one night we can't hide from one another. "We keep dancing around the... *issue* between us."

He steps closer, and prickles run down my body in anticipation.

"We shouldn't give in, but for one night, I don't fucking care." His voice is firm with a sweltering grit.

"What a coincidence. I return the sentiment," I say, flippant.

A gravelly noise rumbles in his throat as his hands cup my face. The moment his lips slam down on mine, I think I'm temporarily blind.

His lips are commanding yet soothing. Repositioning to kiss me better, I murmur from the contact that I've been desperately wanting from this man. I nearly forget that I'm standing on earth until his tongue parts my lips to delve into my mouth. One swirl of tongues and I'm addicted to his kisses.

Only briefly parting, our lips reconnect, and he groans from the contact. This is no longer a first kiss; we're escalating to new heights. His fingers rake through my hair and my fingers fist his shirt.

We slowly subside, and a few quick kisses lead us in all directions. Oliver's mouth abandons my lips to skim along the line of my jaw.

"Do you like that we just kissed?"

I'm almost breathless. "I like it a lot."

"Oh, thank God." Then he bruises my lips with another kiss.

I take a few seconds to enjoy the feeling. Oliver kissing me and treating me like a map to explore makes my pussy throb, and I smile to myself that this is happening.

Deep down, I wanted to believe that one day, even if just once, I would have to confess what I desire, even if the sentiment isn't returned. Except it is, and it's not at all surprising.

We both knew.

My center of gravity has shifted, but before I can stumble, Oliver's strong arms snake around my middle and he pulls me close. I don't waste a second, and I begin to paw at his shirt, searching for the best way to lift it as we begin to walk together with our mouths sealed, circling together, until our legs hit the mattress.

I'm not sure if we are beginning or ending, but it's only when his hand on the back of my neck pulls me close to enable our foreheads to touch that we pause. "Are you sure?" he checks in with a whisper.

My mouth stings in the best possible way from our kisses that have been a long time coming, but one word still manages to leave my lips. "Very."

Softly, he kisses my forehead and my eyelids hood closed as I take a few seconds to let reality sink in. Then we are right back at it.

I'm tugging on his shirt, he's finding the hem of mine. I drop down on the mattress, and he keeps his word and encases my body to ensure he can kiss me whenever the opportunity presents itself.

I've secretly been worshiping his toned body in my head for years, which is why I don't take a moment to linger. Instead, I focus on dragging his shirt up.

He kneels on the bed for a second to yank his shirt over his head, and I do the same with mine. Lying on my back in shorts and a black lace bra, Oliver rakes his eyes all over my body, causing me to clench between my legs.

The subtlest of smirks returns to his face, and he leans down to unzip and drag my shorts down my legs that he holds in the air against his body. He has me pinned with a stare as he softly kisses my ankle before the shorts disappear onto the floor.

Every inch of skin that his eyes explore heats, and I'm desperate for him to touch me everywhere. It feels like time has slowed down, or maybe it's the way I feel as I lift my upper body to unhook my bra, teasing him by sliding each strap down slowly before I toss the bra to the floor too and lie back with my mane of hair splayed across the mattress.

His sound of approval includes a small hiss. "Have I ever told you how beautiful you are?"

Maybe he has said that once or twice when we were at a mutual social gathering, but never like this. Never as a man marveled by what he sees and his eyes powered by hunger.

"I don't recall," I simply reply.

He lies on his side next to me with his head propped against his bent arm. My breath hitches when his fingers arrive right above my belly button and swirl. A new wave of sensation zips straight to my nipples that are already hard and perky.

"I bet if I touch you right here," his fingers barely touch over my lace panties, "that you'll be soaking for me."

I lift my hips, trying to bring his touch closer for friction, anything to relieve a little pressure from my clit, but he doesn't play fair and his palm plants down on my belly to keep me firm on the mattress. With his mission accomplished, he drives his hand up to my breast, two fingers circling around my nipple, and I whimper when he pinches his fingers around the nub.

We both watch what his fingers are doing to me. "Be warned. If we are going to do this then I will be taking advantage of the whole night to fuck you senseless and get you out of my head."

"Yes," I whimper when his tongue darts out to play with my other nipple. "I believe we are in agreement of that plan." My breathing is no longer steady; it's growing heavy from the overload of Oliver around me and touching me. Soon, he'll be in me.

He pops his lips off my nipple and shifts on the bed until

he is on his knees at the end and between my thighs. His mouth trails from my belly button down, and he bites the fabric to taunt me, pulling enough fabric away for the air to hit my clit, and I want even more. He hooks his fingers into the waistband and yanks them down my legs.

The moment he brings the bunched fabric to his nose for a strong inhale, I nearly explode. It's so erotic. He tosses my panties to the side, and his lips make contact with my skin.

Everything inside of me thrums with anticipation. One kiss and then another from my knee up my thigh, tantalizing me as he closes the distance. I keen with a need for more because I'm growing impatient.

I've waited for this moment for far too long.

The room fills with my moans when his mouth touches my pussy. He wastes no time, and his tongue flicks my bundle of nerves, his arms hooking under my thighs to hold me tightly to him. He swipes a few times up and down my slit, only to return to my clit. I can't help but look down, and his eyes are still on my face as his wicked tongue causes my blood to burn and my pussy to grow even more needy.

"You're sweeter than I expected," he says against my thigh as he kisses my sensitive skin.

"Expected?" I whisper.

"Let's not play surprised. You've thought about me fucking you, and I've thought about me fucking you. And now I plan on living out the many ways we can make that happen to prove my theory is correct. Your body is by far more beautiful in the naked flesh." The feeling of his finger sliding inside me causes my hands to clench the duvet. "Your pussy is as tight as I hoped." He adds another finger to lazily stroke me in and out. "And I want to make you come."

His mouth is back on my pussy as he continues to stroke inside of me. Oliver is on a mission that I don't mind one single bit. The room begins to spin as tension around my clit builds. My fingers comb through his hair as he feasts on me. Every one of my moans makes him more persistent to make me come. And it doesn't take long, as I'm under the spell of his magical tongue.

"Oliver," I plead for my orgasm. He follows my cue because it's not long after that my entire body convulses, vibrating against his mouth that refuses to abandon my pussy until I ride out my orgasm.

He holds me down with his hands to ensure I accept every molecule of my orgasm in full force.

When the last wave falls, he pulls away, completely content with his efforts. "Do you know that you are more beautiful when you have a post-orgasm glow?"

I smile drowsily and lift my hand as I'm boneless limbs right now. "I did not know that, but thank you."

"I'm not done with you yet," he warns and quickly searches for his pants and pulls out a condom.

The mere thought of him being fully inside of me pools wetness between my legs. When he lowers his pants, my eyes nearly pop out from his size. I figured he wouldn't fall short, but now I'm scared I can't handle him. He sheathes himself, and since the moment our lips landed on one another, the air calms and acknowledgment floats between us.

"No going back after this," he reminds me.

I draw my toes up the mattress until my knee is pointed up in the air, a sort of sultry pose. "And here I am, still on the bed," I say huskily.

Then he is right between my legs again, and I'm flat on the bed while he kisses me, and my hands drift down his back. I catch my breath while I coat his tip with my desire for him. His soft groan and the anticipation that any second he will be where I've always wanted could make me scream.

Instead, I moan in one long breath as I feel him enter me.

Our eyes haze with lust as he nudges further in until he is fully seated. I bite into his shoulder and wrap my legs around his waist.

"The perfect fit," he whispers into my ear.

My heart constricts, and I'm unsure of what to focus on because I'm completely lost in him.

"Ah." He hits the button inside of me that sends me on a whole new rollercoaster. "You feel good, too good." And addicting.

Our bodies rock together as his thrust is hard and deep.

He's been unleashed, and I like this side of him. Even if his eyes check in every so often that I'm okay, with a caring nature in his eyes that ignites hidden corners inside me.

We both pant as we continue our ride, adjusting position when needed, but we always end up back to our eyes being tied together.

Now we are face to face on our sides with my one leg hooked over his thigh.

He drags his thumb across my lips. "Let me make you come. I'm so close, but I'll only finish if you come again for me."

I chuckle through labored breath. "What a gentleman."

The same thumb travels between us to stroke my clit. "This round, maybe. But I have full intention to use that mouth of yours later."

He circles and flicks while he slams his cock into me.

Bringing my fingers to my nipples, I pinch and play as he picks up his pace. Then it happens.

My vision litters with stars as my body trembles.

Shortly after, he roars a moan as he lets go.

When we both return to earth and end up as two jellyfish in bed, the reality of what we just did sinks in.

We glance at each other but say nothing. It's not bad, just indescribable.

Oliver disappears without a word to go get rid of the condom.

It's then that I examine my surroundings and the clothes on the floor, with me naked on top of a bed, and I can only hope he doesn't regret this.

Because attraction is one thing, but mixing it with genuine affection for the other is a dangerous ledge.

6

OLIVER

I have no regrets.

Should I question that more?

Nope.

Did I finally snap because of my zero resolve?

Abso-fucking-lutely.

Walking back into the room, I see Hailey now under the blanket that is scarcely around her body, and our eyes strike like a match. We say nothing, but there are vague hints of giddiness on her face.

Sliding back into bed, we don't break eye contact until I can't help myself and my sight drifts down to the spot where the fabric is hanging loosely near her nipple.

"Hope you don't mind, I didn't think clothes would be needed for the rest of the night." A temptress she is.

I rest on my side to face her. "That's a very good assumption."

"Good." She, too, eyes me from head to toe with approval before she flops to her back, and I mirror her.

"Want to talk about what just happened?" I offer the option, but I'm not really in the mood to talk.

"Nope." It drags out of her mouth with a popped P. "Well, actually…" *Oh.* "We just sort of both gave in at the same time, right? I'm not imagining it."

I attempt to side-eye her while I face the ceiling. "I'm kind of disappointed that you would need to question if my cock was inside of you. Surely, you must still feel it since you're tight and eager."

She rolls to lie against her propped elbow with her mouth in a theatrical O shape. "Why, Oliver, what a foul mouth you have."

I chuckle to myself. "That's tame compared to what else I could say."

That excites her. "Hmm, my theory about you is right then."

"You've been thinking about this that much that you have theories?" I kind of assumed, but when you get to hear that someone has been fantasizing about you, it's even better.

She pushes me playfully. "Stop it. I'm on to you. You're trying to get me to admit how this has played out in my head a few times."

"Well, Hailey. If you insist that you are on to me, then by all mean get on *top* of me." I rush to throw my arm across her body and drag her over my middle until her legs are settled on either side of my hips and her body is flat against mine, but her head perks up.

Fuck, the entire world has stopped. So much so that I even forgot it was raining.

Hailey bops my nose with her finger because she's always full-on sunshine and cute. "Now, for a lawyer, surely you would want to hash out some details about tonight's events."

My stomach sinks for a millisecond. "If you mean your brother then I would rather not discuss that while you're pressed against me completely naked." I'm not sure I'm going to get away with brushing this aside. I look up at her and comb a few strands of her hair behind her ear. "I've decided that tonight I'm leaving logic at the door. We don't need to make this into more than it is. We let out a little tension, and since we are trapped in a room together, then we can do it all night."

My hands slide straight to her pert ass and squeeze as though I'm about to spank her. It's very tempting. Give me a second more, and I might just…

"But why now?"

She's not going to let this go in this very moment, is she?

"Sometimes, you decide in a moment that you'll take what you shouldn't have," I answer honestly.

Her fingertips tap against my bare chest. "Is that how you see me? Someone you shouldn't have?"

I scoff because she's a smart woman, which means her question was purely to goad me. "Now, you're just trolling me."

She bursts with a laugh that is a song to my ears. "Did you just say trolling? Ah, our straight and narrow lawyer has a funny bone."

I roll my eyes and tickle her sides that causes her to wiggle and laugh, and then I roll us until she is on her back underneath me. "Whoa there, straight and narrow?"

Her cheeks must hurt from her smile. "Nah, but I like joking with you. I know you can have fun. Just didn't expect you to do that while breaking a rule… and say trolling." She bubbles another laugh.

"I'm only this relaxed with you, you know. I mean, sure, with the guys, but with you it's kind of different. Can't really explain it."

She arches, causing her body to press against mine. Fuck, I plan on worshipping her body all night.

"Why did you give in?" I wonder.

A coy look shades her face. "Because you gave me the signal that I could. I know how much you don't want to break some bro code, and maybe I understand. I mean, it's dangerous to hook up with one of my brother's friends. If things go south, then it's a bad situation for all."

I sigh because we're on the same page. "It seems that tonight we are both leaving that fact on the other side of the door. Our little secret."

"Exactly. We can have some fun and forget about it. Be friends, you know." She says it, but I hear uneasiness. Maybe she's waiting for me to say no and that we can be more. But living in a fantasy will get us nowhere.

Except tonight, we *can* leave it all on the other side. I'm going to be a greedy son of a bitch and let us have one night with no questions or reminders of the outside world. It's a dangerous game, but I was faltering all day, for years if I'm being honest.

Now her serene eyes are stabbing into mine. It's been a while since I shared a bed with a woman. But Hailey doesn't compare. She has her own level of class, on a pedestal that is so damn high.

"You're beautiful, you know that?" I whisper. She blushes and attempts to look away, but I hook a finger under her chin and drive her attention straight back to me. "You're not a shy woman, so take the damn truth."

"It's different when you say it… and have seen me naked."

I lean down to kiss her lips. Not soft, instead it's bruising. Inside I'm screaming that I'm the only man who should see her naked, ever. "Naked you is even better, and I'm going to have to memorize every inch of you," I warn as I drag my lips along her jawline.

"Ask me why I wanted you to touch me where you wanted," she requests.

"Why?"

"Because I've thought more than I should about the way you would kiss, the way you would touch me wherever you want, your taste, the way you would fuck me. And not just today has it crossed my mind."

Fuck, she's trying to kill me. My dick is already hardening. I have to pause for a second, wondering if we are teetering on a line of not just a physical connection, but we both know the stakes are too high to explore more.

"I think I need to shut you up now," I warn her just as I sweep up her arms in a quick move and pin them above her head. "I don't want to think. I do that enough on a daily basis, so just let me fucking escape inside of you, whether it be your mouth or your pussy. Will you give that to me?"

She nods in agreement. I dive into the crook of her neck and playfully nip her skin, drowning in her grape perfume in the process. Her body arches up into my touch, and I abandon her wrists to sneak between our bodies to feel her still ready. This is going to be a long night, which won't help with our journey tomorrow, but right now, I'm more concerned about my cock nudging against her thigh, dangerously close to her pussy that I just want to slip right into.

I'm too smart for that, and Hailey is a rebel who croons my name.

"I've decided that if we're going to have tonight then I insist I taste you right now." Her sultry tone informs me that I'm very lucky, especially when her fingertips press against my chest and push me away.

Our bodies twist until I'm on my back and she's on top of me, with her hair wild, the ends hitting just below her nipples.

I tuck my arms behind my head to enjoy watching her with any plan she may have. I'll let her do it all.

She walks her two fingers up my torso to my chest, slowly to prolong the anticipation. "Don't let your ego get too excited, but I was deeply concerned that you wouldn't fit."

"Well, we still have to try your mouth."

"Funny, I was thinking the same thing."

She flicks her hair behind her shoulders and moves to rest between my legs. The moment her mouth is on me, I swear to fucking God that I'm no longer on this planet. A pleasured sound escapes me instantly, and her tongue swirling around my tip like it's a lollipop is a talent that I was hoping she would have.

I reach down to fist her hair, and she takes it as a clue for her mouth to slide down my length. "You're such a good girl. Keep going."

The moment that she gives a signal or I feel that it's too much then I will release her without question. Right now, she seems eager, and I'm one to test limits, which is why I keep her hair tight around my hand to ensure there is only one direction for her.

I groan as I hit the back of her throat with her eyes peering up at me; maybe I see a tear pooling but mostly she's seeking approval.

"It seems my cock fits perfectly in your mouth." My voice strains, and I close my eyes as she begins to suck and bob. "Hailey, I wish I could always shut you up this way."

She continues and gags once. As great as that sound is because it means I'm deep into her throat, and I will be coming down her throat at some point tonight, but right now I need her pussy.

"I want you to sit on me," I instruct.

As she transitions, I reach to the bedside table for a

condom. Her red stretched lips have a droll smile, and when she encases my cock, her arms rest on my shoulders and my hands frame her hips.

"I don't think I'm going to last long," she whispers.

"What a coincidence, I'm the same," I deadpan.

We kiss as I lift her slightly on my cock then push her back down. She learns the rhythm, and our angle seems to ensure that special spot inside of her is hit on every thrust.

Her murmurs mixed with my grunts mingle in the air as we move, and for the pièce de résistance, I move us, linked together, and set her on her back and bring her legs over my shoulders.

The way her breasts jiggle on every move indicates how hard and deep I am inside her. My entire body overheats from our encounter, and I'm positive if I don't lean down to capture her mouth, one of us will scream.

The moment our mouths fuse, I calm only briefly before she tilts her hips to meet my thrusts, and we are in the perfect position for me to rub circles on her clit to get her exactly where I want her before I feel tightness underneath my navel, and I begin to jerk and come.

I'm grateful for my stamina because I don't plan on stopping.

7

OLIVER

Hailey throws a grape at me when I slide on a pair of boxer briefs after our third round. "Cheater. We're not supposed to wear any clothes." Hailey is still draped with a blanket.

I give her a stern eye. "Sorry if I need to refuel, and your bare pussy near me needs a barrier, otherwise we will never rest."

She curls her lip into a pout. "No fun. Speaking of barriers, did you pack like a whole box of condoms or something?"

I hop back onto the bed and my face screws up. "Not exactly a box."

Her jaw drops as she lies on her side. "Were you just going to find some random hookup at my brother's wedding?"

"First off… no. Two, I'm a responsible man who comes prepared. Three, I didn't pack a box which means we need to pick wisely, mouth or pussy later, when you feel the need to have my amazing cock inside of you."

Her shoulders bounce. "Just take me without one." My

eyes pop out from her statement and calm delivery. The corners of her mouth twist. "I mean, I'm on birth control. I normally don't do it, but we trust one another."

I pull her close to me, already knowing I'm not going to resist this turn of events. I never do this, but Hailey is my undoing. "Looks like our marathon can continue then."

"I'm happy I got stuck here with you. Thank goodness for shitty airlines and Midwest storms."

"Me too." I kiss the top of her head. I haven't decided yet if I've ever been a cuddler or why I don't second-guess it with this woman in my arms.

"And thank you for buying the wind chime. I'll have to figure out something to hold onto for you until you have a special occasion. You're not a weird garden gnome person, are you?"

My quirky Hailey. Always random.

I smile. "No garden gnomes, nor indoor plants. Maybe a manly cedar-scented candle."

"Huh, I could see that. I'll hold onto your chime then keep it at my place until there is something for you to celebrate."

"We're not tit for tat."

"No. But I *want* to."

Blowing out a breath, the muscle in my cheek ticks. She cares and I care. We're similar in that way.

The room is quiet but peaceful as we listen to the sounds of the storm outside. "I love the sound of rain," she mentions.

"Me too. My parents have rocking chairs on their porch, and I would just sit and listen to the rain when I was growing up, especially when I was in college and would visit. It's calming."

"It is a sedative, except right now, my entire body is on an adrenaline high because of what has transpired," she admits in a feathery voice.

"Makes sense. We've been walking on glass around one another. We get along, and we laugh together, pretend we are just friends. But the attraction equation comes up with only one answer, and here we find ourselves."

Inside, a pit opens between my heart and stomach. Sexual tension is one thing, but Hailey isn't just that. It's my innate need to feel more. Even if she isn't just any woman, I fear she may be the *only* woman for me. I just can't untangle that thought because there will be consequences.

Squeezing her closer, I still think about the circle we always find ourselves in. "I guess we no longer need to wonder about what happens when we give in."

A short laugh hits my ears. "Yeah, now it's just stamped in our heads what it is actually like to give in to temptation, and I'm not sure what's better, dreaming what it's like or knowing for sure, because both options have my mind spinning."

So true.

"Don't think anymore, Hailey. Maybe we should open the bottle of wine."

"No way. I'm already floating from an orgasm."

"True. I have that effect on people." I sigh proudly.

"Tomorrow's car ride might be a little awkward then," she teases me.

"Nah, we'll be okay, right?" *No. We probably won't be.*

"Sure." Her voice is unsteady. "I've fucked my adult crush, no biggie."

I feel a little cocky. "Crush, eh?"

"Oh, shut up." She jabs me with her fingers. "Would you rather I say that I've been pining for you to strip me and have your way with me?"

"Have you been pining?" I'm no longer volleying back our teasing. I know the answer, but the caveman in me wants to hear it out loud.

The sound of the rain overtakes the room again because no words leave her mouth, and I have my answer.

"Oliver… we click, and any woman would be a fool if they didn't see how you fall into the good-guy category. You're the type of man you bring home to your parents. The kind of man that makes someone feel lucky."

I'm not a good guy.

I only fight for something when it involves sports and law. Maybe I'm protecting a friendship, but I've now crossed a line with my best friend's sister, and in secret, too. And here I am, letting Hailey and me have a taste of something completely forbidden. Not just because of traditional bro-code but also the fact that I don't want to hurt her, and now this might be hard to forget.

"I mean, you're the kind of man whose looks are meh," she jokes.

I softly shake my head. "How do you make life so damn peppy and light? From your humor to your complete randomness at times in general."

"Because my energy is good for the soul. I can't complain about life. Not to mention, being grumpy means fine lines on my face at a young age. I can't have that now, can I? Besides, if I ever want to shift my career a bit, then I need to be ready to rumble with an overload of energy."

Her career aspirations are an honest one. Wholesome, too. It's just right now, in my arms, she is kind of dirty in the best possible way when it involves me.

"You're a good woman."

"We're two peas in a pod then. Can you do me a favor?"

"Anything." I mean it.

"If I give you a hidden signal at the wedding, will you save me? I have a feeling my mother might be sending a pack of single barracudas my way."

I tense at the mere thought. I could slash out anybody's eyes who land on Hailey with non-honorable intentions. Only I get to have those. I'm going to be a selfish prick and steer any protentional guy far away from her. In practicality she doesn't belong to me, but in my head, she is only mine. "Deal."

"Aren't you going to ask me to return the favor? What if a friend from Liam's college days who he hasn't spoken to in years yet somehow got an invite wants to pounce on you?"

Chuckling again, I'm wondering how I'll survive the wedding party table. Hailey with alcohol is always a whole other experience, but add in a happy occasion for her brother and this is going to keep me on my toes.

"I'll tell her that my dick is out of commission, as a beautiful witty woman has left claw marks on my back."

She giggles and it's soothing. "Just don't give me a hickey, I have a dress to wear that shows a little neck."

We both snuggle into one another and that peaceful quiet returns. Her nails brush along my arm, and it feels too natural that my body is willingly her canvas.

"One night," I warn her.

She rests her chin on my chest and her soft eyes stare straight into me. "Are you telling me or reminding yourself?"

This woman knows how to read my mind. We're not strangers after years of orbiting one another, only being intimate is new.

And this once will be the only instance. No matter the thoughts in my head that could cause our own personal apocalypse.

"Shh, and get on your hands and knees," I demand because getting lost in her is my only focus right now.

———

HAILEY and I collapse into the chairs at the dining table that has a whole array of breakfast choices. Instantly, we both begin to stack our plates with muffins, eggs, bacon, anything and everything.

"I'm starving." Hailey sounds exhausted.

"Well… we both need an energy boost after last night and this morning."

"And an ice pack for my thighs… old volleyball injury." It drags out of her mouth as we both see Patricia walk in with a smile and a new jug of orange juice.

She smiles at us brightly. "Good morning. I hope you slept well."

Hailey and I glance to one another. I'm not going to lie. Driving today will be brutal. I basically lived inside of this woman. Her reverse cowgirl is on point.

I scratch the back of my neck awkwardly. "Splendid. Well rested and ready to go."

"Lovely. You can have a late checkout if you like, the next guests won't arrive until 4."

Tipping my head to the side, I ponder, as it means I could bury myself deep into Hailey once more.

"Yes, please." It shoots out of Hailey's mouth with firmness.

My eyes skate to her, and her smile is pasted on to Patricia. It seems Hailey is a smart girl.

"Lovely." A timer goes off in the other room. "Oh, that's the banana bread. Excuse me."

She excuses herself, and I have to admire Hailey while I pop scrambled egg into my mouth with gusto.

Her shoulders lift to her ears when she looks at me. "What? Take advantage of our one-night policy. It only ends when we sit back in the car." She points her fork in the direction of the front door.

"Fair point. We'll have to be quick; we need to get on the road if we want to make it to wedding festivities."

"Okay. It's doable."

"Agreed. Now eat your damn muffin, can't have you weakening on me." *I weaken for you even when I have a full stomach; all the time, actually.*

She takes a large bite into the blueberry muffin with crumbs falling onto the plate.

"What a good girl you are."

"I'm only listening to my master," she quips.

A sound rumbles in the back of my throat in response.

We make good use of our breakfast, and when we go back to the room one last time, I take her as she lies on her stomach. Her skirt is the gift of the clothing gods, it gets us straight to our goal. And I don't give a fuck if I rip her panties in the process.

But now we both linger by the car doors, hesitating to get in. As soon as we do it's over.

"Well… that's that." She avoids any eye contact.

Now reality hits us like a ton of bricks.

The timer is up.

Walking around the car, I surprise her when I grab her arm and wind her into me, take her face in my hands, and kiss her. Not a damaging kiss but a soft affectionate kiss because she isn't just a random one-night stand. It's Hailey. The woman who shines like a comet. Orbiting my life but never touchable.

She deserves the universe.

My gentle kiss deepens against her lips.

One last kiss.

Reluctantly gravitating away from her mouth, my thumb circles her cheek and our foreheads touch.

"I won't forget last night, even if I should," she whispers.

"We don't need to forget it. Just leave it as it is."

She barely nods once in understanding.

"Let's get back in the car. No point standing around," I suggest and hate every syllable of the sentence.

"You're… right."

It's a brutal silence as we settle back into the car. I bite the inside of my cheek as I watch her stretch across the middle to set the navigation. I'm trying to fight the urge to wear down the tension in the air.

But Hailey, the light that she is, saves us both.

The navigation turns on, and I have to laugh. "Really?" I give her a pointed look.

She shrugs at me and can't control her closed-mouth smile.

"You changed our navigation voice to a woman who sounds like Dolly Parton?"

"Fun, right? I mean, I guess we are going to miss the Big Foot museum, so I have to keep the adventure going somehow."

"You're the adventure," I say quietly, but she hears.

Her lids flutter and then she turns away to look out the window.

That's us.

That's it.

We leave it behind.

8

HAILEY

Well, I mean, we're doing what we said we would.

Moving on and going back to the way things were before we decided to have one night that will burn in my head for eternity.

In the car we were quiet but not awkward. We managed to focus on our task at hand which was to get to Colorado. We stopped by the museum for one picture outside by the sign, but that's it. Our ride and time were the priority. I might have also pretended to nap once or twice, but hey, A for effort to keep the vibe going.

Now we're standing in front of a reception desk, aware that we will be receiving separate keys for our rooms this time.

Observing the lobby, a new excitement floods through me. This place is chic, but then again, so is the entire small town of Sage Creek that we drove through. I'm kind of surprised by the modern furnishings considering how classically quaint the town is outside. Still, this hotel seems like a perfect destination for a wedding, as it must be a hot spot for those heading up to the mountains.

My brother is getting married. How can a sister not be excited for that? I hope I don't shed a tear or three. Nor have too many shots of the hard stuff at the reception. There better be some damn good cake, too. I would like to believe that this will be the type of wedding that my brother would want. He's never really voiced his views, and he's too laid-back and probably let Ava choose it all.

Me? Gosh, I have so many ideas for a wedding.

"Okay, that's you two checked in. I'll have someone bring your bags up to your respective rooms. Also, we have something for you," the man our age behind the reception desk says as he slides the keycards to us. He grabs two bags topped with blue tissue paper from below the desk. "For all wedding guests." He smiles.

"Thank you." We each take our present and head to the elevator.

When the doors close and we are all alone, we are finally hit with the dreaded awkward silence, made worse when Oliver hands me my keycard and our fingers graze.

Clearing my throat, I offer him his present. "I wonder what this is." I peek inside my own bag and smile when I pull out a snow globe with a couple inside on a kayak.

"There is no possible way Liam picked that out. But it's a nice touch, though." The corner of Oliver's mouth ticks to the side.

"It's the little things. Anyhow, I guess we made it in time. We have an hour until the rehearsal dinner. I'm starving and might get hangry soon."

"You might be waiting a while. Normally, there are speeches and other BS to sit through."

I let out a disgruntled noise. "Damn it. You're right.

Surely there are appetizers. My brother would never forget a solid food menu."

Oliver peeks up at the number on the elevator. "So true."

The ding informs us that we are on our floor, not that were many. We both walk to the room numbers on our card holders then pause when we both arrive at our doors. Neither one of us can ignore that we will be sleeping in rooms directly across from one another by chance.

Willpower isn't needed though, because we promised that life must go on.

Fuck that.

Let me crank the level of restraint up to a ten.

He clears his throat as we both stand there in the hall for a long beat, staring nearly shyly at one another. "Interesting room designations."

I chuckle nervously. "Right?"

Our eyes hold for a few seconds, and I just want to burst out that we should only need one room, but this all has to be put to the side as it's my brother's weekend and that's what is priority.

"See you in a bit," he whispers.

"Totally." Then I click my card into the door to open it.

———

I HEAR a gentle knock on my door, and Esme saying my name is exactly what the doctor ordered. I open the door.

"There is my little road trip traveler." Esme is quick to pull me into a hug, with her light brown locks resting below her shoulders.

"Here I am." I notice my voice is lacking excitement, and I make a mental note to whip it together.

Esme follows me and stands in the doorway to the bathroom while I continue to apply my mascara in the mirror. "How were the few days of your romantic getaway?" I ask. She and Keats came out early for some alone time.

Her gushing smile is cute but kind of makes me jealous too. "Perfect. I swear if he doesn't ask me to marry him this weekend then I'll do it myself." She would too. Esme can be persistent and feisty around her beau.

"I'll stay out of the way of the bouquet toss tomorrow then." I throw her a grimace.

"Nah, that's too obvious. So, tell me, how was the drive? You and Oliver. Oliver and you. Small, enclosed space." She has a cheeky grin while she twists hair around her finger.

"Fine," I reply simply and continue with my makeup.

"Really?" She sounds doubtful.

"Yep," I lie.

She shrugs. "Okay, same old then. You two just being you two."

"Right." I'm not trying to open the door for a deeper conversation.

"Of course, you two won't be the cliché best man hooking up with one of the bridesmaids."

She's exhausting me now. "Esme, I might just throw something at you."

It only makes her laugh. "Sorry. It's too easy. I just have to say his name and you turn into a woman unhinged."

I throw my blush brush onto the vanity. "Stop it. I really need a best friend right now who will not drive me nuts. I do one crazy thing and then you don't let it go."

Her head cocks to the side and her brows raise. "One crazy thing?"

Ah, shit.

I'm going to burst anyhow. "Oliver and I slept together,

but we agreed to forget it." I say it so fast and string the words together that I'm not sure Esme understood me.

But her lips in an O shape tell me otherwise. "I knew it." She points a finger at me, and she looks like a miner who just struck gold.

I sigh and realize that it feels kind of good to get it off my chest. Then my thoughts drift to images of last night and I feel a giddiness that I'm struggling to keep down. "Don't tell anyone. Especially not Keats."

"Of course not." I give her a warning glare, and she straightens her back. "Really… I promise." She zips her mouth with her fingers.

"Listen, we got out some tension, and we agreed it was a one-night kind of thing. This weekend is for my brother, so we can move on."

Her smile drops. "Is that really what you want?"

I give her a reassuring look. "It's for the best. I would rather have him as a friend than lose him because we don't work out."

"Liar."

"Esme, please, let's just focus on champagne, cake, and watching some distant uncles get drunk on the dance floor."

She crosses her arms over her chest. "Okay, if that is really what you want."

"Yes."

She steps forward to touch my arm. "Then your wish is my command."

"Great. I'm starving and I won't make it a late night. I need energy for tomorrow."

"You do look a little worn out," she taunts.

I bug my eyes out at her, and she holds her hands up by her shoulders. "What?" she squeaks. "I mean it, really. I'm not sure where your mind is at." I'm not sure I believe her but fine. Either way, she's right, which is why I grab my foundation pen for an extra coat under my eyes.

We have a restful silence between us, and because it's out in the open, I can snort a laugh to myself. "I did pack lace pajamas… but they never even left my bag."

She smiles at me. "Naked also works."

"I'm sore, too."

Her mouth curls with a grin. "Most women wouldn't complain about that."

I shrug. "I'm not."

Esme looks in the mirror with me and her face turns serious. "As long as you are happy with your decision to leave it at one night, then I will leave you alone about it."

I push down the thoughts I shouldn't have. The disappointment that the fantasies outside of bed are not realistic. "I am."

"Okay. Then let the wedding weekend begin!"

My mother strides straight to me when I enter the restaurant. Her dark blue dress is clingy yet respectful, and her dyed blonde hair is up in a bun. "There you are." She touches my arms as if she needs to check that I'm here in the flesh.

I paint on a smile. "Yes. I made it."

Her hand finds her heart. "Thank goodness Oliver could drive you. We weren't sure you would get here in time." Oliver is a staple at family dinners and parties. My mom eats up Oliver's over-the-top charm, even though I'm sure he just throws it on to piss Liam off.

"Well, crisis averted. Anything I can do to help?"

My mother huffs. "Ava's parents are micromanaging quite a bit, so I would hate to interrupt that." I hear the annoyance in her tone.

"Just imagine how it will be if Liam and Ava ever have kids. You might have to battle it out for the title of grandparent extraordinaire."

She begins to play with her necklace and a smile appears. "Careful, or I'll remind you that you didn't bring a plus-one."

I smile tightly at her. "Would it matter? I have bridesmaid responsibilities and a speech to give."

She touches my shoulders. "Very true. Just be sure to work the room and dance with who you want." My mother isn't pushy about my dating life, even if she loves to introduce me to potential guys. She is curious about my dating life, though.

My gaze drifts over her shoulder to the bar, and I see Oliver accepting a glass of wine from the bartender while a woman with overdone white teeth seems to be talking his ear off. She's a little too touchy-feely, and he seems so obviously uninterested.

"Did you hear me?" My mother snaps her fingers in front of me, and my attention runs back to her. "I'll throw a BBQ after their honeymoon. Something casual. Just Liam's friends and some family. I think Oliver has a birthday coming up, and I'll bake his favorite angel food cake for the menu."

My lips roll in as I don't dare inform her that Oliver hates that cake and just tries to be polite every time she offers it. Besides, who the hell prefers angel food for a birthday? My mother often gate-crashes any cookout or group dinner at my brother's. It's incredibly funny that she wants to hang with the "cool kids" as she calls us.

"Sounds sweet of you." The scene behind her keeps grabbing my attention. I have an internal instinct to march on over and rip the extensions out of teeth lady's hair. Luckily for us all, I'm classy. "I should probably say hi to everyone and find Liam, okay, Mom?"

"Of course. Don't forget the cousins from Florida are here."

"I'll say hi." Stepping away from her, I approach Oliver and doll lady. He peers up mid-sip from his wine and double-checks when he sees me. He seems pleased by my appearance.

I arrive, and they both look at me curiously. "There you are, Oli." I've never once called him that but maybe that's the indication for him to know that I'm going to try and save him. "I was getting concerned that you overslept from your nap." I set my hand on his shoulder, pretending to brush a piece of lint before I lean into him. Blondie's eyes travel between Oliver and me.

"Aren't you the groom's sister?"

"Yes, I am, and you are?" My smile holds a hint of warning.

"Tracy. I'm Ava's cousin from California. Oliver was telling me about his job. He's successful and easy on the eyes, right?" She winks at Oliver, and I want to claw her eyes out.

Oliver's smile is strained. "Did you need me for something, Hails?" Oliver asks, and I can hear that he is improvising, proven by the fact that he never calls me that either.

"Why yes, I do. I think we're supposed to go practice our speeches for tomorrow. We lost the napkins that we wrote them on... *last night*." I dagger my eyes at Tracy. Last night can be her interpretation, but it gets the message across, as her face falls.

"Right. Oh. Well, I guess I should go find my parents. Good luck, you two." She scurries away, and I hear Oliver chuckling under his breath.

Removing my hand, I step in front of him with a straight face. "She was peachy."

There is a glint in his eyes that informs me that he is on to me. "Saving me?"

"Yes." I cross my arms over my chest.

"Not feeling a little jealous?" He holds up his long finger and thumb to show size.

I swallow, reminding myself of our agreement. "No," I lie. "You're not mine to claim."

He scans the room before stepping dangerously close to me, invading my air. "I wouldn't be asking except my cock was buried deep inside you last night."

There.

That does it. I'm molten and my legs are turning to liquid. I want his breath that dances across my skin to cascade down my body.

"Oliver," I warn him. "It has nothing to do with that." Because I've always been jealous, even before last night.

"I'm calling bullshit on that, but you're right." He sighs. "It shouldn't matter. We're in a room full of people, and I need to detox from you."

I've invaded his thoughts and body that much? I like that.

His eyes meet mine, and it's a tether that we just can't seem to cut. "I'll go schmooze the crowd so we both can cool off."

He nods curtly. "Probably a good idea."

Walking away from him, I feel his eyes on me, and it's a weight. That just means it's harder to run.

THE REHEARSAL DINNER WAS UNEVENTFUL. A few sappy speeches from parents, a buffet, and I worked the room to speak to distant relatives, colleagues of my brother, Ava's family, and probably a cousin of a cousin. It was easy to slip away and go to bed with only a few glances from Oliver during dinner. I escaped unscathed.

But now? As we all stand on the gorgeous rooftop overlooking mountains as my brother recites his vows and the audience of eighty look on, I do the stupidest thing that a single bridesmaid could do.

I catch eyes with the single best man.

The softest stretch of his lips causes the corner of my mouth to tick. He's handsome in a tux, and his eyes review my deep gray gown and burn right through me. I don't think that's his intention, but we can't seem to rip our eyes away until we are broken from our daze by Ava's ordained friend moving on with the ceremony.

My focus returns to my brother who looks utterly happy and Ava who is in a strapless gown. They're officially in the newlywed phase and will enjoy the excitement of their new relationship dynamic. I also know that my brother will be a good husband. He has a strong character and will do anything for her.

A tear pools in the corner of my eye at this special moment for my brother and how fortunate he is to have found his soulmate.

It's a beautiful wedding with bubbles blown as they walk down the aisle, and when it's photo time, I notice the groomsmen already passing out cigars.

"Okay, I need the happy couple in the middle." The photographer indicates with his hands. "Now that we've had a few photos with the wedding parties on each side, let's mix it up so we have groomsmen then bridesmaids and so forth." Everyone shuffles around as he continues to direct us. "You, closer to the best man," he says so easily.

I glance over my shoulder and Oliver doesn't seem to be complaining; in fact, his hand touches my waist, and he pulls me closer because that's what we are instructed to do. My entire core feels as though it just did a summersault.

"You look beautiful," he whispers so only I can hear.

I've heard that many times today but only from his mouth does it feel special and sincere.

"Thanks. You're not too bad yourself," I utter back.

I'm lucky we are only looking forward as there's probably a sinful smirk crawling on his lips.

His hand slides back to touch my hipbone gingerly and keep me in place. I'm beginning to wonder if he is using this innocent opportunity to touch me, maybe even remind me.

After various smiles for the photographer, Oliver has no choice but to drop his hand, leaving a vacant spot.

I refuse to turn around and look at him, and I'm saved by one of Ava's happily married cousins in the bridal party asking Oliver a question.

I'm also spared when Oliver is seated a good distance from me at the table for dinner. I keep myself occupied with conversations with other people until the wedding planner gives me the indication to deliver my speech. I down a sip from my glass of champagne for my big moment and take the microphone in my other hand.

Someone clinks a glass, and the room grows quiet as I stand. I'm not shy in front of people, but this is the one time that I can't mess this up.

"Hello, everyone. For those of you who do not know me, I'm Liam's sister, Hailey." I glance to my brother who has the warmest of smiles, while his arm is draped across the back of his new wife's chair. "My brother has done the unthinkable and actually found a woman who found him bearable past the appetizers." It earns me a little chuckle from the audience.

"But seriously, you two are perfect for one another. A year ago, Liam told me he was going to pop the question, and this guy didn't do traditional. He decided to propose in costume as a gangster from the 20s because Ava loves murder mystery parties. They actually got engaged under different names. Mr. and Mrs. Feathers, I believe it was… and don't worry, they weren't the murderers either."

My brother's grin is ear to ear. "My brother has been my protector, my friend, the guy I can count on, and I see that he can do that for someone else too. Liam wanted everything to be perfect for his new bride. So much so that he demanded I drive across the country the very second my flight was canceled in order to get here." For the briefest of seconds, I catch Oliver staring at me with what I could swear is fondness, but I swing my eyes back to Liam.

"I know you two will have a long life together. Hopefully, you actually remember tonight because I hear a rumor that mezcal is on the menu, and we know how Ava gets. After all, that's how she managed to get past the appetizers with my brother on their first date. To Liam and Ava." I lift my glass, and everyone cheers.

I walk straight to my brother for a big hug. "Your speech was classy enough. I love ya, Sis," he tells me.

Ava smiles when she hugs me. "It was sweet."

I head back to my seat, passing Oliver the microphone as he stands.

The room grows quiet again, and the attention is on Oliver.

"For those of you who haven't met me yet, I'm the best man, Oliver. Liam and I go way back. I believe he chose me as best man because he felt my speech would be safer than if Keats delivered it." Everyone laughs, and Keats shouts out some refute. "Uh, Liam." Oliver turns his attention to my brother. "You have a heart of gold, the mouth of a sailor, and who the hell knows what kind of husband you will be. But I'm certain that you will make us all want to take notes.

You're both about to embark on a road trip across the country. I'm sure Liam would kill a bear for you too, Ava. And I have no clue if you plan on resurrecting Mr. and Mrs. Feathers for…" Oliver glances at my parents who are smiling, "absolutely G-rated activities."

Luckily, my parents find it funny, and my brother buries his face in his hands to hide a giant grin. "The point is, you two have a lot of fun together, and we would all be fools not to see how much you love one another. I have zero experience to back it up, but my guess is that you two are the recipe for a long marriage, and I wish you the best."

I don't take notice when he gives them hugs or when everyone drinks another sip of champagne. It's only when Oliver catches my eye with the same curiosity as my own that my haze breaks.

The music pumps up, and as everyone fills the dance floor, he slowly approaches me.

"Come on." He offers me his hand.

My face screws up, and it causes him to smirk. "You're supposed to be on detox from me."

"I believe it's normal for the bridal party to dance together," he highlights coyly.

My eyes flutter, and I swallow because my mouth feels dry, but reluctantly, I take his hand and we make our way to the dance floor.

"Nice speech. Winged it, huh?" I goad him.

"You did too, and we both kept the room laughing and emotional, so we succeeded."

Immediately, he twirls me around, and the smile that hits me nearly hurts. "Didn't take you for a dancer."

"I'm not. You're drawing attention from the bar, and I thought I would save you." He indicates to the side, and I look to see one of the guys by the bar who I remember mentioned they were a former frat brother of Liam's.

"Ah, here I was thinking that you wanted to dance with me for other reasons."

He tips me back then pulls me tight to him when I come up. "Shh. I'm not supposed to admit that."

It causes me to blush, and I make a mental note to find a shot of something strong soon. "Well… you might be able to convince me to keep that secret," I taunt.

"Oh yeah?" Interest floods his face. "What might that take?"

Before I can answer, my brother appears, still dancing with Ava.

"Your brother's ballroom lessons paid off," Ava gushes.

"I'm happy you found someone decent to dance with," my brother tells me. For a millisecond it sparks my attention.

My eyes travel between Liam and Oliver. Liam is all fun, while I can't help noticing that Oliver's face is more hardened.

"Not so bad," I reply politely.

"Good. He's a keeper." Again, my eyes ignite from his words, only to be deflated when he opens his mouth again. "He's number one on my team to ensure you're closely guarded tonight."

Ava swats him, and Liam winks at Oliver.

They sway away, and the mood to dance vanishes.

"So, that's my brother." I quirk my lips out.

"That he is," Oliver confirms. "We didn't need that reminder," he echoes what I'm thinking, because our few minutes of dancing just had cold water thrown on us. Oliver steps back, and my arms fall from his shoulders in the process. "I think I'm going to grab a drink."

"Oh… right."

He can't get away from me fast enough.

Luckily, Esme arrives with a shot of alcohol for me. "It's lemon-flavored, they say."

I knock the shot back into my throat. "I don't care." It's time to let loose.

"You know he couldn't stop looking at you. During the ceremony, dinner, basically the whole day. I bet if I search over your shoulder, he will be pretending not to be staring at you."

"Who cares. Will you go to the bar for me? Get me another shot or two. This is a celebration."

The song changes to something upbeat, and we both set the glasses on a table nearby then head to the middle of the busy dance floor. I'm not sure how many dances it was until I ditched my shoes, or when I decided that I would rather sip champagne than down shots. And now I'm being dragged to the dance floor where a row of women wait with great enthusiasm while my sister-in-law has her back to us.

"Why am I here? Am I not competition if you want to get the bouquet?" I ask Esme.

She throws me a playful look. "Oh, I'm all good. I don't need flowers to tell me I'm next to be married. But I need to be out here to block others, because you, my friend, are catching those roses."

I laugh at her. "What?"

"You've always told me how much you love weddings and all of the traditions."

I study the overenthusiastic women behind me while the room watches. Looks like I'm joining them in the fun.

Vaguely, I hear my sister-in-law counting, but I'm too distracted by the two women to my left reaching up in the air, trying to block one another. It's only when I look forward that something lands in my hands without much effort.

Glancing down, I see that I caught the bouquet. Or rather, the flowers fell into my hands.

And when I glance up, I see Oliver across the room at the bar with a wry smile and his eyes pinned to me.

OLIVER

Sipping my whiskey as I lean against the bar, I watch as Esme and Hailey whiz away from the dance floor, and I'm wondering why my eyes haven't torn away from the spot where they were just standing.

A nudge of my arm causes me to glance at Keats who is indicating to the barman for the same drink as me.

"I've figured it out, you know." He grins.

"What may that be?" I reply flatly.

He throws me an "oh really" look. "So, when is Liam going to find out?"

Now, that causes my attention to snap to him. "Find out?"

His cheeky smirk tells me enough. "Point proven. Let me guess, you had an eventful road trip."

I can't deny it with him, and I could use an ear. "It was. The road trip, however, is over."

The barman hands him his drink, and we clink glasses. "And?"

Now, I just look at him like he is crazy. "She's Liam's sister."

"And?" he continues to press.

"The guy would kill me, and let's not have him convicted of murder on his wedding weekend. Besides, there are far too many risks if Hailey and I are just that… a little fun."

His hearty chuckle has me scanning the area because it draws attention to us. "A little fun? Are you kidding me? You just spewed out some lies there. But hey, you keep being miserable in that little world of yours."

"I'm not miserable," I defend. "I have work, friends, I might even get a dog."

Keats seems skeptical as he rests against the bar with ankles crossed. "Sure. I'm just saying that maybe let down a wall or two. Liam will be away on his honeymoon for a few weeks, and it's a stressful time at work. It's a good time to have someone make you laugh, and so be it if it involves no clothes."

Glaring at him, I need to wrap this conversation up. "Maybe you should go focus on your girlfriend who didn't catch the bouquet yet will still probably bring up the topic of marriage about ten times tonight."

Keats glimpses cooly down to his drink then back to me. "Not a concern. I'm popping the question next week, actually. Besides, she didn't catch the flowers… Hailey did."

Rolling my eyes, I struggle to keep my smirk from inching wider. "That is the case."

He winces when he sees something over my shoulder. "Eek. I think Sam is about to do the worm on the floor." I follow his line of sight and see one of the groomsmen heading to the floor.

"Hazards of it getting late. I'm going to grab some air." I begin to loosen my tie as I walk through the crowd of people chatting, drinking, dancing, or simply sitting at tables trying to solve world peace.

When I reach the outside roof terrace, I'm relieved with

the breeze and noise floating into the background. A few people are out here chatting quietly, but it's my internal magnet that leads me straight to Hailey who is sitting on a lounge sofa and seems lost in thought.

My feet are already taking the steps before I can even contemplate. "Is the spot next to you free?"

The hanging lights give enough glow that I'm able to see her warm eyes sparkle. "It is."

She scoots over, and I join her, our bodies touching as there is only so much space. Leaning forward, I rest my elbows on my thighs, and my hands hang between my knees. "Good catch."

Hailey glances down to the flowers in her hand. "I wasn't even trying."

"Still. Just a shame that you have about ten women back in there who are not impressed."

"Oh, I know. Who knew it was such a vicious sport."

A few seconds of silence surround us, except it's peaceful. "Are you having fun?"

"Yeah. Why wouldn't I be? It's a happy day for my family."

"Good. It's a party, that's for sure."

She chuckles softly. "Is this you trying to make small talk? We can let certain memories go, it's fine." I hear a little agitation in her voice.

"No. It's not that. Literally, I came out here for some air and you just so happened to be here wanting the same."

"Okay." She bounces her eyes to the flowers in her hand and back to me. "I'm not sure why I'm carrying this around."

"Because you're reflecting on the fact that you will be a beautiful bride one day."

My words cause her eyes to flare slightly, through me even. Maybe she knows that the thought of her with someone else makes me bananas or that she'll… never be *my* bride.

"I'll take the compliment, I guess." She presses her lips together and slides her gaze to the lights hanging over the balcony edge. "You're a good guy, Oliver."

"So I've been told."

She bumps my arm with hers. "It's not a bad thing. Besides, I know you have another side to you."

There is our reminder of our road trip, and she realizes it, too.

Hailey bites the corner of her mouth and pauses for a second. "I think I'm going to go find my brother and say good night. We still have the brunch tomorrow for out-of-town guests."

I glance at my watch and it's nearing midnight which is bordering on questionable. "I might do the same."

She laughs as she stands and offers me her hand to pull me up. "Because that won't be obvious."

Now I want to challenge her. "Obvious of what, Hailey?" I close our distance when I stand, and I notice the movement of her chest because whether we want to say it or not, our sexual tension is still there.

"Oliver, don't overthink everything. I'm not someone on the other side of a contract who needs to be broken down into every little clause. Sometimes, a lack of words sends the message."

I smirk just like I always do when she spews out legal references out of her mouth. Add her confidence and it only gives her another point. And the message that I'm reading now has me teetering on an edge.

It's up to me to act on it or not.

Hailey walks away, leaving me to ponder for a few seconds with my hands in my pockets as I watch her in the distance. A feeling washes over me that I'm not used to. I settle into the heavy feeling for far too long.

It's a few minutes later when I spot Hailey with her brother, giving him a hug. I meander their way and catch the tail end of their declarations of sibling love.

Liam notices me and opens his arms. "There's my guy." He drags me into their hug. "I'm so thankful that you guys made it. I would have freaked out if you didn't."

His words are meaningful but slightly slurred at the end. I'll let it go since it's his celebration. "Anything for you." Including keeping the honor code, except for one misdemeanor.

"One day when Hailey gets married and one day when you get married, I'll be there ready to deliver speeches."

"Liam, you should consider water. I hear it's amazing." Hailey beams as Liam keeps his arms looped around our shoulders.

He points his glass of scotch at his sister. "Where is my wild-spirited sister? We should get you a shot. The entire male population of Ava's family has been warned away from you, but a shot is fine."

Hailey laughs over the music, and it's a good-for-the-soul kind of sound.

"Guys, I'm so happy you are in my life. I would hate if anything came between us." The amusement of his current celebratory state just hit a little too close to home.

"That's my cue to leave. Don't be too hungover tomorrow. You have to endure pancakes and conversation." I slap my hand on his back.

One last hug and Hailey loudly whispers good night into his brother's ear before he moves on to the next group of friends walking by. Hailey abandons walking by my side, and I let it go.

But when I'm about to press the button for the elevator, she appears with a panting breath and heels dangling from her fingers. "Sorry. I didn't mean to be rude and disappear. Forgot these at the table." She holds up her shoes.

My thumb brushes along my jawline, wondering what the hell is the next move for these unusual few days, because the original plan doesn't seem to be a solid one.

"The elevator is super slow right now. Someone from the front desk is looking at it," one of the guests says in passing on his way back to the reception.

"Stairs it is." I cock my head to the side and study Hailey's feet.

"All good. My feet are happy when no straps are involved. They might be a little dirty when I get downstairs, but you've seen me dirty." She smirks slyly with pride. I don't sense she is drunk, tipsy maybe. Either way, enough to be flirty and not freak out.

My head lolls low while I quietly grin to myself. "I think I should kill you for making that comment and taking us there."

"To where?" she says, playing clueless.

She pivots on her feet, and I follow. We get to the stairs and head down.

"In case, you were not worn out enough from the last few days then let's add steps," I comment sarcastically.

"Who cares. I'm going to crash into bed. Sleep is under-rated, and after the brunch tomorrow, I head back to Illinois. You're going on to your hockey meetings, right?"

When we reach our floor, I hold the door open for her. "Correct. I'm not back until next week, so it's a perfect example as to why getting a dog is not in my cards."

We slowly walk down the hall, side by side, the silence

pulling a string from my center up to the ceiling, nipping at my chest in the process.

Our doors are across from one another, and it would be easy to say good night and both enter our rooms at the same time.

Except we reach our destination, and when she pulls out her keycard to swipe, it only takes a second for me to check right and left. There is no one in sight which means we're invisible.

Which is exactly why when that little green light flickers, I urge Hailey forward and follow her into her room while she voices a sound of surprise, only for me to slam the door shut with my foot.

The moment she turns to me, dropping her shoes in the process, our lips crash together.

She rips my loose bow tie away from my neck as I walk her back.

"One more night. I get to have you one more night," I breathe into her ear as my fingers begin to slide the straps of her dress down, giving me ample opportunity to kiss the slope of her shoulder.

"Please," she pleads as she begins to fumble with my belt. "I want you inside of me."

I chuckle sinisterly against the skin of her neck. "What a coincidence. I want that too," I deadpan. "Now turn." I square her shoulders to move her faster.

She lifts her hair while I unzip the dress. I'm cruel to myself and drag the zipper slowly down, admiring her bare back and the curve where her hips meet her waist. I kiss the blade of her shoulder just as the dress pools at her feet.

"Your body is heaven."

Hailey hums a sound as she sneaks her hand behind her and between our bodies. She dives into my boxer briefs to grip my length, and I moan into the back of her neck. "And your body wants me," she whispers.

I'm not gentle when I push her onto the bed, but her squeal and smile inform me that she doesn't mind one single bit. We both hurry to get completely naked, and her thighs part, welcoming me.

We are in too much of a rush for foreplay. Instead, I delve into her with her body lifting on the first thrust. Her warmth around my cock always causes me to stop and soak in the feeling of taking her bare. I get to touch every single hidden corner of her body. When she clenches around my shaft, I feel the connection of how much she wants this too.

"This probably isn't a great idea, but it's also kind of fantastic. You feel so good," she cries out as I hit her deep on my last thrust.

Hovering over her body, I capture her mouth and flick my tongue against hers.

"Tonight, you'll take every last drop from me like the good girl that you are."

Her body bucks, and she murmurs a sound. "Fuck, your words."

I move faster inside of her. "I have plenty more for you."

But none of them convey what I really want.

––––––––

My body stirs, and I feel weight in my arms as I adjust to the daylight peeking through the curtains. It doesn't take long for me to remember last night because I'm spooning against Hailey's body, naked the way she should be.

Either she was already up or we seem to have synced our clocks, because she yawns and begins to wiggle in my hold.

She stills for a second before looking over her shoulder, and her lips part softly when she sees me.

"You're still here." Her voice is far too neutral. Not sure if that was a good or bad statement.

"I am. Or should I have disappeared?"

The corners of her mouth gently pull up as she slides up to sitting. "No, I mean. Wait…" She rubs her forehead as she twists her words. "I meant it more as a statement, not in surprise or disappointment."

I sit up and rest against the headboard. "That's a relief." I reach for my phone, ignoring the new alerts on my home screen of work emails. The time is what I'm after, and it's not in our favor. "We have a brunch to be at in about twenty minutes."

Hailey groans. "Shit. Forgot about that. I need to get ready."

There is no time to dawdle, so I swing my legs out of bed and search for my clothes that are on the floor. "I need to go do my three-foot walk of shame back to my room to shower and get ready."

She scoffs humorously. "Shame? Gee, thanks."

Pulling my boxer briefs up, I'm quick to come sit on the edge of the mattress near her. "It was a joke. I do need a shower, though. Didn't exactly plan on not sleeping in my room."

"Fair point. I would say join me in the shower but that will just add a whole other level of complications to our stellar life choices lately." Her face turns slightly panicked. "This." She gestures to me then back to her with her finger. "We weren't supposed to sleep together last night, and…"

I touch the ends of her hair and comb it behind her shoulder, needing a way to feel her against my skin. "We did what we did. I don't regret it, but we can't—"

"Yeah, I know."

Our eyes tie in a knot of thick silence, but we foolishly accept the situation.

I rub her arm once. "I'll see you later at the brunch, okay?"

She throws me a weak smile. "Yeah, I need to go scrub and throw on clothes."

This is normally when people in a relationship based on mutual benefits normally escape one another, but that's not Hailey. She deserves one more kiss, and I steal that from her.

"Go away. I'll never leave this bed if you do things like that," she warns me with a grin.

I hold my hands up in surrender. "I'll be on good behavior the moment that I stand." Standing up, I half-smile.

But leaving her in bed isn't the highlight of my morning.

———

RACING TO THE ELEVATOR, I adjust my collar. I'm already later than planned. I see Keats and Esme holding the doors open.

"Good morning, you two," I greet them.

"Wait!" The sound of Hailey's voice prevents us from hitting the button to close the doors.

She too joins us. She throws me a nod then gives a lopsided smile to Esme and Keats.

The doors close, and the quiet is unnerving.

I stay intent on staring forward, and in the corner of my eye, I sense that Hailey is doing the same. It also feels like we have watchers, but I refuse to glance at our friends.

"Seems we all had eventful mornings," Keats comments and smiles wryly.

I shoot him a death stare because he is privy on the details of my road trip.

"I hope there are waffles. I'm dying of hunger," Esme says while she no longer takes notice to the rest of us.

Hailey nervously rolls her lips in and seems to study the numbers lighting up above the door.

"I bet Oliver has worked up an appetite." Keats smiles cheekily at me now.

"Keats," I mutter through my teeth.

Hailey zooms her gaze to Esme. "You told him?"

"You told her?" I accuse Keats.

Esme raises her arms. "Told who what?"

We all look at one another, but most of all, I'm stuck in a stare with Hailey and our shoulders fall.

"I told Keats about the road trip," I confess.

She winces. "I told Esme."

Esme begins to chuckle under her breath. "Ah, classic. You think Keats and I told one another that you two might have… well… built up an appetite."

Keats joins in with her laughter, but Hailey and I are not amused.

"Can we just not talk about this? It's Liam's wedding weekend, and I just want to focus on omelets." Hailey huffs.

"I kind of feel that I need to have a bet going on of how long it will be before Liam figures out that you two, well…" Keats goads us.

"It was one night!" Hailey and I say in unison, a little white lie. It was two nights, but semantics.

Esme winces. "*Yeah*… not buying that." The elevator dings open, and Keats follows Esme out who stops to glance over her shoulder at us now standing motionless in the middle of the elevator. "Hailey caught the bouquet last night. If you two are looking for a discussion topic." She grins brazenly.

They disappear, but Hailey and I remain, ignoring the fact the doors just closed again.

"I'm sorry. It just popped out of my mouth to Keats. He doesn't know about last night."

Hailey's shoulders sag. "Likewise with Esme."

"Maybe not our smartest move. They will never let this go."

Her cheeks puff before she exhales a long breath. "No pressure or anything," she adds dryly. "This is why we can't be involved." She snaps her fingers. "*Poof.* There goes our friendship group if we fuck up our sleeping-with-one-another skills."

"And even if we didn't, there is…"

"My brother," she finishes, pointing out the obvious.

Our reasons. We've just repeated them. We're all good again and on the same page.

But she's so damn breathtaking even in a simple summer dress that doesn't show any patches of scandalous skin.

Scratching my cheek, I'm aware that we're late, and we have to tiptoe around Liam. "Look, I'm leaving early. I got an email that the team are flying me out earlier for a few meetings. I'll be away for a week. That'll give us plenty of time to reset and leave it all as is."

"Perfect." She tosses me a smile that feels a little overdone, but I can't study further because Hailey presses the open button with a strong prod of her finger. She can't escape fast enough.

Halfway out of the elevator she stops, sighs, and looks at me. "I need to go spend some time with my folks and uncles, didn't do that enough yesterday. But if I don't see you again then have a good trip. Maybe I'll run into you at Foxy Rox when we're back in Everhope."

It all sounds so simple and lacks emotion. That's what it is supposed to be, right?

"Sure thing," I reply, feeling defeated.

I guess we move on.

● 11

HAILEY

Slurping the final drops of my iced latte with oat milk through the straw, I realize that I haven't done much today. It's summer vacation, and while I involve myself in Lake Spark's summer school two days a week, today is not one of those days. Instead, I'm wallowing in coffee in my living room on a Friday.

It's been unbearable the last week if I'm being honest. The wedding weekend was draining on my energy level. Keats and Esme got engaged, which is great, but they are my neighbors, and I have front-row seats to their new status. They have this weird obsession of hanging around the mailbox at the end of the driveway. Sometimes arguing, sometimes completely content. And right now, I'm not in the mood to be reminded of how two people come together and plan a long life.

I debate staying on the sofa to binge a show or consider if eating lunch is a bright idea. I hear the door open and get hit with a cheery presence.

"Yoo-hoo, neighbor. I've stopped by to check on my favorite tenant." Esme waits for me to holler back that she is welcome before she walks in and heads straight to my current spot and plops down next to me.

Not only is she my best friend but she's technically my landlord since she inherited this Victorian house that's fit for a family. She even uses one of the rooms upstairs for her photoshoots. Just means I pay next to nothing in rent.

"Why the hell are you in here instead of out in the world? It's great weather today. Are you still bothered about the other day when that little shit Clay in your class threw something at your back? I mean, no wonder his parents sent him to summer school, brats need to be re-educated on manners."

That makes me crack a smile. "He didn't throw something at me, per se. He was tossing his ball of paper to the garbage can and missed."

"Right." She doesn't believe me. "Is it the building? I mean the preschool one? I heard the potential buyer backed out."

That grabs my interest. "Oh yeah? Where did you hear that?"

"The real estate agent was talking to Sara at the coffee shop."

She wasn't there when I grabbed my coffee earlier.

"That's great news, except it's also not, unless I can fulfil their clauses too. Besides, fate is telling me to let it go."

Her face floods with understanding and she lifts a shoulder. "Maybe only for now."

"Anyhow, it's nice to just relax. Last week was draining. Weddings cost a lot of energy."

Esme thrums her fingers on the back of the sofa, considering what words she wants to let spill out of her mouth. "*So.*" She drags it out. Ah, crap. I just walked right into the topic that I knew was coming. "I know you don't want to talk about it, but I've noticed that you're not unaffected from last week's… events."

Rolling my eyes with a deep sigh, I have to press my lips together to hold back a lack of smile to show all is well.

Everything is okay. Everything is fine. It's in the past. Repeat it to yourself, Hailey.

"There is nothing to discuss. We had our fun, and we'll leave it in the past. We can be friends for the sake of my brother. I'm sure we'll even be normal next time we run into one another on the street."

She has an odd look on her face as she squints. "I can be honest with you, and I will be… You don't want that one single bit. You're also just assuming Oliver wants to return to 'normal,'" she says, using air quotes.

I shake my head. "He does. He was the most adamant that we had what we did and should leave it there."

Oliver has his rules, and I get it because I have the same issue. He's my brother's friend. Things could go wrong. The loss of their friendship. Awkward neighbor down the street. There's a list.

"We haven't spoken or texted all week while he is away for work."

She offers me a soft smile. "But he'll be back later today. I heard Keats on the phone. Around dinnertime, in case you're interested."

Oh.

"And?"

"Hailey, you're a funny woman, but that's also because you're comfortable around people and that takes confidence. You're always bubbly, and everyone wants you around. Don't let Oliver be a reason that you close up into a shell. That's not you."

Her observations are on point today.

"I'm still all of those things. Not my fault that I have a nosy neighbor who shows up and insists that I feel something that I don't," I say, trying to convince myself.

"But you two at the wedding. Even if I didn't know, I would have to be blind not to have seen the way you two looked at each other."

"We've always been like that," I justify and narrow my eyes at her.

She grabs the drink from my hands and attempts to get the last drop through the straw. "Ugh, you added a coconut shot."

I push her arm playfully and smile. "Don't criticize my summer coffee choice."

"Sorry. That took us off track. Anyhow, I've said my piece. You're being ridiculous, and we're strong women, which means stand up for what you want."

Rising up, I walk to the window for a change of scenery. "Message received."

"Good."

"Why don't we focus on your upcoming nuptials? Have you thought about it?"

A sound of joy thunders out of her throat. "I'm easygoing. We don't want to wait long. We'll keep it not so big and probably over in Lake Spark at the Dizzy Duck Inn since Keats's sister has connections there. You'll have to help me pick a dress."

"Of course," I promise.

Esme hops up. "Perfect. Don't make me toss the bouquet at you. Or cause me to send an invite for a plus-one as a guest."

I wave her off, exhausted yet smiling, entertained. "Leave me be."

"I'm going to run upstairs to grab something from my studio then leave. I'll be quick."

"No worries. I need to head to the grocery store then maybe grade some papers."

Her face screws up. "Eeek, that's a boring Friday. Normally, you insist on going for a drink or you're planning a dinner party. Get it together, I need you back to conquering Everhope with me."

"Yeah, yeah, yeah." I shake my head.

WALKING DOWN THE CEREAL AISLE, I smile politely in greeting when I see a familiar face. "Sheriff Carter."

He tries to suppress his amusement as we cross paths. "Why does everyone insist on adding Sheriff to my name even when I'm off duty?"

"Because you make us all feel a teensy-weensy bit in trouble." I stop my cart and lean against the handle.

He tosses his box of bran and raisins into the cart which causes me to laugh. "Hmm, not exactly a riveting choice there, huh?"

"It's a solid cereal option."

"True that."

"Hey, how was your brother's wedding?"

The mention of last week triggers a spark inside of me. And you know what, in a good kind of way. That's what it is.

I smile. "It was special, and my brother is happy."

"Happy to hear. I haven't had a chance to catch up with Oliver after the wedding but that might be a good thing."

"Why is that?"

He amusingly smirks to himself. "I would have to tell him that for the next family dinner, my parents have invited someone's granddaughter. He hates when our parents do that."

My chin juts up from his comment and jealousy whispers

into my ear. "Nobody wants family meddling in their relationships, right?"

"Most of the population would agree with that. It's my fault, though. They have faith that Oliver will find a wife and stay married. I have an ex-wife and have yet to find someone to settle down with." Sometimes I wonder if he still has feelings for Rosie. For someone who is divorced, in general he brings up that fact a lot the times that I've spoken with him.

"Sorry, I consider her a friend. Even if we don't see one another so much anymore." He lifts his brows and shrugs as if it's nothing. I laugh to myself as I recall a tidbit. "Wait, didn't you also once get set up with the wife of the owner of the Spinners?"

His jaw flexes side to side with an awkward grin. "Violet wasn't his wife yet."

I bring my hand to my heart. "I hope that one day you find Mrs. Sheriff again."

Carter rolls his eyes. "She'll be my deputy." Even he realizes how cheesy his joke is, and we both laugh. "Anyhow, I need to head out. See ya around, and if you see my brother before me, then warn him not to answer if our mom calls."

I give him a little salute. "Of course."

My smile drops like an anchor as soon as he doesn't see me anymore. Can't I have a few hours when I don't think of Oliver? Everything around me reminds me of him.

But it's not a coincidence or the fact that Everhope is a small town. It's because of what I feel for him.

I could try and bury it, but it's been one week and my mind is exactly where it was when I last saw Oliver. My entire body still seems to be consumed by him.

It's because I've always wanted more with him. We've been in orbit around one another that I don't think will ever end.

Then I got a taste of what it would be like. And going along with what we think we should do no longer feels like the road I want to take.

There was only one thing I ever wanted when it comes to Oliver, and I'm no longer choosing to ignore it.

Which is exactly why I speed my cart forward, more determined now than ever.

———

SITTING on the steps of Oliver's house, I wrap my arms around my body as there is a small breeze. The light from the street and Oliver's porch is enough for anyone to see that I've been waiting for a while for him to return home.

I'm confident with my choice.

Honesty is the best policy, right?

When I see a car slowing in front of the house, it's obvious that it's Oliver in a taxi. The patter in my chest rockets to record speed as I watch him thank the driver and grab his suitcase.

Oliver notices me right away and stalls for a second as the car drives away, adjusting his carrier bag on his shoulder. He lifts his chin, and the streetlight catches the smolder in his eyes.

I propel myself up from the steps and wait for him to walk closer.

"I wasn't expecting you," he says in that voice that lacks surprise because he's unreadable for my spontaneous visit, but he doesn't seem to mind if I get any hint of where his mind might be.

I stand there in our face-off, and I'd be lying if I said I wasn't nervous, but when he slowly begins to walk my way, it all vanishes.

"I was waiting because…" My eyes dip down then flick right back up. "I don't want last weekend to end."

He slows his walk with his eyes staking my own. When he stops in front of me, it feels as though I'm about to jump off a cliff because I just revealed my wishes. It's in his hands to make it come true or not.

"Hailey…"

12

OLIVER

S he's standing in front of my house, having waited for who knows how long.

And she's right where she should be.

Hailey is more beautiful when she seems afraid. I'm not sure that's something I should enjoy, but right now, she's anxious because she just admitted something that I very much understand.

"Hailey…" Her eyes grow wider in anticipation. The strap of my bag slides off my shoulder, and I let the bag drop to the ground. "I don't want to forget last week either."

Her face relaxes while a droll smile appears on my own. She takes one step closer, as though she's fearful she might break. "Really?"

It causes me to grin. "Yeah, really."

All week, I've been thinking about her. I thought space would be the escape I needed to move on from the wedding weekend, but it only made me realize how much I don't want to be the good guy who follows rules all the time. I want to be *her* guy.

I glance to my right then left, not forgetting that we are

standing in front of my house on Everhope Road. If we're not careful, someone in the neighborhood will spread gossip like wildfire.

I indicate with my head behind her. "Come on."

Her gentle smile sticks as she follows behind me, and I unlock and open the door.

The moment that we're inside with the door closed, I drop my bag, and we look at one another in a whimsical state. Is it still disbelief?

I swipe my thumb across my end-of-day stubble. "So yeah, I don't want to stop sleeping with you or kissing you. But this isn't going to be simple."

Hailey hesitates but treads slowly toward me. "My brother," she states simply.

Our eye contact doesn't break. "He's on his honeymoon for a while. We don't need to worry about that now, right?" I'm trying to convince myself of the logic. Now it's me who takes one foot forward to curl my arms swiftly around her middle to pull her against my body.

"You've been thinking about this?" She's asking a silly question, but I hear the doubt deep underneath.

Smirking, I'm going to have to snap us out of the disbelief that we are on the same page. "All the fucking time for way too long. Only made worse in the last week." I cage her face between my palms and lift her lips to ensure I can perfectly capture them when I lean my mouth down.

It's a deep welcoming kiss. This isn't passion, just purely a kiss of truth. We have a connection beyond the bedroom, and this is our reminder. Our reunion is only a week later, but it feels like way too long.

She runs her hands up my back until they're hanging over my shoulders. Our mouths slant and we mumble calming noises in our mingling breaths. My tongue sneaks between her lips for one circle of her tongue right before we begin to part, only to quickly magnetize back into another kiss. Finally, we pull away, with our lips gently tracing the other.

"I couldn't wait so I sat on your steps," she whispers.

I drag my thumb up the line of her cheekbone. "I noticed. It's a good way to arrive home, to be honest."

"I'm not sure what happens next." She captures my thumb between her teeth before planting a kiss on my thumbprint.

"I've been on a plane all afternoon. Let me shower and we can talk after. You can wait in my bed."

Hailey retreats her head back, her lips in one line, attempting to keep her smile locked away. "Ah, I see how it is. We're going straight to that part."

My long finger lands on her lips to shush her. "One, talking after reunion sex is always a great way to communicate. Two, I don't exactly expect you to leave my bed tonight, so you might as well get comfortable. Three, when I say wait in bed then you wait in bed." I'm half-joking.

She croaks a laugh and blows my finger away. "I can speak and decide for myself, thank you very much... just so happens that *I* want to do all of those things. That's because *I* want to, not because Oliver is demanding." She's teasing me, and I can get used to this.

"But seriously, give me five minutes or just join me in the shower," I suggest.

"I think you know that answer."

And two minutes later we are standing under the stream of hot water with my bathroom steaming up. We face one another with our bodies pressed together and her smile permanently painted on her lips.

"Is this where we are having our conversation?" Her voice floats, echoing in the shower.

I swipe water through my hair as if this is a normal shower, even though there is a woman right in front of me who I get to have for another night.

"Where shall we begin? The part where for a long time I've done things to you in my head that even I couldn't get myself out of jail for, and I'm a damn good lawyer."

"You're not a defense lawyer," she deadpans before she grabs the bottle of shampoo.

"Feisty," I retort.

She flashes me a look of feigned annoyed. "I meant the discussion about the reality of our situation."

I sigh as I switch my demeanor to being more serious. "Your brother is away on his honeymoon for three more weeks," I remind her again.

Hailey focuses on rubbing suds on my chest. "And? What about when he returns?"

"I'm not sure, but he doesn't need to discover our new dynamic, not now. We'll figure out our direction in our own time." I'm a little scared my choice of words lacks optimism.

But then she nods once. "Agreed. We can do that. I also think it's better that we don't tell *anyone* that we've entered fuck-buddy territory." My eyes gawk at her choice of words, and she notices. "We don't have a label, okay? It's hard to title it. But we can keep it quiet. Esme knows about the road trip, but she has no clue about the wedding night or the fact that I've been waiting on your step."

"Likewise for Keats. Plus, I'm not particularly fond of the idea of both of them watching from the sidelines giving commentary."

She bubbles a laugh. "Even when you and I were platonic they gave their views. But yes, let's not give them more ammunition."

"Then there is the neighbor factor," I add to our list while

I rub her slick back with soap, causing her to be tightly glued to my body.

"We live on opposite ends of the street. We'll just get creative on sneaking around. I haven't jumped fences since I was twenty and needed to escape a party, but I'm sure I still have that skill in me."

I study her for a second. "Do I want to know that story?"

"No." She's blunt.

A calm silence fills the air as we look at one another, our eyes in a trance, the smell of mountain-fresh shampoo wafting to our noses and our bodies slippery.

"Now, tell me about your bed? I've never been in your room. Is the mattress up to my high standards? How's the thread count of your sheets?" Here is entertaining Hailey which means we can close the serious discussion and move on.

I walk her back against the tile wall, hooking my hand under knee to raise her leg, and I encourage her to keep it right where I want it and create the perfect opportunity for me to drive straight into her. She flinches but her face remains coy, right until I give her an open-mouthed kiss.

"Silly girl, we need to try the shower first." I give her one vicious thrust which causes her nails to dig into my shoulders to hold on tighter.

"Oliver," she gasps, and it's music when it mixes with the sound of running water.

"Tonight you're mine. Understand?" I'm buried deep inside of her and refrain from pulling out until she answers me.

Her moan causes her to search for her voice because my grip on her hips tugs her harder against me.

"Yes," she whispers.

Satisfied, I begin to move again.

With plans to do this all weekend.

———

HAILEY WAS in a deep sleep when I woke at eight. Peaceful and maybe a little sore from our all-night fuck fest, but it's all worth it. As much as sleeping in should be a hobby for me, it isn't. I don't even know how. It's often that my phone goes off at six with an urgent need to get a player on the team or do a trade. Saturday is usually less work, and luckily, today nothing. I left a note for Hailey that I would be right back because I had no supplies in my house for breakfast.

Now, I'm exiting Foxy Rox with a tray of coffees and a bag of bagels. The place is packed, as I expected for the weekend, which is why I'm in luck that a man holds the door open for me. The sun is shining, clear blue skies, and my mood is fucking peachy, even if I couldn't get a parking spot on Main Street close to the coffee house.

When I walk by the building with the for-sale sign, I stop as soon as I accidentally overhear the real estate agent outside on the phone. I'm trying not to listen, but it'd be obvious if she took any notice. Also, why in the world does she have her phone on speaker?

"Truthfully, I wish that girl who wanted to open a preschool could manage to buy this place. When you brought her through the open house, she was the only one who seemed to be in love with the space. The other offers were nothing of interest. I don't want that couple who is keen on opening a brewery. There are already enough cute places for food and drinks in Everhope."

Molly hums in understanding. "Hailey would be a great move-in. But as I mentioned, she most definitely can't fulfill the clause about marriage."

I can hear the woman on the other end crack a sound. "I know. It's just my grandfather had the clause, then my father, and now it feels it would be taking away tradition."

"I'm not sure what to say. I mean, there is the orthodontist who would like to open his second office. That's a great offer."

It's a few sentences more and I've heard enough, know enough, and hate the situation enough.

Sighing, I need to get out of here. It's just, I continue to mull over the conversation on the drive back to my house. It bothers me. A lot, apparently. Everyone sees the potential, but nobody will move the rocks in the way.

I park my car in the driveway and quickly, with my hands full, attempt to wave to the tired couple next door who are watching their preschool-aged girls draw on the sidewalk with chalk. I can tell they have had an early morning, and I internally wince for them.

Hurrying, I get inside before the coffees get too cold. I can already hear the movement of cupboard doors. Hailey must be up.

A smile quickly hits me when I slow my stride into the kitchen to find her back to me, on her tippy toes, in my shirt and giving me a glimpse of her panties.

I'm an idiot for not giving in to this woman years ago. She's part of the picture of my kitchen, and I want to walk right to her and wrap my arms around her like a warm blanket.

"Not a bad view."

She closes the door and turns to smile at me. "There you are."

I hold up the tray and bag. "Replenishments."

"Oh, thank the heavens." She rushes straight to me and snatches the bag from my hands. She fishes into the bag and pulls out a bagel. "Are you joking with me? Is this your way of trolling me? I don't need the reminder of my kitchen failures."

I laugh, as I didn't think about it. "No way. I just know you like bagels. There's a variety and a container of cream cheese, too."

She squinches her eyes to appraise me to check my sincerity then grins ear to ear before sliding onto a stool at the counter.

"I guess breakfast is more important than a good-morning kiss?"

"Kind of," she jokes.

When I hand her the coffee, I give her a quick peck then circle the counter to grab plates.

"What's on the agenda for today? Boardgames? Knitting? Giving G-rated kisses."

I pause and have to laugh to myself again. This woman brightens every moment.

"None of my ideas include those."

"Good."

There is a brief quiet while she focuses on food, and I grab a knife.

"You know, I ran into your brother yesterday. He mentioned I should probably warn you that your parents might have a new prospect for you on the housewife hunt," she says and smirks to herself, even with her mouth full.

Instantly, my shoulders sink at the reminder of the world's expectations. "Swell." I'm being sarcastic. I'll do things my own way in my own time. "You don't need to worry about that. It's been their scheme for years. I just never had the heart to lie and say that I already had somebody who was by chance always too busy to attend family dinners."

Her head wobbles side to side. "That's one strategy."

I take a sip of my coffee while Hailey chomps down her breakfast. Did I really wear her out that much?

"We can stay locked away in this humble abode all weekend, but I need to grade papers tomorrow night. I have the generation who feel a teacher isn't needed when they have social media to teach them the facts of the world."

She's always upbeat, and I hate to dial it down. "Speaking of teaching…" Awkward lines must appear on my face. "I overheard the owner of that building with the agent. They might have a buyer, an orthodontist or someone like that."

Her chew slows. "Oh." A frown takes over her. "I thought he backed out. Not that it matters."

I'm not sure why I just shared the information or why watching her contemplate all of the ideas in her head feels somber. Probably because it's all in earnest good what she wants. I even briefly think of the kids next door; I think my neighbors mentioned once that they drive two towns over for their girls' school.

Hailey begins to play with her bagel before taking a nimble bite.

I swivel side to side on my stool as a thought deep within whispers, and it builds like a storm brewing until it is large enough to be a tornado that spins right out of my mouth.

"Marry me." My tone is firm.

Hailey's eyes snap to me, and the bagel in her hands drops to the counter in one thud while her eyes grow into saucers.

"Say what now?" Her mouth hangs open.

"You heard me. Marry me."

13

HAILEY

y eyes flicker as I replay in my mind what I just heard, and register that Oliver is standing in front of me with no sign that he's joking.

"Really, what did you just say?"

The only part of my frozen face that moves is my tongue swiping across my bottom lip to capture a bagel crumb, because of course, this strange turn of events happens when I just stuffed loaded carbs into my mouth.

Oliver hops off his stool and steps closer but stops mid-distance to me. "Marry me, Hailey."

It's a few heartbeats of silence. I examine him only to realize that this is apparently a conversation that we're about to have. In that moment, my eyes fire disbelief and I square my shoulders.

"Uhm… we just kind of established last night that you and I can't really define what is transpiring between us and decided to maybe see where things will go, and now we're speeding into marriage?" My face puzzles from confusion. "Dating." I hold one hand up level with my chest. "Marriage." My other hand soars above my head. "Dating.

Marriage. Marriage. Dating." I adjust my measurements through my arms.

That's when a hint of a smile crosses his face, and then he rushes to me while I stay seated. His firm hands cup my face, with his eyes anchoring my own. My entire body races because I can't count the number of times this fantasy has crossed my mind. I'm a hopeless woman with a crush. But right now, something feels as though dream weddings will remain in a box.

"You'll get the building," he states.

Oh, convenience.

"Huh?" That's what I manage to say.

"We can get married and then the owner will give you the building and you can open the preschool. I overheard the owner speak with the realtor. You're so close."

My breath gets caught in my throat. Oliver has so much conviction right now.

"B-but it's m-marriage," I stammer. "What happens… you know… later?"

"We'll get a di— Once everything is officially yours, then we'll figure it out. Hell, I could give you the money, I have it." I shoot him an unimpressed glare because I'm never a fan of flaunting, but it makes him smile because he's aware. "But you need a husband to get this one thing, and you can't do that on your own."

I should stand and break our contact, create distance instead of letting my body and mind sink into the idea. "Getting something because of marriage isn't… I don't know."

"It's also the only way to get the building. Maybe the bank will give you the loan if we're married. Either way, I won't interfere. It's all yours."

Am I in some odd dream that I'll wake up from?

Gathering strength, I break our connection to stand and

walk to the middle of the room, feeling his heated eyes on me the whole time. "Marriage is marriage. What happens in the long run?" I repeat.

His head drops low. "Di— That will be awhile in the future." He didn't finish the word divorce for the second time, but for some crazy indescribable reason, I don't question it. I shove the idea that maybe we'll never get a divorce deep into a dark corner in my mind where a dream has been locked away.

"What's in it for you?" I examine him warily.

He lifts both of his hands and cradles the back of his head as he blows out a breath. Damn it, now I see his chest flexed, and it's distracting.

"Everhope will be happy, everybody thinks it's a great idea. The preschool, I mean. I'll see you hap— Nobody needs to know the details or the fact you have a husband. Of course, maybe once everything is done and dusted then it might reach the public and my parents won't bother me anymore about trying to find me a date, but by then, you will have the building."

I stifle one laugh from that thought. He didn't seem pleased when I reminded him what Carter said about being set up. But it's such a minimal issue, too. Very marginal.

"My brother? Our friends? We literally said last night that we don't need others interfering until we are confident with what we are. Remember? Climbing fences, pretending to borrow cups of sugar, you know, that kind of thing." A grin of bewilderment graces my face.

A lazy smile is painted onto his face before he lifts his shoulders. "Nobody needs to know that we're married."

I titter. "How the hell does that work?"

He saunters my way with what I can only describe as

swagger. Why must he look so damn sexy when he's talking insanity?

He takes hold of a long strand of my hair and twists my lock around his finger. I'm too focused on his lips to meet his eyes.

"You know you can be married without living together. And in Illinois, we can get the license then marry the next day. I'm sure the county courthouse will have openings; they seem kind of bored these days anyhow, with permits for quilt markets."

My throat bobs then I crackle a sound while I mull over this situation.

"People accidentally get married in Vegas all the time. Sometimes to someone they don't even know. You don't always need a logical reason to get married. It's a wild adventure."

No, Hailey. Do not contemplate this.

"You're making no sense, Oliver. Isn't there some law for this that might get us in trouble?"

Then he melts my uncertainty away. He snakes his arm around my middle and abruptly pulls me close. My belly presses against his center, and Oliver has a strange aura of persistence that feels unfamiliar to me. It's heated and tense. Is this what he is like at work? No. It can't be. Because I'm not that to him. Attraction aside, I know I'm not a contract he files away.

"For financial gain, you mean? This isn't exactly that. Plus, it's hard to prove, and besides, there is enough on paper to make it seem that our marriage is real. The thing is, Hailey, most people assume I'm going with the flow of things, not a huge risk-taker."

"Really? Didn't notice since you took so long to kiss me," I reply dryly.

He slants a smirk on the right side of his mouth. "Don't rile me up right now. I have no problem putting a pin in that subject only to punish you later with my hand."

My mouth gapes open because there is no humor in his tone, and admittedly, it's not a bad image.

He continues. "I am a risk-taker. It's just I don't until I cross a line, and then I'm kind of hard to reel in. I've crossed the line with you, so I'm not afraid to get a little spontaneous on this. Take it up a notch."

Well, fuck me. This is what I get now? Oliver leaving me in awe of his tenacity that I've never experienced before with him?

It would be hard for any woman to turn away from this.

The man's eyes are cloudy with a sweltering command.

I breathe through my pursed lips, and he doesn't let me escape his hold, not that I'm trying.

"A secret marriage can't last that long in this town. We have snooping neighbors too."

He plants his long finger against my lips. "I'll make the owner and the agent sign an NDA. We can say the owner dropped the marriage clause if anyone gets wind. I doubt anyone knows about the clause except us and those close to us. It will buy us time, at least until the bureaucracy is in order and you have the keys. Maybe people will find out later —or not." He shrugs.

"Then they will wonder what the fuck we do with our marriage next?" I nearly screech.

He grabs the back of my neck to pull me in, and his warm breath crawls down my skin. "We can play the part until we have clarity about u— It will be easier then," he whispers, and it causes a ripple to dive down my body to between my legs.

"Playing a part isn't what we wanted last night." Disappointment is apparent in my reply.

"I do want us to discover what we are… just… this is a little unconventional."

His lips skirt to my temple. "You've always been the spontaneous one. An explorer. Don't stop now."

The answer is dancing around inside of me. The moves getting heavier, a turn coming natural to the rhythm. Your body sways alone or with someone, it's a flow.

…one that flows out of my mouth.

"Yes," I whisper. Then all the uncertainty of this unusual breakfast morning fades, and I surrender to him with confidence. "Let's get married."

14

HAILEY

Pacing outside the courthouse, I wonder what the hell I'm doing. I stop mid-stride and pull out my lip balm to spread a layer onto my lips. It's sunny out, mid-afternoon, and a weekday. Some county clerk just walked by and dropped a paper and smiled hello when he swooped down to pick it up. This is a normal workday.

Except for me. It's my wedding day.

This isn't how I planned to get married. Not in a million years. It isn't me. I'm missing the long white dress; instead, I'm in a short white cotton dress that I would wear to a BBQ, paired with a light jean jacket. I get points for the white, right? My parents and brother aren't here. Nor friends. My macaroon cake is nowhere to be seen. Sadly, no dog carrying rings, either.

It's all okay because this isn't supposed to be real.

Still, leave it to Oliver to handle everything, and it took only a few days for today to happen.

During the last few days, every time my mind would rocket a thousand thoughts a minute, including backing out, my feelings took over.

I begin to pivot back and forth from nerves, an explosion of adrenaline littering my insides. All I have to do is say one word to stop this, but it also only takes one word to ensure it happens.

That's what has me concerned, perhaps. It's the latter that is screaming inside of me of what I should do.

Oliver has offered me the key to a dream, but it's my dream. I'm not sure why he is insistent if he gets nothing out of this except an escapade and a wife that he can add to his health insurance policy if he wanted. He has hammered me to a wall with no way to run… and I wouldn't want to anyhow.

Fanning my face, I remind myself that we are just two people who enjoy one another, and we're still going at our own pace. Marriage is just on paper. We can even ignore that little detail, right?

My eyes zip toward the sound of fast steps to find Oliver with a swaggering grin highlighted from the sun, and his appearance sweeps away any concerns that I have. He's wearing dark jeans and light blue button-up with his sleeves rolled. It's an image, that's for sure.

"Sorry I'm late. There was a family of ducks stuck on the road halfway between Everhope and my office in Lake Spark. The police officer didn't seem so concerned that people had places to be."

"Not everyone is Sheriff Carter," I wisecrack.

Oliver is a man who is so calm that it spreads straight to me. "True. I would say that I miss his presence right now, but that's not what this is." Right, it's not the real deal, just a logistical marriage. "Ready?" he asks.

"Sure."

His eyes narrow to observe me as his fingertips cup my elbows. "Everything okay? We don't have to do this."

One beat. Two. Three is only for him.

My smile grows. "I'm fine. A secret marriage is something that I always wanted to cross off my bucket list," I joke and nudge his arm.

"Funny. Shall we head in?" He offers me his arm like the gentleman he is, and I hook my own into his. "Just maybe, you know, don't mention the fake-marriage part, just to cover our bases," he mutters.

I shake my head because he doesn't need to highlight that.

We walk together into the room to find an older judge behind a desk wearing a saccharine smile. In Illinois, witnesses are not required, which means one less thing to worry about.

"Hi, Oliver, seems you are already walking her down the aisle," he jokes. It doesn't faze me that Oliver works in law and his brother is police royalty. But I guess a judge can't say what happens inside this room… right?

"Now, Judge Daniels, I know better than to let go of the one for me, no matter what." I notice in my peripheral view that Oliver winked at him.

I laugh inside because Oliver is so over-the-top ridiculous, except he just glanced sidelong at me with his eyes anything but. It strikes behind my heart.

"We'll do the quick version," the judge informs us.

"Kind of like the engagement," I mutter to myself, and Oliver throws me a smirk.

"Wait." Oliver holds a finger up and his other hand probes into his pocket. I'm confused about what he's doing until he pulls out two rings.

My eyes bug out as this didn't cross my mind, or rather I forgot about this detail. In my dream book, a man would have a ring when he actually asks, preferably on his knee in a field with wildflowers.

But then I smile to myself because that would all be

predictable. Oliver is anything but lately, especially as I have no idea what he picked out. I tip my nose up and transfer my weight to one foot to evaluate.

Ah, damn it, they're silver, and one has a little sparkle embedded in the band, and by sparkle, I mean a little stone of the diamond variety.

"Those are a little obvious, and we are supposed to be sec —" My voice goes uneven as my word trail off, and I was just about to admit in front a government official the tiny detail of my marriage. I throw on a smile. "I mean, we're just not a ring couple. It's all the new rage not to wear one."

"That's not us," Oliver chides as he holds up my ring. "You can wear it on a necklace underneath your clothes, and I'll keep mine in my pocket." His smile is contrite because he only wants to win.

I smile tightly. "Clever." And that's kind of a hopelessly romantic idea, which isn't safe for us right now. He slides the ring on my finger, and we both get a look at my finger no longer bare. That will have to go around my neck later for sure. I'll also have to question more why he is so adamant that I have a ring, but perhaps he is right, and we have to keep up the pretenses with the owner of the building.

The judge seems unfazed by our unusual behavior. "Let's get you two married then."

There is a problem when I stand face to face with Oliver and his eyes are glazed with a fondness that feels is only for me. I know my face must be a wistful display of how much I've thought of this.

Even if my brother or our families aren't here, or I'm lacking a dress or a delicious tower of cookies as a cake for the reception. All of that is a speck in this moment because happiness swirls inside of me, even if this type of marriage is not what I intended when I always thought of Oliver.

Being lost in his eyes while he holds my hands is just as good, or it's at least something that isn't bad. Except for the fact that being lost in this moment means that I haven't heard a word of what the judge just said. I think it was something to do with not entering marriage lightly.

Doesn't matter, as we're already at the part where we say I do.

"Vows?" the judge asks.

Oliver and I look at one another awkwardly.

"Legal version will work. We're not a bells-and-whistles kind of couple, unless there is a wind chime around," Oliver responds.

I beam a smile at his reference because it's sweet. It's a little detail that shows that I'm not a stranger from the street.

"So be it." The judge continues.

My head tilts slightly as I lock my eyes with Oliver and feel content. He makes me feel content.

This is going to be one wild story someday.

"Oliver Oaks, do you take Hailey O'Shae to be your wife? To have and to hold in sickness and health. For richer or poorer, as long as you both shall live?"

"I do," Oliver is quick to answer, our eyes not breaking our line.

"And do you, Hailey O'Shae, take Oliver Oaks to be your husband? To have and to hold in sickness and health. For richer or poorer, as long as you both shall live?"

For a millisecond the magnitude of what I'm doing hits. It shouldn't be taken lightly, yet I seem to do just that. I attempt to hide my smirk. "Of course, he saves me from bagels. Yes, I do." Now he is the one with a grin.

"Then I pronounce you husband and wife."

There are no claps or bubbles being blown, only an earie

silence. That is until Oliver kisses me, when a symphony plays in my mind.

I deepen our kiss, my tongue delving into his mouth, and our kiss isn't the same as a day ago. It scares the hell out of me because it's strong and keeps me rooted to the ground. His lips engulf mine, and it isn't until we hear the clearing of a throat that we slowly pull away, remembering where we are.

"I wish you both the best," the judge says.

"Thank you." I smile.

"Thanks. Also appreciate that we keep this between us."

The judge waves Oliver off. "You know I can't say anything. Besides, I'll be too busy focusing on my golf game next time I hit the green with your father."

Inside I curse to myself from how silly that sentence was. Everhope elite at their finest.

"Come on, we need to celebrate." Oliver wraps his arm around my shoulders to guide me away.

When we are outside on the sidewalk, we look at one another, our faces light and nearly blushing.

"That's us married." He clucks his tongue.

"It is." We each appraise the other, trying to figure out what the other is thinking, but it's a fail. "*So…* there is a no-return policy on this, right? No 24-hour window, in case I wake up deciding that you might be a horrible husband," I say in jest, but no line on his face flinches. Not even a smidgen.

"Probably should have asked that before saying 'I do.'" Then the corner of his mouth tilts up, and I know that he's teasing me. "I'll see you at my place since we came in separate cars?" he adds as if it's a normal day.

Still, I nod once in answer. "I'll leave my car at my place

then walk over. Pretend to be power walking for a new form of exercise."

Something gnaws inside of me, grinding down a curiosity of what comes next. Order in food? Watch a movie? Take photos of this blessed union? How funny this day is. There are no rules or guidelines for this.

But I like the new tradition of Oliver kissing my forehead with a chaste kiss but his hands on my arms firm with a warning.

Except we probably shouldn't mix getting physical with a marriage entered into for practicality. In fact, we should keep intimacy out of the equation. It's safer that way, right?

———

"I'M HERE," I call out as I walk into Oliver's house. I breathe to myself because everything *does* feel different, that's already obvious.

It's quiet, and I lift a shoulder. "Hmm, must have already run away from his wife."

But I hear shuffling upstairs, and Oliver must be changing in his room. I guess we can have a normal night just like a few days ago.

I go find him, with nerves swimming in my stomach. When I find him, he's by his dresser unbuttoning her shirt. "Oh good, you figured the front door was unlocked, I forgot to mention." He glances up with a smoldering look, his eyes hypnotizing. "You should have waited outside so I could carry you over the threshold, Mrs. Oliver Oaks."

I crack a small smile. "I'm not even living with you, so I'm not sure it would be traditional."

He throws his shirt to the chair in the corner and now he is shirtless. I tear my eyes away because him being half naked won't help this situation. It only takes a quick glance back to see that he looks curious.

"Everything okay?"

"I think we need to talk about something." Phew, I've started the entry point.

"What might that be?"

My head tilts to the side as I draw my line of sight back to him. "It would be better if we're not physical while we are married." It spews out of my mouth.

His eyes nearly pop out before amusement floods his face. "Funny. Now we're supposed to consummate the marriage, otherwise this isn't real."

"It's not supposed to be a real marriage," I say, flippant.

He studies me, and he seems to be grasping my request as I cross my arms. "Is it really what you want?" His voice thins.

"It's… no… yes. I mean, it's safer. We can't confuse where we drew the lines."

Oliver rolls his lips in and tries to steady his neutral look, but his effort fails. "Hailey, your idea is as horrible as me suggesting we get married, but we're running with it. I'll follow your lead on this one, but I'd be lying if I said you're right. It's not in us anymore to restrain ourselves." He's now sincere.

Oh, fuck it. He's right.

"I'm just scared of what we're doing." My eyes bow down. "This can really mess with us."

"Perhaps, but we were already in that territory when we decided to sleep with each other on our road trip. I'm helping you because I care, and that's where we are right now."

I sigh, and my energy to debate it is gone. "Okay. You make a point. This is just me throwing caution to us, you know?"

"I know."

Our eyes lock in mutual understanding, and then in a split moment, we return to where we were when I entered the room.

Oliver begins to work his belt. If he's going to get comfortable then so can I; I'll just grab one of his shirts. I throw my jean jacket to the side and begin to take off my earrings and proceed with my ring.

"Don't." His tone is sharp.

I glance down then draw my sight back up to him. "I can't let the world see this."

He approaches me with his fierce determination impaling me, and a shiver hits me instantly. "But not right now. I believe it's our wedding night? And I plan on fucking *my wife.*"

Hailey's eyes gleam with blazing interest, while I'm a man with a desire within that's roaring to come out.

Her attempt to end our intimacy failed. I would have followed if it was what she truly wanted, but I saw through her. She is scared that we will mess up any potential that we might have for more. But that theory gets pushed away by my current need.

I take one step and then one more. "Dress off," I demand with a firm voice.

The dress is a problem for many reasons. Besides being the perfect fit that accentuates every slope of her body that I plan to draw on with my tongue, but the dress is white. Wedding dresses are white. I've imagined her always in a dress that she would have spent hours picking out, with a veil, something long, too. I'd be a fool to think that she didn't have a dream wedding somewhere in her head.

But the main problem of a white dress? It reminds me that I married Hailey today, because something inside of me stirred and I asked her to be mine.

Now I have a wife.

I meant what I said the other day. Once I finally cross a line that I've been desperate to cross, then there is no going back, and I go all in. That's probably why I've never touched her; I knew it would unleash me. A decision not to stop with whatever we started the other week was the tipping point. Marriage, however, shouldn't have been on my radar. It's full speed ahead, even for me.

Yet here I am with a beautiful wife.

Pushing away all logic in a situation that I suggested, with indescribable reason as to why I didn't backtrack.

Nonetheless, I kind of want to rip that dress to shreds. Naked or not, Hailey is gorgeous, and naming her my wife doesn't sound bad at all.

Call me traditional but her listening to her husband is how this is all going to go right now.

A sultry smirk ghosts her face as she slides her fingers underneath the straps that are already loose below the curve of her shoulders. She slowly drags one strap off and then the other, until the dress pools on my floor by her feet and she's left wearing only white lace panties.

White.

That color is beginning to taunt me as a memento of today, which to most is kind of fucked up for normal standards, and I treated today like a normal day at the office.

Until I said I do.

A sudden possessiveness and twist of satisfaction that I get to be her husband briskly breezes through me. Surely, it's because I care for her, always have, and even when she makes no effort, she's always painfully beautiful.

And now she's unconventionally my wife.

With our eyes not breaking contact, she steps out of the dress, waiting for further instruction.

I grip her arms and turn her to press her back against my front in a flash, causing her to release a quiet yelp.

"You'll listen like the good wife that you are," I whisper heavily into her ear, and her body sinks into my touch.

"Yes, Husband." I hear the smug smirk in her voice because she's playing along.

But I'm not playing a game right now.

I widen my stance, encouraging her to wobble forward as I keep our bodies glued. Her legs touch the foot of the bed, and I nudge her calf, causing her knees to drop onto the mattress. She is now on all fours.

Planting one palm splayed down by her belly button, my other hand cups her breast to fondle, and her nipples are hard as pebbles. She draws in an audible breath from the touch.

"I wonder if you're needy in a different way now," I say against the back of her neck, causing her head to ease down.

"Oliver," she softly grits out.

Abandoning her nipple that I twist once, I skate my fingers up to gingerly brush her hair to the side, and my lips feather kisses down the curve of her shoulder. "Is that a yes, Husband, I want your cock even more?"

I half-circle around her head and kiss her because she meets me halfway. It's a firm kiss, and her tongue delves into my mouth for our tongues to duel. I don't waste a second as soon as our kiss breaks.

I slide my palm down her belly to let her panties glove my hand, allowing my fingers to swipe along her pussy, surprised at the way her juices coat my skin.

"Ahh, so you do want me even more. You're soaking," I rasp. I guide her up to her knees, bringing her back against my front. My other hand returns to her breast, and I have her still firm in my grasp with her breath thick with pleasure.

Circling her clit, she attempts to find stability and touches the sides of my body. "Tsk-tsk, Wifey. Those arms need to be up and circled around my neck." She doesn't hesitate, and the moment her arms wrap around me, her body elongates, making it even easier to drive her crazy.

I slip one finger inside of her, and she squeezes instantly around my flesh.

"That feels too good," she hums. "More."

I'm so thankful that Hailey isn't shy in the bedroom because I keep going. Another finger and I lick and kiss her neck, and I pinch her nipple with a little extra force which causes her to yelp then moan.

"There is something about you right now that has me about to lose it." I push her forward until she is on her hands and knees. Lowering myself, I lick her from behind over the lace of her panties with one sweep of my tongue.

"Fuck, Oliver."

I still mid flick of my tongue. "Yes, Wife?"

"Can my husband just skip this? I need you inside me." It's a torturous plea.

Gently spanking her once, I dig my fingers into the skin of her ass. "I haven't even done anything yet," I say as I skim her panties down her thighs with urgency before pushing her back to all fours and kissing her pussy and returning to exactly where I was, this time my tongue diving inside of her to flick against her walls.

I'm completely drowning in wanting to do everything with her.

Noticing that her hands are clawing the bed, I smirk to myself with pride. "There is something about you writhing under me that's dangerous. I might take you to the edge then stop as punishment."

"No. Don't do that," she weeps and pants. "I want to come on your cock."

With that, I lean forward and stuff my fingers into her dirty mouth, and she sucks instantly. "I want that too, but it's our wedding night," I taunt her.

I kiss down her back, appreciating every inch of her dewy soft skin, pausing at the bottom of her spine and feathering her skin with my lips. My fingers find home on her pussy again, and I can't help but tilt my head to examine her. "Hailey, you're glistening wet."

"Isn't that how I'm supposed to be on my wedding night?" she coyly reminds me.

Taking hold of her hips, I flip her body so she's on her back staring straight into me. Her eyes are hazy with lust, and I'm beginning to wonder if we should really be playing this game of wedding night. It's roleplay, isn't it?

But fuck it. I'm going to reap every second of getting to call her my wife.

She nibbles on the tip of her finger with a lazy smile painted on her lips, watching me as I strip naked from any clothes that I still have on. I'm between her legs in no time, abruptly shackling her one arm above her head against the mattress. She reaches between us to stroke my cock, and my eyes close for a second, only to see her soft eyes speaking to me in a silent language.

Her body rocks up and rolls against my length as we slow our pursuit of exploring each other's bodies. Our lips chase one another, tracing an unknown path.

Something inside of me ignites, and suddenly, my wish to fuck her senseless is replaced with a tenderness that is confusing.

I hover over her and rest on my forearms against the mattress to frame her face. She attempts to kiss me while I settle between her legs that she butterflies out. I trail my mouth down to the base of her throat and feel her pulse pounding.

"Oliver," she begs, her words scraping from her throat.

"Shh," I tell her in a long hush as my lips drag until I latch onto a nipple. Both nipples get the attention they deserve as I take my time.

But I feel the tip of my cock press against her center and gravitating toward entering her drenched pussy.

She guides me straight into her, and we sync on the first thrust, with her mouth softly biting into my arm causing me to let go of her breast.

I start slowly but speed us up, with Hailey breathing into my neck. Our bodies mold as we move together, and our kisses are randomly placed.

Her moan is a driving force for me to begin to slam inside her, filling her to the hilt. I do this for a bit then rise slightly on my knees when I pull out, to enable me to hook my arms under her knees to jolt her forward. Lifting her legs while I lean in, I kiss her ankle, her calf, her knee, working my way up until I reach her apex and align my cock with her, entering with a reverence that surprises me.

"Deep. That's how I'm going to fuck you, until you're filled up with your husband's cum."

Her jaw hangs low in fake surprise from my choice of words, but then she smirks to herself, her hands attempting to paw my stomach. I hold onto one of her bent legs to keep her wide, but I bring my other hand down to interlace with hers.

Perhaps this is the best way to fuck your wife. Blunt thrusts but holding her hand?

I can't help it, and I quickly scoop my head down to capture her welcoming lips for a kiss before returning to my position to ensure we both burst from pleasure.

I still just as she murmurs and clamps around my cock,

bringing her fingers to her clit. "That's it. I'm giving you what you wanted. You can come all over my cock now."

She nearly screams as her body thrashes and her pussy convulses.

I don't wait, I pick up my speed and chase her orgasm until reaching my own, and I empty into her.

My vision is blurred and the room is spinning, but still I manage to see that our hands didn't let go.

We're still connected when I leave her warmth and collapse on the bed next to her.

I also notice that we both still have rings on.

———

HAILEY LIES naked on the middle of the bed on top of the sheets. Propped on her elbow, she watches me as I emerge from the bathroom. Her closed mouth is slanted to the side due to approval of how this night is going.

"I mean, I guess we're following the tradition of fucking like crazy on your wedding night, even if this wedding is, well…" Her brows furrow. "Something different."

I scoff to myself, as that is some way of putting it. Joining her on the bed, she instantly swirls the back of her fingers along my torso.

"I'll walk home in the morning if that's okay?"

Glancing to her, taken aback, I realize she is almost checking with me about our rules.

My hand covers hers. "Did you seriously just ask if it's okay to spend the night?" I want to laugh.

She instantly pinches me and grins. "I don't know. I mean, we're not living together."

"I didn't mind that we spent the night together the other night."

"Before we got married."

Now I chuckle to myself. "On paper… and possibly when I want to fuck you into another galaxy."

Hailey sighs. "Very true on both counts." She turns onto her side to stare at me. "You know, since I've known you, sometimes you're quiet. But in the bedroom…" She clucks her tongue. "You're a dark horse that is even better than the dirty dreams I've always had about you."

I nod slowly to myself, getting an ego boost if I'm honest. "Lucky you then."

"Indeed. But I'm also lucky or crazy that I've agreed to your out-of-this-world plan that now has me with a ring." Her lips roll in and her cheeks tighten because she wants to smile, and it might be so damn big that my not-so-shy wife may blush.

"Trust me, this is a surprise turn of events, but I meant what I said. Once I cross a line, then things just…"

"What?" She's melodramatic. "You have ex-wives because you've crossed lines before and things just…?"

I roll my eyes and shift to my side, taking hold of her leg to swing over my hip. "Ha-ha. Crossing *this* line is new, so we're going to have to just roll with this situation."

Her eyes strike to mine but there is something peculiar in the gleam. What is it?

"Oliver, really." Her voice is serious. "It's because of your insanity that I have a real chance in opening the preschool. But what happens if the time comes and poof." She gestures with her hands. "What if I play the part of the best wife possible, the kind that you never want to let go of, even if I decide that's what I want in the end?"

Oh.

Yeah, right.

This marriage thing is for convenience.

This isn't the clear-cut version of marriage. Not quite fake nor real. I wonder what she would give if I had gotten on one knee and promised a long future with kids, two dogs, and the best safe bagel cutter there is?

Instead, I skipped a few steps.

Maybe it's possible that we can grow into a marriage that could be…

No. I need to focus on the present.

"What is the wife version of Hailey like?"

"This is a preview of… hmm, a wife in training? Nah, huh, I'm not sure." She smiles widely. "But wife-me is someone who cares a lot and hopes you kiss me right now. We don't have any champagne, so strong kisses will have to do."

It's her who initiates the kiss. A cementing kiss that won't let me go. The kind of kiss that roots me down.

Because we're just going with the moment, and right now, it's just Hailey and me in our own little world.

Perusing around the small groups of students huddled around the classroom, I cross my arms as I slowly tread around the room. Every time a middle-schooler lifts their gaze to me, I smile. For the most part, the kids in summer school are sweet. Some need extra help, and summer ensures they can catch up with their classmates for the year.

Others, well… are a pain in my ass.

My eyes dart to one group in the corner near a globe with three students engrossed in the workgroup and one boy insisting that he just watch.

Sighing, I'll give him a few minutes more to change his attitude before I have a word. I hate being stern Hailey, it royally sucks. I'm supposed to be the teacher that kids like and would rather see than Mr. Smythe in Algebra. Social Studies rocks, it's everything rolled into one. Geography, world history, the creation of country, and a few boring sections on law. What more can you want?

Oh yeah, a different age and manner of teaching.

Sliding onto the chair behind my desk, I begin to play

with my necklace between my fingers. Four-year-olds are curious in a hands-on kind of way. Sure, I assign projects that let my early teenagers get creative. However, it's not cute little messy finger paints and drawings that you can't quite figure out but still smile when a little pigtailed girl says it's a dog and then you agree.

Numbers and alphabets are new, and their eyes are opened to a whole new world. It's a lot of balance between play and learning. Not ripping away cell phones and hoping your students completed their homework.

Noticing that I'm playing with the ring on a chain that I've been hiding under my shirt, I quickly let go.

I'm wearing a ring. I'm not sure I meant to keep wearing it.

I have a husband.

The sentiment repeats for the thousandth time in my head.

It's not real, yet I do things subconsciously such as wear a necklace with a ring that isn't exactly needed for a fake yet legally real marriage.

Oliver is my husband.

All over again, the thought causes the corner of my mouth to lift from that fact.

He's making my dream come true, and it's because he wanted to. So what if I eagerly agreed because deep down I was jumping at the chance to fulfill a fantasy that's taken real estate in my mind for way too long. It makes this all risky for my heart, but his eyes were pure reverence and I knew he wouldn't accept no for an answer, and his kisses entrapped me. I'm in quicksand and couldn't run away if I tried.

One day it will all make sense why he is going to such great lengths to help me. Gratefulness isn't even the right word for what I feel.

But a flicker in a tiny corner within me twists, warning

me that we are just playing the part, it's only legal. Fucking endlessly for a few nights before we jumped into marriage doesn't always make a marriage of love and a long-lasting future.

And there lies my dilemma. We wanted to try and see where things go, embarking down an unknown path. Then we added a detour.

I'm a wife. Oliver's wife. Mrs. Oaks.

"This is useless." A cranky teenager's voice causes me to break out of my daze.

I shutter my eyes a few times to bring my focus to my student in the front row, and I frown. "Why would that be, Danny?" This is going to be a few soul-crushing minutes, I feel it.

"It happened so long ago, we don't need to learn about this stuff. We should be focusing on the future. You know we'll probably be living on Mars in a few years."

Tapping my fingers on my desk and smiling tightly, I remind myself that his mind is still impressionable. "*Well*, Danny. Learning about migration to the west of the country and how the settlers lived their life upon arrival is important in understanding American history."

"But it's like what, thirty years ago or something."

Breathing to myself, I push down the fact that I keep repeating myself. "Or 175-ish years ago," I correct him. "Look, I know this is the last place you want to be, but not only your parents sent you to summer school; you also got Ds in my class last year. I truly believe that you have more in you and we can get that grade up. In order for that to happen, you need to work with your group."

"It's just boring. It's summer, I shouldn't be preparing a presentation with a group of bookworms. I'm missing the parties by the river. I have a social calendar to maintain."

My eyes enlarge at this kid's audacity, but his parents donate enough to the school that I've been warned to go easy. With preschoolers, their little brains are fresh and your patience strong because they haven't even figured out what school is. But the seventh-grader in front of me with attitude? He's putting in no effort, and I feel exasperated that I've tried all the ways to get through to him but failed. That's not the feeling I want to have as a teacher. I care.

"You have the gold rush to study, and that's a topic that might draw your interest."

"Or I can just search about it on the internet and no longer use a book. You know books won't be around in like ten years. Only our parents use them. We have apps and social media now."

Now I take hold of my desk. "Well, books it shall be today. Because our fine state of Illinois has a curriculum to follow," I deadpan. I fear for when we reach the civics unit in the book.

"Whatever." He huffs and turns to face a fellow student.

I hear a ding and my hand dives into the drawer of my desk. My phone is on top of the pile of cell phones that I make the kids leave on my desk at the start of the day. Using my thumbprint, I unlock my screen and read the email.

Hi Hailey,

Thanks for your email and sorry for the delay. I was out of town. We can have a call later or I'll see you in town. My office is open until five. Hopefully, you have some information that will change the situation for the building on Main.

Molly

Everhope Real Estate

This is happening, it can really happen. The whole reason that Oliver and I got married is at my fingertips. I quickly shoot a text off to Oliver, and a few minutes later, I get a reply.

OLIVER

I can make it for 4pm. Does that work?

ME

Yes! 😊 I'm out from school at 3pm so will be back in Everhope on time.

My fingers slide across the keyboard then stall when I bite my lip. This isn't the setting to ask, but I do.

Are you sure this is okay? I mean, this is a big step. You helping me in this way.

I can't exactly walk away… we're already married. ;)

How ridiculous, a freaking emoji calms me.

————

I PACE back and forth on Main Street, nervous yet excited. The street is quiet for a weekday, which is a blessing as it means less chance to be seen with Oliver and raise suspicion, even though before we used to stop and talk as friends all the time.

The spot in front of me next to a parking meter that no longer works is now occupied as Oliver parks his sports car.

My heart speeds up, and when he slides out of his car with papers in his hand and a sweltering grin, I nearly forget why I'm here.

"Just on time. Sorry, I'm nearly late. A player wanted out of his contract to return to the European league."

"Sure."

He walks to me and steps forward to lower his head for a kiss, but I quickly duck back.

"Nobody is supposed to know that we're fucking each other's brains out, remember?" I mumble.

His smug look doesn't help the need that I'm hammering down to kiss the hell out of him.

His face squinches. "Fair point. Should we head in?"

I nod once.

"By the way. The Spinners have a really good insurance policy. Did you want me to add you to my plan since you're my spouse? Maybe you need it when you leave your current job. We have a good one when you work for the Spinners, and we can add our spouses to it." He says it as though it's everyday conversation.

Creases form on my forehead. "That's a little over the top, no? Considering our dynamics. Besides, I have good insurance at Lake Spark Academy for now, and we'll figure the rest out later."

His lips quirk out, and he cocks his head to the side. "I would say building purchases are a step above insurance on the over-the-top scale."

Ruefully, I shake my head as he opens the door, and I go in first. It's a small office, and Molly looks up from her desk where she's typing on her laptop and smiles brightly.

"Wonderful. I'm happy to see you again." Her gaze skims to Oliver, and she's clearly confused. "Hello, Oliver. I wasn't expecting you."

Oliver is now in work mode, I sense it. Proven by the fact that he whips out a paper and hands it to her. "A good surprise, I hope."

Molly reads the top line and now she's even more confused. "An NDA?"

"Yes. A non-disclosure agreement is needed if Hailey is going to discuss the building."

Her chin tips up as she remains bewildered. "Uhm, I guess that I can do that. Just a little unusual for Everhope."

"All the more reason. News spreads fast here," he clarifies.

She shrugs her shoulders but reluctantly grabs a pen from her desk and quickly signs it then hands it back. "There." Her smile returns and she circles around her desk, indicating for us to have a seat.

I feel the excitement about to burst out of me. "Tell the owners that I want the building. I've fulfilled all of the requirements."

Molly seems taken aback. "Hailey, it's great if you get the financing, but there is still one more out-of-this-world requirement that I'm not too pleased with myself."

Glancing to my side, I see Oliver smiling wryly.

"I'm married now," I tell her. Right on cue, Oliver sweeps up my hand to hold, even places a small peck of a kiss near my knuckles.

Molly's jaw hangs low. "M-married?"

I nod proudly. "Yes. Oliver and I are married. So put in the offer and hand me those keys." Confidence fills me that this is all falling into place.

She sways her finger side to side between us. "You. Him. Married?"

"Sure are." Oliver's grin is cheeky. "And I remind you that you just signed an NDA. So, I'm sure you'll keep this to yourself until we are ready to share the news of our blessed union."

Molly scrubs a hand across her mouth as she digests the news. "Since when?"

"Does it matter? Everything is in order," I reiterate.

"Your parents, brothers, friends have no clue?" She can't let this go. "No cake from Foxy Rox?"

Oliver breaths out a sigh and rolls his eyes, getting exhausted. "No clue. No cake. So let's wrap this up."

Molly tilts her head side to side, raising her brows then her shoulders go slack. "Okay. It seems I can inform the seller. I'll go give her a call. You're just in time because she just got another offer this morning, but I know you are her first choice."

I sit up straight from that knowledge and watch Molly disappear to the corner of the office for a little privacy.

Immediately, I squeeze the hand that I forgot I'm holding. "If they don't agree then you have a wife for nothing," I whisper and crane my neck in an attempt to examine Molly's facial expressions.

He muffles a noise, but it's not a response.

"It won't be for nothing." I zip my gaze to him because his words have sincerity underneath, I can sense it. "You'll get it," he assures me. But I could have sworn that he meant something else.

The sound of Molly ending her call brings my attention back to her. Her demeanor seems positive, so that's a start.

"Okay."

"Okay what?" I ask.

"Okay. It seems it is yours."

My entire body slouches from tension evaporating. "Really?"

She nods her head with a bright smile. "Yes… you just both need to meet Ingrid for high tea."

"W-what?" My face squinches.

Molly shrugs. "She's a little traditional, I guess. Or just sentimental."

"No shit. But fine." Oliver holds his palm up. "She wouldn't be the first to want to hash out details over a meal with a signature for dessert. High tea will be a first. Does Hailey need to wear a bonnet or something? This feels a little older than our times."

She looks sympathetically between us. "I'm sure you newlyweds can handle a high tea together, right?" I hear skepticism and sass in her tone.

My head tilts to the side from her brazen change but also find it amusing. "Of course we can. Send the details and we'll be there. Oliver needs to check his calendar because it's still the hockey trade season."

"And newlywed season, that blocks out my schedule during the evenings if you get my drift," he retorts and challenges her.

She laughs weakly, and I sputter from his boldness. "Well then, perhaps leave me the details for your assistant and I can contact her."

"Perfect." I clap my hands together. "I guess I can read through all the paperwork and speak with my bank beforehand?"

"I don't see why not." She uses the mouse on her laptop to take a glimpse at something. "I'll send a draft to you later today or tomorrow morning. You can only sign the final documents after you meet with Ingrid. She still needs to fully agree."

"Alright then." I am completely relieved that all my ducks are falling in a row.

Oliver leaves his seat, and he throws Molly a warning glare. "NDA."

She breathes out, frustrated. "Yes, I know. What about your brother? Doesn't the sheriff overrule that document? So if he were to ask then I would have to tell him?" Her hypothetical is not likely at all, she probably just wants to stir the pot in a non-malicious way.

"I doubt my brother would specifically ask that question."

She throws her hands up at a loss. "Okay, okay."

I interlink Oliver's arm with my own. "Come on. I think you are getting hangry." I yank Oliver with me. "Thanks again, Molly," I call out as we leave.

The moment we are out in the warm summer air, I ignore all logic and throw my arms around Oliver for a hug. "It's happening."

He slings his arm around me. I'm beginning to think that he left a print on my body already a few days ago which means his arm knows exactly where to mold.

"It is. You're almost there." The genuine look on his face that lightens, pings in my chest as I look at him affectionately. His eyes trail down, and he notices something on my neck. "Hey, you're wearing the ring." He seems pleased by that.

I glance down, pull out the chain, and the ring appears from under the fabric. "I am. Silly, huh? I needed something to remind me of this whirlwind week while I dealt with Social Studies and unenthusiastic summer school kids." *And because I like that you gave it to me.* Playing the part of wife isn't bad at all, either.

"Good."

"Come on. I'll attempt to cook dinner."

Oliver unlocks his car. "Sure. I'll drop my car at home and leave my laptop then head to your place."

"Nuh-uh. Keats and Esme are next door. Too many questions."

His head lolls to the side as he contemplates. "Solid point. I'll see you at mine then."

"Yep."

Because I don't live with you.
And it stings a little.

17

HAILEY

As soon as I turn from my front path onto the sidewalk heading down the street, I hear my name being called.

"Hailey." Esme prances toward me. "Where are you going? Want to order in with me? Keats went to see his sister."

"Uh, I can't."

"Okay. Plans? And why are you in yoga pants and sneakers?" She assesses my outfit.

"Because…" *Think.* "I thought I would start power walking. Yep. A great form of exercise."

She looks at me oddly. "Power walking? You?"

"Totally. Try new things, right?"

Esme ogles me then lifts her nose to look over my shoulder. "You know, a certain someone lives in that direction." She smiles playfully.

Shit. Do not blow your cover, Hailey.

"Oh? Well, I do need to power walk along the sidewalk."

She throws a thumb over her shoulder. "But not that way?"

"Esme, seriously. No need to play detective. Nothing is going on, and if I need to see Oliver it's because we are in charge of watering my brother's plants while he is away and we only have one key." Phew, good story.

She brings her hands to her hips, trying to figure out if I'm lying or not. I passed high school drama class on the honor roll, so I think I've succeeded.

"Okay. Enjoy your walk. Is this like an everyday exercise regime?"

"Yep."

"Cool. Alright, well, careful with the mosquitos." When she wanders away, I sigh in relief.

Cover story one out of the way. I guess I'm now having daily power walks. That isn't exactly a bad thing, it's great for your health.

I embark on my stroll and wave to a neighbor mowing the lawn and another going for their evening jog. The sun is out but rain will come, I smell it in the air. Or rather, the humidity indicates that a storm will burst and bring a breeze.

It always interests me how lots of ancient cultures connect spirits with nature, weather in particular. It can be very telling about current life events. Right now, my energy is shifting.

Arriving at Oliver's house, I double-check that nobody is taking notice. Oliver sent me the code for the door, as he wanted to stop by the grocery store.

The moment I'm inside and clicking the door closed, a new smile graces my lips. It's a manly home, could use a little color. Gray and navy-blue throw pillows. Everything is new, with Scandinavian design, and an open floor plan. I notice the wind chime that he got me on our road trip. It's lying on the long side table along the wall where a few hockey-related copper statues rest and a big bowl in the middle. Gravity pulls me straight to the chime, and I pick it up with the sound of the bamboo sticks bumping.

It mixes with the sound of Oliver entering from the garage at the end of the hallway. He stops near the kitchen island to set the grocery bag on the counter, only to then lean against it. He crosses his ankles and arms as he observes me.

My eyes flick up to greet him. "You said you would hang it at your house so I don't jinx my dreams, but now I wonder what are your dreams." Vulnerability is thick in my voice.

It has dawned on me that he is doing so much for me, but I'm not sure what ambitions he has in life or what he could want that might feel out of reach.

He scratches his cheek, perhaps contemplating or simply not wanting to share. "I haven't put it outside, sorry. I mentioned I would when we got it." Ah, so he is avoiding my question.

I'll let it go. I spin on my feet and teeter straight to the sliding door. "Then we must hang it. Maybe something will come to you with the breeze that will bring signs through the chimes." It sounds silly, but I mean it. I want him to be happy with whatever that may be.

Well, maybe not another woman, because that would just… I guess… cause a crack inside of me now that I've crossed the line with Oliver involving things I've only fanta-sized about.

I can't see him, but I know he's approaching, and every step he takes is like walking up stairs, except it's up my spine with a tingling wave.

"I think there is a hook near the patio light. For hanging plants or bird feeders. Can't say that I've used it. Otherwise, I might have to find the hammer and a hook."

Crossing the frame of the door, I search and then spot

exactly what we need, and I nearly march straight there before I stand on my tippytoes and stretch my body up to hang the wind chime.

From behind, a pair of warm and strong hands brace the sides of my body as I lower my heels to find earth. I'm getting tucked into his arms that loop in front, and I lean back into his body.

This is heaven.

In his hold. Me and him. Our own quiet world.

He kisses my hair right next to my sensitive earlobe. "You can take it home. You're getting what you imagined."

"Not yet. Besides, we need to unlock what you've been waiting for. The world has many roads."

"And your body is my map." His ragged tone breathes along my neck as he is clearly in the mood to ravish me, and although it's in my favor, something nags at me.

"Well, before you strip me naked, can we establish that I'm well aware that you're avoiding any effort from me to discuss you?"

The moment that he abandons me, I regret that I pressed because being in his embrace is by far better.

He rakes his hands through his hair. "Not avoiding. Just not sure what to say. I barely think past next week. Why don't we just leave it that I'm happy that you're a step closer to your preschool."

Gently I shake my head. "But that's me. I want some attention on you so we can make your non-dirty wishes happen."

Oliver lolls his head to the side. He's the opposite of annoyed, appreciative perhaps. "Hailey, really. Right now, there is no need to push the topic. I'm content. Even when I got approached again the other day about a job in New York, I said I wasn't interested."

"You got a job offer?" I'm surprised. "I remember you mentioning on our drive to the wedding that you got an offer way back, I just didn't think it was still a factor."

He shrugs a shoulder. "It would be a big opportunity working for the league at headquarters. Maybe if the terms and package were right I would consider, but to be honest, I don't think I would want to leave Everhope because I'm content here."

I still feel like he's holding back something, but I can't pinpoint it.

"Well, if you say so." My lips pinch, and I give up because I'm not entirely convinced but he doesn't want to budge. So, I give up. "Okay. Little things then. Dinner? I can cook simple things."

"No, you can't. Remember, we're not strangers."

My sight drifts up to the sky. "Exactly, so you know that I love rain, and it will be here soon. Last time, I was stuck with you in a storm, we created our own."

Oliver instantly sputters a laugh. "That is one hell of a line." He hooks his arm around my shoulders and walks by my side to guide me back into the house.

"It is, isn't it," I proudly admit.

I help him unpack the grocery bags, and I determine that a roast veggie and couscous dish it will be. When I'm distracted grabbing various dishes, Oliver grabs my wrist to stop me.

"Maybe dinner can wait? You have two options. Kitchen table or we actually make it to my bedroom." That cocky grin causes me to forget that humans need to eat.

Dropping the wooden spoon onto the counter, I throw my arms around his neck and kiss him longingly because his plan works too.

"Whatever you say, Husband."

It only encourages his hunger for me. He lifts me, and my legs tie around his waist. His intention is to carry me upstairs.

It is still my intention to break away the pieces to discover what Oliver is thinking.

But I'm not sure that day is today.

HAILEY

Nervously, I bite the end of my thumbnail as I watch the woman behind the desk typing. The middle-aged woman with a friendly smile and Jane on her name tag is busy inputting my data into the system. With everything online these days, I had to head two towns over to the nearest bank branch.

"My preliminary application online seemed to be okay," I mention.

Her tiny smile returns as she clicks and examines the screen. Dread wants to boil inside me, and the moment she turns slightly, she abandons the keyboard, causing me to sit straight in anticipation. "I can see that. The application is from more than thirty days ago, so you will need to complete another one."

"Of course, I did it before purely to check my possibilities. Now, I seem to be on the road to buying a building. I've seen the paperwork, but the process will only continue once I meet with the owner as she was doubting to sell."

To me in particular or anyone who isn't married. Some

audacity. Now, I have a husband. I'm lucky. Problem solved, and it's with Oliver, too.

Our high tea got pushed back to next week as Ingrid is sick with a flu.

"Okay, and you mentioned that you recently got married which needs to be clarified on the application next to your social security. It's a good idea that he co-signs as you will be in a far better position for the mortgage if he does, even though you have the downpayment already. Will he co-sign?"

Hmm, I want to say no. This is why I avoided asking my brother. This isn't a small favor. It's a big ask of Oliver, even though he would. He already mentioned it. It's my last resort though, but the option is on the table. The woman seems to notice that I'm slightly uncomfortable.

"If you're married then it's not a requirement, but I can also use his income statements to get you a higher mortgage on the place. It will probably be a must if you want to guarantee the mortgage rate."

I tuck hair behind my ear. "That makes sense, but it's for business and I am trying not to mix business with pleasure."

Really, Hailey? Did that just fly out of my mouth?

She tries not to bubble a laugh, but luckily, she doesn't seem to mind my slip.

"What does your husband do?"

"You know, we are kind of private people. Keep things on the down low." As in live in different homes and fuck like crazy when the opportunity arises. "But he's a lawyer."

"Let me guess, he will review every document you sign."

I smile to myself at the thought. He will whether I like it or not. I'm sure he would have done it before all of this transpired, too. It's a sort of protectiveness, a steel wall unable to break through. He has his mind set.

"Maybe. Next time we sign and dust the documents then

he will join me. He's busy now, as hockey players enjoy their contracts this time of year."

Her face puzzles, and I realize I shared a tidbit of information about my secret husband. It's because I'm proud of him. Always have been. His career is one that many who study law dream of.

"He works for the Spinners," I clarify. Everyone around here knows about hockey.

Her whole face lights up. "Really? I bet you get some great seats and tickets."

My brow arches, and I contemplate testing the waters. "Is… that something that interests you?" My words stretch.

"My son always asks for season tickets."

I whirl my finger around. "Would that put me favorably in line for my application?" I smile quickly to pretend I'm joking.

In truth, I have no shame in bribery right now.

She chuckles. "Probably, but you don't need to sway me. It would be no good. Everything is down to what I put in the computer. I'm not sure I would worry so much, you have you have everything well prepared."

That's a relief, and I smile confidently. "Okay. Then I guess I'm done here. I'll call when we can move on to the next step." I stand from my chair and slide the strap of my purse over my shoulder.

"Yep. Nice talking with you, Hailey, and we'll see one another soon."

"Thanks again." We shake hands, and I nearly skip out of the bank.

I'm one step closer to my dream.

———

MY DRY-CLEANING HANGS from my finger as I walk out the door onto Main Street. Errands are the theme of the day, and my smile hasn't wilted one bit since the bank. The sun is out too. If I'm feeling adventurous then I might even grab a tub of ice cream from the store to have later while I work on grading papers.

"Hailey." I hear a familiar voice call my name to grab my attention.

That smile I have? It now wilts.

My lips roll in, and I slowly pivot on my heel while pasting on a new tight smile. "Nancy." Oliver's mother, my husband's mother, my mother-in-law, except she doesn't know that.

"It's good to see you. I haven't seen you since before the wedding."

I blink a few times as a small blip flies in my stomach. "Wedding?"

"Your brother's." Right. Of course that's what she means. "I really wish we didn't miss it. I'm sure Oliver knocked it out of the park with his speech. He sent a video that someone made, and I can't wait to see the newlywed couple when they're back. Such a special time."

Newlyweds are a special sort of species. I'm beginning to feel that.

Nancy gives me a once-over and seems to approve. "You look different. Your hair?"

"No."

"Did you get a tan?"

"No."

"Hmm. Been working out more?"

"Definitely not in the gym," I quip because the reality is that it's in bed with her son.

She snaps her fingers. "Ah, you just seem… happier. Is

there a new man in your life?" She steps forward and nudges my shoulder with her arm. "I'll keep the gossip down."

What is with our parents all trying to pretend they're thirty and part of the crowd?

"Not exactly." Wrong choice of words but also the truth.

Nancy winks at me. "Fair enough. I'll wait and listen for any developments."

A wave of warmth, the kind I sometimes get when dizzy, washes over me. I feel incredibly guilty right now that she doesn't know that I'm officially her daughter-in-law. I wonder if that would make her happy or if she believes that I'm deserving of her son. Not that her opinion matters.

I inhale a deep breath and remember that marriage aside, I have ideas in my head that involve her. "Since my brother is away, I'll ask if he needs for help with Oliver's birthday party. Normally the guys plan birthdays for one another. Maybe something with just family and friends, nothing crazy but not a BBQ either."

Her entire demeanor softens, and her eyes stake into me, her smile so incredibly warm. "That's great. You're always a little party planner. I'm sure it will be wonderful. I remember the murder mystery you planned. I heard about it for weeks."

I chuckle to myself. "No murders for this one."

"Just send me the details. We'll be there. We're not traveling again until next month."

"Perfect. Well, I need to get home. I need to grade papers and all that jazz."

Her eyes almost sparkle in admiration. "You are something special, you know. Being a teacher isn't easy."

I shrug. "Someone has to do it. Besides, it might change a bit now that I have a h—...homework. Yep, issuing less homework and that cuts my workload." Holy crap that was a close one. Nearly said husband who is helping me get the building for a preschool.

"Hopefully. It was nice to run into you." She touches my shoulder in passing.

All the fear erases from me as she walks away.

A little reminder of my unusual situation.

———

SITTING ON MY COUCH, I go over my lesson plans for next week. With my pen in one hand, the fingers on my other hand play with the necklace with the ring along my collarbone. It's a struggle, as my thoughts keep lingering back to Oliver. The other night, he closed off when I pried for details of what he wants in life.

I just want to do something for him as I'm so indebted. It's also the fact that I've never wanted to make someone so happy in my life. He deserves it, and it's the only way that I'll smile.

Reviewing the calendar, my eyes still on a date.

Husband or not, I would have been involved in planning Oliver's birthday. Everyone seems to come to me for help in that department.

That also means that nobody will bat an eye if I organize one. I'll make it his best birthday yet and nobody will need to know that it's because I'm completely besotted with the man.

A dinner down at the River Bell with a group of friends and family. Simple decorations. A drink menu with a specialty cocktail, and after the party, I'll throw on something for his eyes only.

You only turn 34 once.

Still, I need to cover my bases, and I grab my phone and quickly type a message to my brother.

ME

> Hey! Sorry to interrupt your honeymoon but just wanted to check if you needed me to do anything for Oliver's birthday? I remembered that it's soon and normally you plan a gathering or something. I can imagine you have been occupied. Should I just take that off your hands?

I will play it cool because this is nothing unusual, and a few minutes later, I get a text back to confirm my theory.

LIAM

> Oh yeah, I was going to handle that when I got back. You'd be my favorite sister if you can take over since you are a party wizard.

> No problem.

Alright, that's solved, and I can go ahead with my plans.

I hear a sound of something hitting my kitchen window, but it must be a bird as there is a bird feeder near there. However, the sound continues. Woodpeckers don't attack windows, do they? Call it my sixth sense, but I rush straight to the kitchen because I know who is outside standing at the bottom of the deck step, waiting.

Smiling, I quickly go to the back door to let Oliver in. I look side to side to ensure we have no watchers as he rushes inside.

I close the door and have to ask. "What's with the pebble throwing? You could have just knocked on the door."

"What's the fun in that? I'm not supposed to be here so better go all out on the sneaking around." He steps to me, and his hands rake through my hair only to fist it at the back of my head to drive my mouth straight to his.

It's a fervent kiss that has me closing my eyes to

completely inhale his breath and dip my tongue into his mouth. I'm already gone. He could slide my pajama shorts right down and I'd be ready.

I pull back and scrape my teeth along his stubbled jaw. "Are you sure Keats and Esme didn't see you? I feel as though they are watching this place like hawks."

"Nah, I walked through the backyard of that new family that just moved in next door. Their dog was inside which gave me a clear path." We both meander to the couch, and Oliver sets my papers onto the coffee table before we have a seat.

I snort a laugh at his effort to fly under the radar. So far, we've used power walks, Liam's key, neighbors' yards, and me showing up to say they mixed up our mail as excuses. For the most part, we stay at his place since Esme and Keats are live next door. Carter has random shifts, and to be honest, he is the least of our worries.

"I wasn't expecting you; I thought you were working late." Getting comfortable, I tuck my legs under and love how his arm rests on the back of the couch behind me. It gives him ample opportunity to take his long finger and stroke my arm. I was hoping he would touch me.

"Managed to get out early. I might have to dash into a call later since the player's agent is on Pacific time. Sorry if I'm interrupting your teacher stuff. Did that little punk have a better attitude today?" Because we do talk about things as our whirlwind has worn off, and now, we are in reality.

"Actually, a little. However, the excitement of my day was running into your mom in town. It was hard. It nearly burst out of me a few times that she's my new mother-in-law."

Oliver rubs his chin and seems to be in deep thought. "I

haven't seen her since they got back. I'm not sure how I'll handle it."

"I guess it's the same boat as when Liam gets back. We have to get our nerves in check and stories straight. It's just …" My eyes find his. "We're deceiving everyone, and I know it's what we walked into, and it will be temporary, but still…"

He cups my cheek, giving me that feeling of comfort. "It will all fall into place," he promises.

I nod repeatedly, and he leans down to kiss the tip of my nose.

But he doesn't succeed because the front door swings open, with the sound of feet quickly walking in. Oliver and I are quick to scramble apart.

"Oh hey, I didn't know you were ho…" Esme stops mid-sentence when she stands in the entryway to the living room and notices Oliver sitting on the other end of the couch and still doing his best to sit straight. "Home." Esme finishes her sentence and smirks gently to herself, and it's almost sly because she seems to enjoy this awkward moment.

I swipe my hair behind my ear. "Yeah, grading papers."

Esme bounces her eyes between me and Oliver. "Not alone, I see. Didn't know Oliver loved to grade essays on the industrial era."

My cheeks hurt from my tight smile.

"Actually, I stopped by because…" Oliver glances at me while he thinks before sliding his gaze back to Esme. "We were just talking about Liam's plants. One of us forgot to water them. We were debating if we needed to buy a new one," Oliver attempts to cover the situation and could in no possible way fool anyone with that lie.

"Sure you were." Esme sounds completely unfazed before she sharply turns her attention to me. "Sorry to bother you. I sent you a text earlier that a client forgot her sweater by the door, so I was going to pick it up. You said cool. Remember?"

Ah shit, I did. Still, I need to reset some boundaries about knocking.

She uses her hand to cover her eyes and pretends to look away. "Well… nothing to see here. I'll be on my merry way." Then she scurries away.

When we hear the door close, my body eases because it was tense. "Fuck." My eyes zip up to Oliver. "She knows."

He rubs the back of his neck with a pained look. "Nah." He takes a few beats. "Maybe."

I shake my head before it falls into my hand before I swat him. "Liam's plants, really?"

We look at one another and our serious looks drop into a wide grin, and I chirp a laugh. Because it is ridiculous and he knows it.

Oliver lifts a shoulder, confident. "I mean, it could be true."

I sigh. "Well, she didn't exactly see anything, and we didn't confess. She is probably jumping to conclusions in her head, and she's always had those."

He reaches out to yank me flush to him. "Let's not worry about it."

"I guess you're right."

After a few calming breaths and acceptance of nearly getting caught, I decide that we should move on with our night. "Anyways, I went to the bank after school, and it seems everything really will work out."

He squeezes my arm attentively. "I'll make sure of it."

The way he says it feels as though there is so much more underlying. It's heavy, not said in jest.

Ignoring the thought, I touch his thigh and grin ear to ear.

"And I'll make sure you have a birthday worthy of cele-brating."

He groans and sinks back onto the sofa. "Don't remind me. I'm getting old."

I crawl on top of him and straddle his hips, instantly grabbing his interest. "No, you're not, and I'm planning a party whether you want it or not."

"Hailey." I can hear that he is pretending to hate the idea.

"Oliver." I return the tone and smile smugly.

His head falls forward, and he nuzzles his nose between my breasts as he growls annoyance. "Fine," he grits out.

I bounce with her hands showing excitement. "Excellent. Because I would have done it anyhow."

Oliver relaxes again, and he wets his lips while his hands begin to run along my thighs. "You're taunting my cock with all of your movements."

I bring a finger to my chin and pretend to consider. "Hmm, how can I rectify that situation?"

"I have about 1000 ways and 99% of those are dirty as fuck."

I throw my head back in laughter. "We should make a list and we can work our way through them," I suggest.

"That's a pretty long list and will require a long time… very long." He has my eyes pinned and suddenly the air in the room shifts. It shouts in my head how much I want this to be foreshadowing.

This time it's me demanding a kiss, and I ensure I get it when I dive straight to his mouth for a hard kiss. It takes him by surprise, the force, but he doesn't mind because his hands wander around my body, and we both murmur as our kiss doesn't break and our bodies glue together.

I hate air.

You need to breathe and have no choice but to part for air.

A thought that's been floating in my head recently enters into the situation. I wipe his lips with my thumb and swallow to prep myself. "Kind of wild that we went from a one-night stand to spouses at the speed of light." My voice thins, delicate, as my eyes slide away only to return.

He's patiently waiting for me to continue because he knows I have more to say, and the sly smirk barely visibly on his face tells me that he is partly entertained about my sudden shyness.

"We kind of missed a step, and I was thinking… maybe… since we haven't, you know… gone on a date. A real one." Am I nervous right now? That would be silly. This man has already gone a step above to care for me.

A date is a small speck on the scale.

"Blisswood winery or Dizzy Duck Inn in Lake Spark?" He's very on board, even if his face is set in an unreadable mask, but his voice is cool and smooth.

"Uh, isn't the Blisswood winery your brother's ex in-laws'?"

"There are no hard feelings. So it's the Dizzy Duck? Dinner or should we just stay the night. Wait…" He holds up a finger. "Scratch that. Keats is there a lot as his sister works there. Too risky."

My shoulders lift then sag. "Probably anywhere in a 20-mile radius is out of bounds." I almost frown because I'm not enjoying this obstacle. But being out in the open with all to see is a whole new ballgame.

Oliver's lips quirk out and then ease into a coy look. "I've got it."

"What?"

"You'll see."

I'm curious, but I'll accept that it's a surprise. "No pressure or anything but my expectations are high," I tease him.

He grips my hips and in one swift move shifts us until I'm on my back and he's hovering over me. "Don't you worry. Now be a good wife and open those thighs. I'm starving for you."

Heat prickles all over my body and my arm snakes between us so I can touch him, and he isn't lying.

I would say he only came over for sex except you show feelings through actions and everything he keeps doing for me erases that thought.

"Oliver, I want hard and fast." My breath is already heavy and my voice scrapes.

"Whatever you say."

He kneels with one leg between my thighs. Watching him unbuckle his pants causes my pussy to pulse with need.

His sight stalls on me, and the promise of fast turns into Oliver sliding over me to slowly brush his lips on mine with intention.

"My wife." His whisper cascades down my neck until he plants a soft kiss on my shoulder and slides down the strap of my tank top before his teeth capture the ring on the chain.

This man is feral most the time, but this time the glint in his eyes is a promise.

19

OLIVER

Liam stares back at me through the screen on my phone as I stand in the parking lot of the park outside of town. This is the worst possible time for him to video call, but I already let him go to voicemail earlier when I was in the grocery store buying a few items.

"You're on your honeymoon. Why the hell are you calling me?" I'm slightly bewildered as he stands in kayaking gear and pines are the backdrop. "You should be MIA to anyone you know."

He has a sheepish grin from that fact. "We only have a few days more before we drive back east. I was wondering if you could maybe tone down my sister."

I flinch and crane my neck. "Oh? How so?"

"Judging by my call with her earlier and her peppy tone, I'm positive she's going to decorate my house or some shit like that as our welcome home, but that's just not us. A simple bouquet of flowers or fruit basket will do. Knowing Hailey, she will probably spread flower petals somewhere and that stuff is a pain in the ass to clean up. She already mentioned she is organizing a birthday party for you since

I'm not around to do it. Again, she's lost her marbles. Like is she on some drug I'm not aware of? Changed her coffee order? Anyhow, you probably know more than me since you see her a lot."

My stomach sinks and I swallow, trying to figure out what he is implying. "See her a lot? Nah, no more than normal."

"Really? I mean, you live on the same street."

I scratch the back of my neck and play it cool, even though guilt cuts through me due to the complexity of the situation or the fact that every time he brings up Hailey my heart jumps. "Opposite ends. Plus, I'm normally at work until late."

Then screw your sister senseless because she's my wife.

"Oh, okay, cool." He seems to buy it, and he looks over his shoulder. "Our instructor is telling us it's time. I gotta go."

"Yes! Please. You're newlyweds and shouldn't even have left your hotel room, but fine, go kayak." I smirk. Their idea of a honeymoon is hiking and adventure sports.

I would say that I'm a hypocrite for roasting his ideas of what the newlywed phase should look like, but I now have my own.

Not exactly conventional, but on the calendar, the newlywed phase began a week ago when we said I do. No honeymoon for us, but I'll give her the closest thing possible.

The sound of wheels on gravel brightens my smile as I lean against the car and wait for Hailey. Ideally, I would have picked her up, but I needed to be here to set up a few things.

When she parks her car next to mine, I open her door for her, and she slides out of her seat in good spirits, giving me a quick peck on the lips as I close the door. I told her to come casual, and she nailed it with jeans and a black tee, with her dark red sneakers.

"Sorry I'm late. We had a staff meeting and it went overtime due to the science teacher from hell, but apparently, he is moving next month, so that's a win for us all."

"It's fine. I was occupied with your brother on the phone."

Her face drops, color even slightly washing away. "What? I spoke to him earlier, but it was quick, and I didn't even have time to process that I'm keeping a big secret from him. Maybe he found out. He was grilling you or tricking you or I don't know…" She's about to have a meltdown.

"Relax. As much as I had a few moments of internally cursing *oh shit,* we're fine. Just wanted to check about the key and ensure that you don't go overboard with decorating his house."

She theatrically wipes a hand across her forehead. "Thank goodness. We're really going to need to rehearse this until the time is right. But I don't want to think about that now. They can enjoy their honeymoon, and I'm here." She steps forward and her arms circle around my middle.

"You know…" I cock my head to the side and cluck my tongue. "Technically, we're in the newlywed phase, and I know we are going backwards on the timeline with now actually having a date, but I think I have us in the middle." I step back and hold my hand out to her. "This way, please."

The moment her palm greets mine, I feel a sting near my heart. She almost appears shy with anticipation in her delicate smile. In truth, I'm the one who's a little nervous. It's been a long time since I've been romantic in this way. Okay, maybe I've never gone this far off the scale, but it's for someone well deserving.

"We are walking toward the river," she notes.

"Someone is observant." We walk through the woods with no path. It's only a three-minute walk from the car, but still, it feels like we may get lost.

"Mosquitos might be a pain. The sun will set soon, and those little pesky things come out in full swing," she notes.

The corner of my mouth lifts because she isn't complaining, she's joking around with me. "Don't worry, I'll rub aloe vera on every little bite when I take you back to my place."

"What an offer."

In the corner of my eye, she searches around us for clues of what our date entails. It's only a minute more and our steps slow until she completely freezes, and her mouth hangs so far open that those mosquitos may just fly in.

I patiently wait for her to say something, and when she side-eyes me, her slack mouth flows into an angelic smile.

"Oliver, I-I," she stammers. "What the hell?" She shoves me playfully. "This is beyond expectations. This is beyond, well… you might be doing all the talking because I'll be too quiet from shock." She continues to soak in the setting.

In front of us along the river, in a private spot, there's a small table and chairs, with a jar of flowers and a candle. Plates and wine glasses are already set, too. I bought the whole shelf of solar lights at the store, which are now hanging between the trees, along with a few tiny wind chimes and those plastic pinwheels that move in the wind. I also threw pillows on the chairs and ground to give us options. Quickly, I pull out my phone and swipe my thumb to turn on the Bluetooth with my mix of soft indie and country music.

"Don't worry, the candle is citronella. As much as I would love to kiss every tiny mosquito bite, I'm not a monster and don't want to end up spreading ointment because you itch."

She sputters out a laugh. "You really have thought of everything."

I extend my arm to indicate for her to go to the table. She looks up at me as I tuck her chair under the table, and I grab a bottle of wine from the cooler.

"We needed a private spot." The pop of the cork on cue makes me feel like a magician, and it causes her smile to grow.

"The walk back might scare the hell out of me when it's dark."

I pour the white wine into her goblet. "I'm smart, remember? I have flashlights."

"And all of this stuff?" She looks at her surroundings.

I chuckle because again, I think I might have nailed this. "There is actually a chef who has the night off from the River Bell who delivered the food, and he will take care of the cleanup later."

Her jaw drops again. "What?" she nearly shrieks.

I set the bottle on the table and pick up a covered plate by the cooler and deliver it to the table and sit down across from her.

"Relax. Everything is thought out," I promise her and lift the cover at the same time.

Her eyes bug out and again her entire face lights up. I'm 90% positive that she might just cry, but that just means that my grand gesture has touched her within.

"Bagels," she says. There are spreads too, but the bagels are more significant.

"Dinner rolls are not for us, baby, and I've taken the knife away from you too," I tease her then hold out my glass to her for a toast.

She meets me in the middle. "To Oliver, for throwing on the charm and setting unrealistic expectations for every date going forward."

I chuckle and then we toast. Sipping my wine, I revel in the view. She nearly blushes, even when her fingers play with the stem of the glass that she looks into, and a beat of silence stretches.

"You okay there?"

Her eyes flick up to lock with mine. "It's just… nobody has done something like this for me. I'm wondering if I need to pinch myself to see if it's real."

Resting my forearms on the table, I'm conflicted because I wish someone had treated her like a gift, but then I'm happy they didn't because I want to be the first and set the standard. One that will never be as special as this.

My stomach dips because I'm well aware that I'm so infatuated with her now that I have her in some way.

"It's real."

She cracks a smile and her head lolls to the side. "Well, some of it." Her eyes narrow on my finger. "You're wearing the ring."

"And if I were to tuck my fingers into your shirt then I would find yours too." My voice is steady because this isn't us volleying back and forth. She silently gasps a breath because she knows it too.

"Look at us going on our first real date and already married."

Now we both have ridiculous grins on our faces.

I give us a few more moments then break us from our daze. "Hungry?"

She shifts on her chair and takes another sip. "I nearly forgot about the food, but I'm absolutely starving."

"They are garlic and onion bagels, with butter and hummus options. We have a salad with figs and goat cheese on a bed of some vegetable that I have no clue the name."

Her fingers are already ripping off a piece of bagel, and she shakes her head. "I'm not going to be able to focus tomorrow. This whole set-up is out of this world."

"Mind-blowing probably when I tell you that we also have chocolate mousse and strawberries."

Hailey points her bagel at me, still unable to contain her smile. "Now that's just a little cheesy."

I spread some hummus on my bagel and finally relax now that my date idea seems to be a success.

"I have to say that you are a wild card. I never would have guessed this is on your romance list. It's interesting seeing you in this light."

"How so?"

She rolls a shoulder back. "I've had ideas in my head of what you might be like when you are with a woman. I just couldn't figure out what way you would be." She bites her bottom lip for a second. "Or rather, I don't think I wanted to know. It kind of stung that it wasn't me who would be sitting on the opposite side of the table as you."

My eyes widen. "Whoa, we are not doing the whole past relationship convo this evening."

She cracks a laugh. "No, that's not what I mean. It's more like it was safer for me to block out the options of what you could be."

"And? Now that you know?"

"I'm happy I didn't know. It would have made life a little miserable every time I ran into you."

I wasn't expecting her to explain it like that, but it makes sense, and it just confirms that I was in her head as much as she occupied my own.

"We're totally doing everything the wrong way." I make the statement in a monotone.

She giggles and throws a tiny piece of food at me. "No, really? I'm having my first dinner date with my husband."

My lips purse, and I bite the inside of my cheek to hide my grin of satisfaction about that, but she must notice.

"So, tell me, young Oliver, what is it that you've always

wanted in your future?" She crosses her arms and rests against the back of her chair.

Hailey wants to pick at my brain, and in all honesty, other than being consumed by the woman sitting across from me, I haven't taken a moment to think about what I want in life. I'm beginning to think that I've thrown this upon us in order to figure it out.

"Success."

Her lips press together and her eyes squint. "You're not happy with your job, are you?"

"I am. Really, I am. It's never the same. Like I said a few times, I've been asked to work for the hockey league at their office in New York. That's gotta mean that I'm doing something right."

"I remember when we were younger and you would hang around Liam how you always wanted to be a lawyer. I think you had even already looked up questions for the bar and you weren't even seventeen. Therefore, I believe you. What else?"

My hand swipes across my face as I think about it. "At some point, I want to settle down. Everyone around me is."

"Doesn't mean you need to," she challenges.

"Or it just reminds me that I want those things."

Her mouth slants to the side. "Ah, you're using me so you can get a dog and then have me babysit when you have a business trip."

I grin at her banter again. "You figured it out."

"You had that adorable Saint Bernard growing up."

My face screws up. "You remember that?"

"Well, yeah. We remember the little things about the people we want in our life." She slays me every single fucking time. "Just like you don't want to admit how much you love the backyard of your parents' ridiculous-sized house, but you just like to say the opposite of whatever they say."

"Don't be too clever on me now." I'm enjoying this light conversation.

"Truthfully, that back patio with the river view is stunning and worthy of elegant festivities. I might endure one of your mother's gossip sessions just so I can sit outside there."

My brows furrow at her seriousness in that. "I didn't realize. Otherwise, I would have done all of this there."

"This is better. It's original. Plus, no prying eyes."

We talk a little more until I grab the main course from the warm bag. Then I place the plates in front of us, with chicken and rosemary potato roulade.

"Thank you so much. It looks delicious." Hailey skates her sight between the plate and me.

"Smells good too. We can eat slow, so no rush for dessert."

Hailey gives me a pointed look as she seems to be impressed. "Any other plans?"

I bob my head side to side. "Maybe."

The early-evening sun turns to the night sky that covers us. Our discussion was about various things, mostly what her preschool will be like. At some point we navigated away from the table to the blanket closer to the water. I'm lying propped against the pillows while her head rests on my stomach and she lies sideways with the sound of the chimes gently blowing.

"Of course I see my house as a home," I refute her challenge, as she said I live in only a house.

"It doesn't look loved inside. It's very… plain."

I begin to stroke her hair as the hue of the candlelight glows on her face. "Sorry it's not up to your standards," I say, sarcastic. "I guess it's because I'm not always home or I just work."

"You need the house to feel as though people actually cook there, relax with a movie, or even better, have little things that show your personality. It should feel warm and welcoming."

"Uh, it is." But I think she means that someone should be waiting when I open the door. A place where one day if I ever have kids, we pencil their growth on the wall, and right now, I'm stuck because in that thought, it's with her.

"I mean, I guess. I just can't help feeling that it could use a little something to complete the puzzle."

I've been formulating theories in my head the whole night. Mostly, that I've been living life, following the grind of the world. The times when it hadn't felt like a routine were when I was around Hailey. Every time she made everyone laugh, every moment when we would shamelessly flirt or the way we clicked without thought. Maybe that's why I've been a little mute every time she steers conversations to being about me.

She snuggles closer to me, as the temperature has fallen a few degrees, and her peaceful sigh has me worried that we won't leave this place tonight, and we need to.

"Want to go swimming?" she suggests, and there is no humor in her tone.

"Nope." My P is sharp. "I can't see what the hell is in the water this time of night, nor during the day, either."

Her fingers crawl up my arm. "But you always talk about going tubing on a river in Texas."

Creases break out on my forehead. "You remember that?"

"Sure. Like I said, it's the little things."

I guess it is, and it's not a one-way street between us.

"Plus, the moon is out." She pouts.

I chuckle and hold her closer. "Perfect for snakes."

"Eww, then no naked swimming."

"How about you come back to my house, though? Tomorrow is Saturday, so we get a few extra hours in bed."

She plants a kiss on my arm that's across her chest. "I mean, I guess. My neighbor down the street is kind of legally married to me, so I might as well hop into bed with him."

"That you shall."

We both shuffle in our spots and sit up. "Hey, Oliver." Her voice is soft, and her eyes shimmer in the candlelight. The sound of locusts are the background noise to our brief silence.

"Hey, Hailey."

She places her hand against my cheek. "Thanks for making this a special night. I never would have imagined this, and it was perfect." Her thumb strokes my skin once before she gives me a decent kiss that is worthy of a moan into one another's mouth.

"It's easy when the person it's for is already perfect." I'm not sure if it's me trying to be cheesy or if it's the reality, but her mouth twitches from my reply.

We scurry up, and I grab the flashlights near the cooler and offer her one. "Come on, before the deer or beavers attack us. I heard they get hungry this time of night."

After cleaning up as much as we can, she follows closely behind me, gripping my arm for dear life. "Seriously, if some animal appears that isn't cute and fuzzy then this date's rating drops."

I halt us and kneel down. "Get on my back."

"What?"

"On my back," I order. "I'll ensure nothing attacks you, including snakes and opossums. Now get on my back."

She listens and jumps on for her piggyback ride. "You're crazy."

I boost her up on my back as I stand. "Someone is speaking from experience," I rebuke.

She laughs and tightens her hold around my neck. "What a match we are then. I guess there will be a second date."

Hailey can't see, but I roll my eyes and half-grin. "Our date isn't finished yet. We have part two when I take you on the stairs after I rip your clothes off as soon as I close the front door."

And because I need to get inside of her and not for just physical gratification.

It's because we are in a confusing situation, and when I don't want to think, I would rather be lost in the woman who probably has more power over me then she realizes.

The woman wearing the chain with a ring around her neck.

Blowing out a long breath, I lean back on the patio chair at my parents' house. It was my home growing up, and when I return, it is as though I never left. My parents, despite their tennis matches at the country club, are down to earth, and my mother isn't afraid to be bold with her words.

It's not that I've been avoiding them, it's simply that they were away and then I was just kind of occupied. Okay, quite possibly avoiding my mother might be slightly correct.

Swiping off my sunglasses, I toss them on the table next to a bowl of nuts and pitcher of lemonade. My mother smiles, clearly happy that I'm here.

"You look well. I'm so glad that you stopped by."

"You would have chased me down, anyhow," I remark, and it earns me a lopsided smile.

"What would you like for your birthday coming up?"

I snicker a sound. "I'm not eight. You don't need to ask as though I have a wish list of toys."

She chuckles, and it's nice that she enjoys my presence because I do feel like family is important. That's probably why that sharp pinch in my stomach hits because I'm lying straight to her face.

"Okay, I'll figure something out. I ran into Hailey, and she mentioned arranging a party. I guess that makes sense with Liam away, and I know you boys always plan things for one another. But if you have a say in the invite list, Kale's daughter just moved back and it would be good if she could connect with new friends."

That just translates to "Honey, I have a potential dating option for you." This is the moment where I want everything to spill out of my mouth that I have a wife, and the ring is in my pocket because I'm the guy who takes marriage of convenience up a notch.

She accepts my warning glare that I will not be taking her up on her suggestion. "I'll stop," she lies with a smile. She extends her arm across the table and squeezes my forearm for a shake. "I'm so happy that you are here, have I mentioned that?"

"Yeah, and if you call me adorable or try to pinch my cheeks then I'm abandoning ship as fast as possible," I mundanely say which causes her to howl a laugh and let me go.

"A mother occupies herself with wanting the best for her children, and that's something I will never stop," she reminds me.

Taking a sip of my drink, I appreciate the ice cubes on this warm summer day. My eyes narrow to the sound of a chime. There is one hanging near the roses that grow against a trellis. I never noticed the chime before. It causes my cheek to tick because I think of Hailey. The sound calms me but doesn't take me away from the conversation.

"How's Dad? He seemed to be in a conference call when I arrived."

My mom almost frowns because she's supportive of him and they do love one another, but it must get tiring when your husband is so occupied with work.

Ooh, touché to me.

I see similarities between us in that aspect, but at the same time, Hailey mellows me out. I pay a little more attention to work-life balance, and this woman has only been legally bound to me for two weeks.

"Everything okay, my favorite youngest son?" I'm her only youngest son. "You seem lost in your thoughts."

I lift a shoulder and brush her off. "Nah, it's nothing."

Her cheeks lift and her nose raises as she looks over my ear. "There's my eldest son."

I glance to see Carter arrive, and his face is hardened with an indescribable mood, except when he looks to my mother and he softens. But when he plops himself on the chair across from me, I feel uneasy.

"Lemonade?" My mom offers my brother the pitcher.

"I won't be here long. Just wanted to stop by when you mentioned Oliver would be here for a little bit."

I squint at my brother whose eyes are a death stare.

"You know, I heard on the grapevine that Rose's horse died. She loved Astro."

I can hear my brother mutter under his breath. "Probably more than me."

My mom seems oblivious. "Perhaps you should phone her your condolences."

Wowza, this is a tough one to watch. "Or maybe not… it's a horse," I intercept.

Her fake smile swings my way. "Funny. I'll go grab some chips and dip from inside. You boys behave."

The moment she stands and is out of sight, a gust of

discomfort and confusion washes over me when I catch my brother's steely demeanor.

He snaps his fingers then points at me. "You. Me. Now," he snipes.

Carter abruptly stands, and his urgency causes me to not even second-guess before I follow him. His pace is fast and direct, causing me to trail behind as he heads straight to the other side of the yard, no longer in earshot of the house. Not caring about the immaculate cut grass, he storms straight to the spot where the woods meet the lawn on the side yard.

"What the hell?" I clench my jaw.

He crosses his arms and his face is fuming. "I should be asking you that." My eyes pop out as I wait for him to explain further. "How is marriage treating you?"

Oh fuck.

Everything inside me tumbles down from my head to my toes, and my Adam's apple bobs from the swallow of dry air that is causing my throat to strain. My mouth opens, and I search for words but fail.

"Yeah, for someone who works in law then you didn't do a good job of covering your tracks. You remember that when you request to seal a public record that it doesn't happen overnight, right?"

"Yes, and you only look when you have a reason to look. I doubt our friends and family are thinking, 'Oh, Oliver and Hailey probably secretly got married and let me go check.'"

"You see, the thing about being sheriff is you are at the courthouse a lot. Harold mentioned he saw Hailey there the other week, and then a funny thing is that he mentioned he saw you there too, heading into the judge's office together." He brings his finger to his chin. "Hmm, I thought. That's a little strange coincidence, and imagine my surprise when I played detective. So, I'm going to repeat myself. What the hell?"

I throw my hands up in the air and my entire body sags. "You can't tell anybody."

He looks at me as though I'm crazy then points back in the direction of the house. "Oh, you mean I shouldn't mention this to Mom back there, or Dad? Hell, I'm sure Liam would love this little tidbit of info. A simple FYI that you can tell him on your evening jog along the street after you remind him that it's garbage day tomorrow."

Stepping closer to him, I roll my eyes, now getting aggravated with his over-the-top lecture. "Especially don't tell him. Can you just let this go?" A wishful request, but I need to start somewhere.

"Why? Did I miss the memo that you two were even dating? I literally ran into her in the cereal aisle a few weeks back and she didn't mention her abundance of joy that I'm now her brother-in-law." Nothing about his current state is cracking.

My palms fly up to calm him. "It's new, so technically you were just Sheriff Carter to her, and please just let us figure this out. She needs to be married in order to get the building for her new preschool."

The explanation seems to exhaust him. "Are you fucking kidding me? Now I'm in a shitty position because I'm supposed to be enforcing the law. You're committing fraud."

Now I just dagger him with my stare, and if I had a pitchfork then I would stab him. "When you put it like that then *maybe* it appears that way. Marrying for financial gain isn't exactly ideal. But it's not like we *don't* care for one another. Therefore, Hailey and I have done no crime. Thank. You. Very. Much," I correct him smugly.

"Tell that to yourself. You're lucky that I'm looking past

the skeptical ethics of your marriage and it's only because I know my little brother has been a lovesick puppy for that woman. What is the long-run plan? Join me on the divorce train? Move in together? Pop out a kid? Oh wait, I have a great idea… don't lie to all of us!" He continues to raise his voice, and I have to step closer.

"Will you calm it down?" I lower my voice and grit out the words, scanning the area in the process to ensure that we are still alone.

He waves that damn finger at me again. "Wake the fuck up. This is the most twisted situation. Either someone gets hurt, or you end up in an everlasting marriage with our parents pissed off that they couldn't throw a wedding here at the house with fucking candles floating in the swimming pool."

Rubbing my temples, I'm now thoroughly annoyed. "Just can you stop?" I plead.

"Why? My brother is completely deranged and took his crush to a whole new level."

"Just let us figure it out ourselves. We have options of how this could go." She'll never give me that ring back is my favorite option.

His nostrils flare and his head retreats while he pauses to study me. "You don't get it, do you?" I stare blankly at him. He sighs heavily and locks his eyes on me, seeming to be debating something internally. But he gives up. "Fine."

Now my entire face screws up, as that was too easy. "Fine?"

Carter drags his hand across his jaw, and he subtly nods once. "Yeah. Only because I'm going to sit back, shut my mouth, and watch until this explodes. Because it will," he warns me. "No marriage is easy. Whether it's starting or ending." I can sense his own feelings and views bubbling to the surface. Fair enough. He has experience. "But I swear if this drags on then it might slip from my mouth at family dinner when I ask for someone to pass me the salad."

My jaw flexes side to side, accepting my fate. "Okay."

We both square our shoulders and enter a faceoff for a long minute.

"I'm out of here. No way am I listening to Dad and Mom talk about their fantasy of their son being mayor. I would say informing them of their son's blessed union will deter that conversation, but you're my brother and I won't do that… yet." He turns and walks away without a further glance to me.

I don't flinch an inch and stew in the complexity of life happening right now.

NOT MY PROUDEST moment but I'm adding coward to my title.

Hailey doesn't know that my brother is aware of our legal status because I didn't tell her. I've had a solid 24 hours to do that, and I haven't.

Now I'm entering Foxy Rox to pick up Hailey for our meeting with the owner of the building. She wanted an extra caffeine fix which won't calm her jitters, but I relent. Her dress has short sleeves, and the blue fabric reaches her knees. Completely elegant.

Right away when I open the door, I see her chatting with Esme at the counter who instantly sees me and dodges her head around Hailey's shoulder.

"Oh, look at that. Oliver is here." Her smile is unreadable, but there is a sense of something wicked.

Hailey turns and flicks her sight to meet my own, and her eyes flash at me so Esme can't see. "Hey, wasn't expecting you here. It's like I run in for a coffee and meet everyone on Everhope Road. First Esme and now you." She laughs nervously at her excuse.

"Guess so."

Esme's eyes travel between Hailey and me. "Coincidence," she states simply then focuses her attention on the barista.

Hailey mouths to me *fuck,* and I'm nearly distracted that the letters cause her mouth to open into the shape in which she takes my cock. Immediately, I shake that thought away and attempt to focus.

"I should order that coffee I came in for. I have a meeting soon." I step to the counter to order a coffee I don't need.

"When did you get that?" Esme asks as she stirs the stick in her coffee and grabs a lid.

I have no idea what her question is until I do a double take when I see Hailey innocently playing with something around her neck.

Not exactly subtle.

Hailey's eyes drop down and she realizes her error. She lets go and tucks it into her shirt, but it's too little too late. "My grandmother," she spits out. "Yeah, my grandmother gave it to me since Liam got Ava a new ring. Thought it's something nice to wear every now and then," she lies nervously.

"Yeah, it's nice." Esme finishes securing the lid and then turns to us both, fortunately not interested in pressing further. "Okay, well, see you guys around. Gotta run to a photoshoot."

Hailey sighs in relief as soon as Esme leaves. "Shit. I

totally forgot that was still around my neck. I wasn't even thinking." Because it seems to be human nature for her and that's not a bad thing.

"She didn't take any notice."

"Are you sure?" She blows out an audible breath. "We should be more careful. It feels as though we are hanging on by a thread to keep this all together."

"It was one question," I assure her.

Hailey gawks at me. "She thinks I power walk for fun and talk about dead plants."

A smirk dances on my lips because it's kind of hilarious.

"Forget about it. You have a bigger issue right now." And it isn't my brother. "Ready for the meeting?"

Her facial muscles ease. "I think so. I now check all the boxes, plus you will be there. That's already a relief."

"Okay, then let's get out of here." I throw some bills at the barista and inform her that we don't actually need coffee. She looks at us strangely but then shrugs and accepts it.

When we are out on the sidewalk of Main Street, it's a temptation to touch Hailey. Whether it be my hand on her lower back or interlinking her arm with mine. The way she lifts her sunglasses on her head is the same as at the start of theater when the curtain rises, making me feel curiosity and excitement.

"This shouldn't last long," she says as the ring around her neck finds a new home on her finger.

I pull out my own ring to slide onto my finger for appearances with this old lady. "It's fine. I've cleared my schedule."

She throws me an appreciative look. "Thank you. Not just for schedule adjustments but also everything that you are doing."

"It's nothing."

"Neither one of us believe that, but we'll have to assess that at another point. Now come on, Husband." She nudges my shoulder as we walk side by side.

On some levels we think the same, which is why I know she's right.

21

HAILEY

This is it.

An old lady sipping her tea and eating cucumber sandwiches will decide my fate. I should be nervous, and I am. It's just…

Oliver walking next to me with his fingers grazing my arms scares me more.

For the past few days my mind has drifted away from real estate, and in place, it's about my husband. The one that has me feeling as though we are on a shaky boat.

Which is perhaps fitting as we now walk down the hall on a river boat, albeit no longer functional. Still, my feelings shake. They bounce back and forth between my belly that does somersaults before rocketing right back to that place between my breasts that stores a message in my heart.

"It's fine," Oliver whispers to me with that gentle smile that sometimes doesn't appear as just affection; it's something more powerful. A determination to ensure me that he won't fail me. And no longer on the side of best friend's little sister, we crossed that line a few weeks ago.

His commitment to this meeting has him wearing a mint-green polo shirt that is fit for a golf club, but that is beside the point.

I smile weakly at him as we enter the private corner room overlooking the river.

The older lady immediately smiles at us. She has gray hair that stops at her shoulders, and she's sporting a sequined sweater even though it's the middle of summer. "Hello. You must be Mr. and Mrs. Oaks. Please, have a seat."

Nobody has called us that yet. It's an odd sound to my ears but not in a bad way.

"Hello, it's nice to meet you."

"We're happy to be here." Oliver pulls out my chair, and I get comfortable while he sits in the chair next to me.

I have to blink a few times as I take in the items on the table. A pyramid tray with an array of little triangle sandwiches, fudge in cupcake paper, lemon bars, little muffins, a pot of tea, and the list could go on. My lips roll in to stop my laugh, purely because this must be Oliver's idea of hell.

The waiter arrives as fast as light to pour some tea into the cups on our saucers. Truthfully, I never knew the River Bell did high tea. I guess they will cater to any requests.

"This must be a little traditional, but my father always told me to become acquainted with whomever you conduct business with, even if it's for a sale of property. And my grandmother insisted that it should be over afternoon tea."

"It's a wonderful idea," I say, and in principle, it is. But right now? This is a pain-in-the-ass request that has uprooted my life.

But then Oliver throws on the charm and offers Ingrid the pot of sugar with that suave smile that has my mother wrapped around his finger, and quite frankly, many women. He has no problem going overboard, hence why there is a ring on my finger.

"We understand that you live down near Decatur. It must be a bit of a drive," Oliver says.

"I went to an antique market in the area so the drive would be worth it." She scoops a spoon of sugar into her tea, stirring it, then sets her spoon down and glides her sight between Oliver and me. "I must say that this is a pleasant surprise. When Molly phoned to tell me that you're married, it made me excited that we could perhaps proceed with the sale. I'm just surprised. I was under the impression that you were not which is why I needed to seriously consider the orthodontist who would like to set up his private office."

"Well…" I smile tightly.

The sudden feeling of a warm hand on mine that is resting on the table near my fork relieves me.

"We're private people and have been dating for a while. We've always wanted a low-key wedding, and we've kept it to ourselves. Romance, right?" Oliver explains.

"Well, that is true. Tell me about yourselves."

I grab a sandwich from the bottom of the tray to set on my plate, it appears to be egg salad. "I'm a teacher over at Lake Spark Academy, and Oliver works in law. I've kind of had my eye on starting a preschool. Teaching middle-school social studies is fun and all, but four- and five-year-olds have a different type of curiosity, with playful ways to discover things."

Ingrid beams a smile. "That's wonderful to hear. You've always lived in Everhope?"

I nod. "Mostly. I went away for college and then worked at a school in the Chicago suburbs before returning."

"And I'm the fool who ignored her when we were younger but then noticed her when she returned. The moment I saw her walk into Foxy Rox, I knew I was a goner." Oliver's words strike me, partly because it's not a lie, I can tell, and I love hearing it.

"What will you do in the summer when it's school vacation?" she asks before she sips her tea.

"I want to run a summer camp perhaps. Preschool in a way but more games. It's really so parents don't get stuck without somewhere for their kids to go during the summer while they still work. Oliver is always busy, especially June and July, so it would keep me occupied." Because clearly, I've apparently been planning the logistics with a husband that might divorce me once my name is on that contract.

He rubs my shoulder with one hand. "Hockey season is over, but it's when we acquire and trade most players."

"Hockey?" Her ears perk up.

"Yeah, I work for the Spinners."

Her hands find her heart. "Believe it or not but this old lady loves hockey. That Connor Spears is such a looker," she gushes.

Oliver chuckles, and a laugh clogs my throat.

"And kids? I know I shouldn't be asking that since times have changed, but I'm trying to understand the long-term. I'm aware that the sale would mean that my family no longer owns the building, but it would break my parents' and my late grandparents' hearts if I sold to a couple that would only end up selling again soon. Even marriages end, but when you are married then you have another wall to break before you can give up."

Please, Hailey, don't throw up. It's completely true, and hearing the obvious brings chaos inside of me.

"Uh, wow, what a question." Oliver clears his throat. "If it happens then probably two." He cocks his head to the side. "Three is a better number. We have to get a dog before that, and Hailey has to first mov—ah." He quickly realizes he was about to say that I need to change my address to his. "Move all of her crafts sitting in the living room to the new preschool. Yep, a lot of crafts." Before he can say anything else, he picks up his drink.

My face, thankfully, remains poised. "It drives him crazy. Clay, markers, crayons, paints. Did you know there is glitter paper these days?"

Ingrid studies the little cakes before taking her pick. "I have grandchildren, so yes. But business—I'd need to discuss my decision with my family, but we could get paperwork in order and then you would have the building quite soon." Her attention turns to Oliver, ignoring me. "I would assume you will handle the finances."

My mouth nearly drops. What time warp am I in? Did I get shipped back a few decades?

Oliver controls his own disbelief and rolls his lips into his mouth to give himself a second. "You know, I do enjoy taking care of Hailey. Anything she needs."

Ingrid is satisfied with his answer and takes a bite from her little sandwich. "That's wonderful to hear."

"*But,*" I intervene. "That also means that I take care of Oliver, which is all the more reason that the preschool will be a success. He won't have to worry about me and the stress that entails. I'll do it all, and he can swoop in with a cape when I need a hand."

I'm independent and I want her to know that. However, everything that I just said is support that I believe I have. A balance, I guess.

It's impossible to read Ingrid's face right now. I'm not sure she even heard me as she seems more occupied with her sandwich.

"That's what I love about her."

My head whips in Oliver's direction, and maybe my eyes

turn into the size of baby saucers. *Love.* Except, he meant it as a figure of speech. Nothing special. No different than someone who loves flowers or the color blue.

Now isn't the time to remember the number of times over the years that I've dreamt of this guy and every possible way he could say those words I wanted to hear, and touch my skin the only way that would make me come alive.

How is this meeting about a damn building untangling me?

Did the devil just want to pop in and say hello? Because his powers are coming through in the form of Oliver's fingers under the table feathering my skin, right above my knee. He probably wants to soothe me, but I just tremble.

"As mentioned, I need to discuss with my family and then I'll be in touch with Molly."

Taking a deep breath, I pull my concentration forward. "Do you have a timeframe for that?"

"Is there a rush, dear?"

I nibble my bottom lip as I bow my head with one shake. "I guess not. Even if the sale goes through, I still plan to return to Lake Spark Academy in September. It will be a while, anyhow, until renovations and all of the registrations and checks with the state go through." Oh shit, did I just ruin my chance? "I mean, the renovations are to spruce things up and ensure the space is utilized correctly for teaching and kids. It is a lot of space." Flattery might not get me far.

Ingrid tips her chin up with a little hum. "Would you keep the original features?"

I hold my palm up to encourage her to relax. "Everywhere I can. It's just the building has been empty for a little while and electrical will probably have to be updated, along with windows."

"My family was not ready to let it go."

"And I appreciate the sentimental value. I promise, I'll do all I can. The garden will be the same, just a little sprucing up."

"Will the gargoyle stay? It's impossible to move." Her tone is a little tart.

My brows rise, as I forgot about that. "It might scare the children," I reply mundanely. Also, it's probably cursed and scares the shit out of me. She doesn't seem impressed. Hmm. "But." I snap my fingers and rustle up some enthusiasm. "I could dress him according to our current themes. A little mascot maybe."

That seems to help.

"Hailey will actually add a lot of wind chimes to the garden. It sweeps in luck and fortune," Oliver adds.

I turn my view to my husband and my eyes lighten. It's the way he says it that uplifts me. Sweet and reflective. A flashback from our road trip comes to me, and I cling to how the excitement felt then and how the fondness for him now mixes with that.

He winks at me, and I half-smile.

"Well, you two. I really do appreciate meeting face to face. You'll hear from me next week. Now, shall we leave business aside and enjoy all of this food?"

All I can do is hope, as there is nothing I can do now.

———

OLIVER BLOWS out a long breath as I enter through his garage. After another hour of listening to Ingrid talk about her time in England and her grandkids, I feel extremely bad that he got dragged along.

He went home, and five minutes later, here I am after dropping my car off at my house and now sneaking through the garage. Oliver is in the kitchen grabbing two beers from the fridge. He's now in a different pair of jeans and a dark tee.

"Again, I'm so incredibly sorry." I've been apologizing profusely.

His cheek lifts from his amusement. "Why? It was funny and also a necessity. You don't need to apologize."

I take my spot leaning against the counter, hearing the pop of the bottle caps and click of them on the counter. "Still… anyhow. I don't want to talk about Ingrid anymore, as I've done all I can do."

He hands me a beer, and we clink our bottles before taking sips. "That's a good approach."

His gaze feels heavy, and it causes my brows to lift in caution. "Why do I feel like there is something you want to tell me?"

The rumble in his throat doesn't sound comforting. "Right, so funny thing." He sets the bottle on the counter and wets his lips before tilting his head to the side. "My brother knows."

"Knows?"

"About us… the marriage part."

"What?" I squeak.

He steps forward and touches my arm to calm me. "Relax, he won't tell anyone… I think. No, he won't." Oliver is trying to convince himself; then again, Carter doesn't seem like someone who would particularly want to involve himself with spreading the latest gossip.

I stand still, pondering what to do or say. "Okay. And?"

Oliver gentle tilts his head to the side. "It doesn't matter. We go on as usual. I just thought you should know, and soon you will get your preschool, anyhow. By then, we will have everything figured out."

"What exactly?" I dare raise the question, and it's a

dangerous one. We both keep getting lost lately in thoughts that neither of us want to share with each other.

Right now, we both seem to still take that stance.

"Hailey, let's not think. Just celebrate that we survived a high tea with an old lady who probably has a cat at home and plays bridge."

That does make me smile. "A story that will stay with us."

Oliver steps in front of me and in a flash raises his hands to plant home on the sides of my face, holding me in place to ensure my eyes can't escape his. That pounding in my chest returns with a pattern only for him.

The heat in his eyes will cause me to simmer all night.

He enjoys being in control, but this time, I won't let him have the first word. "It will stay with us," I rasp.

The corner of his lips pull an inch from my words before he slams his mouth down on mine, the flames inside me now on full blast.

My tongue delves into his mouth for a flick while I wrap my arms around his neck. My insides are turning to liquid because his hand is running down the side of my body and stopping right at the hem of my dress. His fingers drag the fabric up, causing agony because I want him to move faster. The ache between my legs is pounding because we've escalated at record speed.

His lips rip away from mine, and he spins me around with a little force. Pushing against my back, enough for me to fall forward with my hands landing on the counter. This is the position of his choice, and I love it, which is why I tilt my ass back and place my forearms on the counter.

I feel the snap of my panties as he pulls the waistband. A little murmur escapes me, and I bite my bottom lip. My hair is wild and becoming a mess around my face. It's distracting but not enough, because Oliver just managed to rip my lace panties.

Sensitivity overloads, and there's a tingle in my nipples, wanting to be traced. I try to reach behind me, to touch him, but I fail and my upper body flattens against the surface with his hand between my legs.

"You drive me fucking crazy. You know that?" His lips graze the back of my neck, and I let a moan escape when his finger swipes along my pussy.

It's an inferno. An uncontrollable rage that is a passion I've never felt before.

I tilt my ass to press against him, offering more space to touch my clit and make me wild.

He notices, and I hear a chuckle buried in his throat.

"Oliver." I feel my pulse soaring.

Oliver encases my body when he leans over. His stomach to my back and his hand shackling my wrists above my head. I ignore the feeling of the cool quartz underneath me or the fact it's hard and pressing a little against my hip bones. It's all forgotten when I attempt to glance over my shoulder, but halfway our mouths fuse for a kiss. Slowing us down as his fingers play with me, stroking me. I'm surviving on his touch alone.

"Please," I beg.

"Please what?" he husks then draws his mouth down my neck, sending a tickle down to my toes.

"Fuck me." I'm breathless.

He surprises me when he lets my arms go and stands up, leaving my body in a 90-degree angle. He squares my hips only to give my ass a little pat, as though it's the ending of what is transpiring in here. He says nothing, but I get the drift and stand up, slowly turning to see his stoic face.

I can't question what is happening because he answers me

by returning his hand to my waist. "Tell me and answer me honestly," he says, adamant. "Do you prefer that I fuck you right here on the kitchen counter because we are trapped in a moment, or would you rather we go to my bedroom where I lay you down because we're trapped in something else that we are too scared to admit?"

That's my option. Hard and fast. Or slow because it means something.

It's an answer that I'm scared to admit, but he wants the truth. "Your room," I whisper and attempt to avoid his gaze that spears into me.

He places a finger under my chin to lift my gaze back up. "Then don't make me ask."

I sweep up his other hand and intertwine our fingers. With no words, I lead the way. Every step to his room builds the anticipation.

The moment that we're in his room, I turn to see his eyes gleaming with a look I haven't seen before. He steps forward, and I step back, then he steps forward and again I step back. All the way until the back of my knees hit the mattress and I drop down to sitting. I'm unable to tear my eyes away from his fierce gaze that has me entranced.

Oliver pulls up his shirt and throws it off to the side. I don't wait for instruction or his hands, I strip until I'm naked. Lying back, my hair splays against the duvet, and I watch intently as he undoes his jeans.

The moment he is over me with my thighs resting against his hips, I realize that this won't be like the other times.

My hands float around his back, occasionally brushing his skin, our mouths chase, and we're in no rush.

His cock rests against my pussy, and although desperate to lead him inside me, that's not what this is.

There's a slow and silent awareness of indescribable feelings we share, yet an unwillingness to say a word except one another's names.

The feeling of his palm covering my breast only makes me needier and drenched. He pinches one nipple, and it nearly sends me over the edge.

We do this for a few minutes, taking our time to explore one another. Finally, when he guides my thighs wider, I know we'll be rewarded for our patience.

I shift my upper body up and lean against my elbows to watch him align with my pussy then slide in. My head falls back, a gasp leaving my lips because it feels good to be filled up by him.

He groans once then begins to find a pace as he drives in and out of me, his cock glistening from my arousal.

"A fucking perfect fit."

"Mmm. Deeper," I request.

He listens, and I wail when he hits me so deep I think I might break in two.

As our skin slaps against one another with every thrust, our foreheads meet, and our open mouths don't touch; instead, we are sealed by our eyes.

The feeling of something clamped around my finger reminds me that I'm wearing a ring.

"Hailey, I plan on doing this all night. Do you understand?" His voice is thick, and I hear the firmness of his tone.

"Yes," I whisper.

Tonight is ours, which is why I reach behind his neck to pull him down to me. He stays inside me but stills as we kiss.

"You're something, you know that?" he says softly against my lips.

I squeeze tighter around his length. "Only because I'm with you."

Our eyes connect in recognition of the underlying meaning.

Which only leads us into moving in sync with one another, hips rolling and our skin beginning to shine with sweat. We continue this way with no perception of time.

I've never taken ecstasy, but I would assume it's like this.

It feels as though the room is floating colors, but I'm in the safety of his arms as my entire body begins to shake, and I'm so incredibly lost in the feeling that I have no idea what is around me or grasping that I'm going blind.

I'm not sure that I'm even in my body.

It's only when I come back down to earth and steady my breathing, I remember that the man resting his head against my chest, with the pounding of his heartbeat against my skin, doesn't just have a wife.

He has me.

Every single part.

I wonder if he grasps the magnitude of that.

●
22

OLIVER

I'm not sure that Hailey realizes how hard this is. She's bouncing around like a kid in an ice cream shop. She's always loved party planning, so much so that it seemed to slip her mind that we are in a room surrounded by everyone we've been lying to.

This is the ultimate test.

Then again, I think we are all distracted by the blue decorations on the deck of the River Bell. It's early evening and the river is still, but the conversation amongst friends and family is buzzing.

A table of buffet food is along one side, a chocolate cake with who knows how many candles or perhaps one of those sparkler things is coming out later. Everyone has a drink and they're all busy with a conversation with someone next to them.

Looking across, I see that Hailey is talking to one of the young bar staff members with tattoos on his arm who I'm positive is eyeing her up in her casual summer dress that covers all the right places, which fuels me with annoyance, but when Hailey glances my way with a small smile, then it reminds me that she has no interest in him.

My brother interrupts my thoughts and dread fills me.

"Happy birthday, little brother. All the none wiser." It sounds like he is taking pleasure in my predicament.

"Carter." My tone is curt.

He takes a long sip from his gin and tonic and surveys the party. "Liam arrived. Back from his honeymoon. Hmm, I wonder if he will notice anything new." He has the balls to smile contritely at me on my birthday.

I glimpse down to the ice cubes in my own drink, and I swirl the glass. "Would you like me to bring up your ex-wife? Because you're being a little bit of an ass right now."

Before he can reply, Liam smiles and heads my way.

"Going to say hi to Mom since Dad is away on business again. Have *fun*," Carter taunts and leaves me to face my good friend.

"Hey there. How was the honeymoon?" I ask as Liam approaches.

The guy is near giddy. "Great. Nice to be in our own little world. Now it's back to reality."

I search over his shoulder. "Where is your wife? Already run away?"

He laughs. "Nah, she's under the weather at home. Happy birthday! I'm so grateful that my sister did this. Don't hate me but I wouldn't have been able to swing this. Just too much going on."

"Say no more. It's cool."

Keats joins us and clinks his glass with ours. "What did I miss? Hopefully no sordid details of honeymoon escapades."

"Funny. You have a wedding coming up, so be nice, otherwise you are getting a dirty-as-fuck speech at dinner," Liam warns him.

"Eek. Someone's a little grouchy," he replies in good humor.

I can't seem to control how my eyes keep drifting back to Hailey who is now talking with Esme near the bar, both laughing. I'm still not thrilled by the barman who seems to insert himself into their conversation, though.

"You okay there, buddy? You seem a little distant considering it's your birthday," Keats comments and looks at me strangely. He follows the direction of where my sight leads, and his lips can't help but twist before he takes a sip of his drink.

It's my birthday, and my brain seems to take that as the memo that the birthday boy gets to do what he wants. And apparently, what I want rolls up inside me and straight off my tongue.

"Hailey and I are together," I spit out.

Liam's eyes laser in on me, as if he's checking that he heard me correctly.

"Yikes. You just ripped that band-aid off," Keats mutters and can't help but take amusement.

"What did you just say?" Liam's voice is sharp.

I sigh, about to lay out some truths onto the table. "Hailey and me. We've been seeing one another. I know it goes against all of the rules friends have, but it is what it is."

He puffs his shoulders and gives me the death stare.

"Are you fucking kidding me right now?" he grits out, and I see the fume boiling.

I stand taller, because I'm no longer scared of his reaction. I've already said it.

"You heard me. I've been seeing your sister."

In the corner of my eye, I see Hailey and Esme arrive, oblivious.

Esme rests her hand on Keats's shoulder. "Catching up?"

Liam doesn't flinch, and his gaze remains directed at me. Hailey skates her eyes between her brother and me, her smile fading.

"Hailey, you're dating Oliver?" Liam doesn't bother glancing at her.

Esme lets out a big sigh and hangs off her fiancé's shoulder. "Oh, thank God, the obvious is out in the open. I was waiting for this." We all turn our attention to her, and she is quick to sip her wine. "I mean, I totally didn't know, and this is such a surprise," she utters as she looks away and takes another sip.

"Obvious?" Hailey sounds puzzled.

Keats shrugs. "Well yeah, I mean the whole neighborhood is aware that Hailey suddenly power walks after parking her car, and then sometimes Oliver throws bones at the new neighbor's dog so he can walk through their yard. Doesn't take a rocket scientist."

"You knew?" Hailey is still confused.

"Sure," Esme answers as if it's all nothing.

But Liam doesn't seem to follow that sentiment.

"Liam, please don't go brother bear on me. I'm old enough to make my own decisions," Hailey implores.

He takes notice of her, only to slide his set eyes on me. It's a few seconds of silence and then his demeanor melts and a smile begins to form.

What the hell? I was waiting for him to throw me off the boat.

"I knew it would happen eventually. Finally, you two."

Hailey's jaw drops, and I freeze for a moment.

"What do you mean?" I'm still weary.

He slaps a hand on my shoulder, his grin getting wider. "I was hoping this would happen. I mean, we all obviously knew it would eventually."

"Wait, what?" Hailey is still suspicious of her brother. "You're not mad?"

"Yeah, what she said," I deadpan.

Liam chuckles and his grin stays pasted to his face. "Don't get me wrong. Hailey, I've always had the rule that friends can't go after you. Up until recently, I would have killed Oliver. But it's Oliver. He's a good guy. I haven't been blind that you two have had eyes for one another for a while. Maybe it was planning my wedding that softened my rules, but I kind of began to accept it. I just thought I shouldn't push you two or raise that point in case it all went wrong. Didn't want to rock the boat. You two kids needed to figure it out for yourselves."

"What the fuck?" I swipe my hands through my hair. "Are you saying we didn't need to hide behind your back?"

We made this whole situation harder than it needed to be. We've been worrying about nothing.

"No." He shrugs. "The road trip probably made you two realize. I had no issue insisting she tag along."

"Truthfully, we thought you would be pissed. But kudos to you for forcing them on a road trip," Esme comments from the sidelines and lifts her glass in the air.

"I mean, my best friend and my little sister. It can't be fucked up, but it's pretty cool."

"Again, what?" Hailey is still in awe.

Liam holds his hands up as if his sister might throw something at him, and quite frankly, I want to throw something myself.

"Chill. All is fine," he repeats his sentiment. "I'm not that blind. At Sunday's brunch at my wedding, you had the same look on your faces: guilty. Besides, just add the clues together then it isn't rocket science. Road trip, the rehearsal dinner, and yeah, I fucking noticed the looks across the room."

"Why didn't you say anything? Let us know that it didn't bother you?" she implores, because, like me, she's a mix of annoyed and angry that he could have made one of our challenges disappear.

But I'm not sure it would have altered the fact I have a wife now; it just would have made it a hell of a lot easier to be out in the open.

Liam holds up his ring finger. "Oh, let me see. I was in the middle of my own fucking wedding weekend. A little occupied there, Sis."

Fair enough.

She shoves her brother, now visibly annoyed. "You made us think that we could never happen, and this whole time it wasn't a big deal!" she shrieks then jabs her finger at his shoulder.

He fakes pain and just finds it funny. I blow out a breath, trying to refrain from committing murder. He could have given us a fucking clue of his thoughts long ago.

Our tense air is interrupted by the tattooed bartender personally delivering a new tray of drinks. Esme and Keats happily take another.

"We'll be needing these. This is fun." Keats is having the time of his life.

Hailey grabs a glass and chugs down the wine until it's half empty then sets it back on the tray, and asshole bartender gives her that look again.

"Seriously, can you stop looking at my wife like that!" I nearly shout.

Then it happens.

The entire party grows quiet, to the point someone dropping a fork is the only sound. All eyes are now on Hailey, Liam, and me. Hailey appears to wince, and I feel the weight of attention on us.

"Excuse me. Did I hear that right?" Liam's happy demeanor vanishes into thin air.

Silence stretches, and my jaw flexes side to side as I gather composure. "We're married," I mumble.

"You're what?" He blinks repeatedly.

"Whoa, I did not have this on my bingo card for the year," Keats mentions, one-toned, to himself but loud enough for us to hear.

My brother joins the circle as the whole party watches. "Uh-oh. Cat is out of the bag." He grins and seems to take satisfaction in this.

Liam ignores them all.

"We're married," I repeat, this time with more firmness.

He laughs to himself. "Funny. This is a joke, right?" He bends his head in different ways to examine Hailey's and my fingers. "I mean, no rings on your fingers. Nice try."

Hailey pops her lips and tucks her fingers into her dress to pull out her necklace. "I mean… technically it's on my neck, *so…*" She drags it out.

Esme gasps theatrically. "It's not your grandmother's ring? Not cool. You lied to me." Esme shakes her head, but her voice isn't angry.

Liam's anger returns, and he steps forward. "What the fuck!"

"You just said you don't mind us being together," I reiterate.

"Married is a whole different level. So what fucking game did you drag my sister into?"

"It's not a game." Hailey grabs his arm, but he shakes her off.

He looks at both of us as if we are insane, and we probably are.

Hailey is receiving the brunt of his brazen face. "Not a

game? You've been together for a hot second and you're already married?" His voice rises an octave. Hailey grows quiet, and he directs his attention back to me with his nostrils flaring. "You," he seethes.

Liam's palms shove into my chest, causing me to stumble back a step, and instantly I retaliate. Hailey and our friends make a commotion, and Keats intervenes with his arms separating Liam and me. "Come on, no need for this."

"He crossed a line," Liam booms his statement.

"We're adults," I point out.

He pinches the bridge of his nose as if he is dealing with a headache, and truthfully, we all are having one right now.

Carter intervenes and presses his hand against Liam to keep him at bay. "Allow me to handle this." My brother steps to the side and turns his focus to me. "Secret's out, so allow me to voice what we should all be thinking. This is some twisted shit. Who even suggested this marriage? Because the thing is, marriage plays with emotions. You shouldn't just jump into marriage with no expectations for the consequences. You're supposed to go in with the view of forever."

Liam's face screws up, and I attempt to listen patiently because I sense a bit of underlying anger in my brother, and I'm not entirely sure if it has to do with me or his own life. Which is probably why our friends watch on, doing their best to hide their apparent shared sentiment that my brother is ranting about his own emotions.

My mother appears out of thin air with a bright smile. "What's going on, boys? I return from the ladies' room and everyone is in a circle. Did we already do toasts?"

Carter snickers. "Not yet. We've taken a detour and need to change the toasts to a new marriage." He steals the glass of scotch from Keats's hand and takes a decent swallow.

My mother doesn't understand. "But it's Oliver's birthday."

"And your son is deranged and married my sister without any of us knowing." Liam glares at my mother whose smile wilts.

"Huh?"

Hailey steps next to me and swoops up my hand to hold. "If we want to look at the law then you're my mother-in-law now." She smiles weakly at her.

My mother begins to grasp the situation, her eyes traveling between me and my wife. "Married?"

I blow out a deep breath and look up to the sky for a second. "Yes. Now everyone knows the fact. You heard us, and we don't need to keep repeating it."

"I was supposed to set you up with the James's daughter next week!" My mother sounds inconvenienced, but then she looks to Hailey and her smile returns with her hand on her heart. "But my son is no longer a bachelor." She pretends to pray to thank some spiritual force for her wish having come true.

Carter glances to her strangely. "Your son deceived us all and has a wife," he says dryly.

Her sour face scowls at me. "Oh, don't you worry, young man, we will be discussing this tomorrow." But then she retraces her line of sight to my wife and her smile returns. "Welcome to the family. I knew you looked different the other week. I just thought you were pregnant or something."

"Is she pregnant?" Liam screeches in horror and points to his sister.

Hailey holds her hands up, eager to stop this chaos. "No. I'm not pregnant." She mocks her brother. "We're married and that's that."

If she's holding down under these hurricane-force winds, then so am I.

"Accept it," I demand to Liam.

"No."

"Yes."

"I mean, maybe." It's apparent that he is still digesting the news and calming. "I guess if I was okay with you and her together then marriage is just, well... you're my brother-in-law now. It's just fast." He's coming around, I can tell.

My brother? He's growing irritated. He stares coldly at me before his gaze drops to our hands where we don't let go of one another. "Marriage. Seriously, playing with her emotions because sometimes you're going too fast you forget to use your brain." He snaps his eyes to me. "Who even woke up suggesting that a quickie wedding while nobody even knew you two were together was a great idea?"

Hailey attempts to open her mouth but only a scratchy sound escapes from her throat.

"Does it matter?"

My brother tilts his head to the side to examine me. "Ah, it's my brother who lives in a fantasy where marriage can be taken lightly."

"Should we intervene?" I hear Keats ask Esme from the side as they look on.

I throw him a glance. "Don't. If my brother would like to voice his views, then by all means, let him." I drive my sight back to Carter and give him a pointed look.

"You're a coward. At least let your wife know the real reason you asked her to marry you, and don't give me some bullshit about necessity. You've had strong feelings for her for God knows how long."

Hailey touches my arm, encouraging me to give up. "Just leave it. I think he needs the news to sink in."

Carter takes another drink and sets the glass down. "No, Hailey, it's perfectly sunk and anchored into my brain that you two should confront reality before you decide that signing divorce papers is the only way, only to regret it later."

"*Yeah*, I'm sensing this isn't about my sister anymore," I hear Liam comment to Keats.

I drop Hailey's hand, and my palms face forward in front of Liam's chest. "Take it down a notch. It's not like we woke up in Vegas with no recollection of the ceremony. We were sober and well aware of what we were doing."

"You both have no clue what you are doing. Zero to a hundred in the span of fuck knows how long. Are you telling me that you two are so in love that it couldn't wait to, I don't know… let all of your friends and family know that you are even together first? Because up until fifteen minutes ago, you two had some secret marriage that you hid behind. Trust me, you two might want to have a little more honesty with everyone, most of all yourselves."

"Wait. You two aren't even living together." Keats still seems to be trying to adjust to the news. He lifts a shoulder. "Meh. To each their own." He cooly takes another sip from his drink.

Hailey blows out an exhausting breath before she claws her hair from exasperation.

We knew this was probably coming, it's just sitting through the experience is a little excruciating, even if it will soon be over and we get the hell out of here.

"You two are so unhinged that I don't even what to do right now." Carter isn't cooling off in the slightest.

"What am I supposed to do in this moment?" Liam asks, slightly bewildered.

Hailey's eyes bug out as her hands fall, causing hair to cascade behind her shoulders. "Nothing. You need to do nothing. I'm a big girl who makes her own decisions. Oliver is my husband, and I'm his wife"

Rubbing my face with my hands, we're going in circles. The sun is disappearing over the tree line due to sunset, but I'm beginning to believe the sun is running away from watching this scene unfold.

"Don't make me disappointed in you for your choices," Carter drills into me.

Our mom begins to tug his arm. "Come on, stop it."

I hold my palm up to encourage my mom to leave it. "It's fine. I'm a man. I can handle what my brother would like to voice so openly. After all, he's the one so wise on the topic of marriage."

Fuck, that was a little low for my standards.

The boiling anger on Carter's face turns fuming at record speed and fists form at his sides. If he had it in him, he would shove me right now, but that's just not him. Instead, his nostrils flare before he pivots and storms off.

My mom lifts a finger in the air. "I should probably follow him." She scans the area and pauses on Hailey, a smile tugging on my mother's mouth. "I guess I'll be setting an extra plate at our next family dinner." She attempts to make a joke, but it falls flat. Realizing that, she adds, "I think we should all give the apparent newlyweds some space and interrogate them another time. Well, actually, sooner than later, but not now." She offers Hailey a sympathetic look before she walks away.

I turn to face Hailey in the still silence of the boat. "I'm sorry, I think the party mood has changed."

She musters up a tiny smile on her face. "It's okay. At least, my brother isn't going to murder you."

Liam scoffs from the sidelines. "Still debatable, but I'm not going to have a meltdown at least."

"This has been unexpected." Esme hums a sound as she leans against the railing, and she looks into the empty glasses in her hands before setting them on the nearby table. "What a honeymoon you two have found yourselves in. We can all agree that the party is over. Oliver, your birthday present is over by the bar." She propels herself off the railing and gestures her hand as a phone and mouths something to Hailey.

Liam takes a few steps to us, and he has softened to us. "I think… just give it some time… for me, I mean. Carter?" His face turns contorted. "That's going to take a little more maybe. I'll be in touch and maybe then I can congratulate you both."

"Thanks." Hailey sighs. Liam touches her shoulder gently in passing as he leaves.

With guests dispersing, Hailey and I face one another.

"I'm sorry. Being married just kind of spilled out of my mouth."

Her shoulders lift, and she touches my upper arms with a little squeeze for reassurance which puts me in admiration because she should be a complete mess right now.

"Bound to happen. And I don't think you and I go as planned. That seems to be our thing." The way she describes us causes me to tighten the line on my mouth with an urge to smile. "Well, that was confronting." She is trying to lighten the mood, even if it's the truth. "Probably time to address our situation."

"I, uh, guess we have a lot to talk about, but I'm not sure my energy is there."

She nods in understanding. We both grow quiet until it seems a lightbulb goes off in her head. "I'll be right back."

"Not going anywhere, especially the parking lot," I retort.

While she is away, I take the opportunity to look out on

the river that is slowly turning dark from the change of daylight. The sound of the current sending tiny little waves is a comforting noise.

It's all unraveling.

The mess I got us in. I had to go and make it so complicated. At least it's one thing off my chest. It's a few minutes later when I'm now alone on the empty deck that I hear Hailey approaching from behind me.

"Turn around," she requests.

Instantly, I smile as she is holding a chocolate cake that seems to have seen hell, topped with a lit candle. Her hand is cupped around one side so the wind won't ruin her attempts to turn this evening around.

"It's still your birthday, and you have a wish to make."

My brows knit together when she is close enough for me to study the cake.

"I dropped it on the table. Three-second rule. We're fine. Now make your wish," she presses.

"Don't get bossy on me," I tease her and do as directed by leaning over to blow out the flame, silently wishing that I can admit to her that I'm insanely in love with her and won't let her even contemplate divorce. One puff and then the smoke from the candle dances in the air.

She proudly holds the cake up. "That wasn't hard, was it? I would say tell me what you wished, but it's bad luck. I just hope it was a good one."

Very good, it's about you. I'm just waiting for the sign that you won't walk away and will tell me the same.

"Okay, let's eat cake." She sets the cake on a nearby high table and notices that there are no forks. "Hmm. We don't need them." She digs her fingers into the icing and offers me a piece crumbling between her fingers. She's unpredictable this one, slightly eccentric at random moments, too.

I wrap my lips around her fingers, and the taste of the moist chocolate cake mixed with the subtle saltness from her skin is electrifying. Slowly, I pull my lips from her finger, moaning in the process as our eyes latch. I take my time until my lips pop off.

"That's good cake. Perhaps the best birthday cake yet." I mirror her actions and bring cake to her mouth.

This woman knows how to suck, and I think I would pay every waiter in sight to all disappear so I can take Hailey against the railing of the boat.

But for now, this is the next best thing.

Her eyes are sultry when she licks my fingers clean; she knows she's turning me on.

But then her face turns delicate. "Oliver…"

"Yes."

"My head is spinning from tonight, but you're eating your birthday cake and made a wish. That's all that matters." She is hopelessly beautiful because she also cares and wants me to be happy.

I have the urge to cup her face and slam my lips down on hers, but we will both be covered in cake.

I do the next best thing. I close our distance, and I swipe against her nose with mine to leave a small mark of chocolate. "It only matters if it's with you."

It earns me her yearning eyes to illuminate and her lips to tug. "I guess I won't need to sneak around anymore. I'll be able to walk right into your house with you."

"Is that your plan for tonight?"

"It is. I don't want the birthday boy to have a bad evening that has been a colossal experience. But most of all, I don't want *my husband* to be alone on his birthday."

I dip my head down to place a chaste peck on the tip of her nose before I kiss her lips softly but intently. Pulling away, I whisper, "And I wouldn't want *my wife* to go anywhere else but with me."

"Come on. I want to escape the world for a while. Everything can wait until tomorrow." She eagerly walks away, only to quickly pivot and pick up the cake. "We can get a doggy bag for this." Her smile is infectious.

She's right. Everything can wait until tomorrow.

We just don't know if it's the clarity we need.

HAILEY

I stretch, my naked body lengthening against the soft cotton sheets and mattress while I yawn blissfully. Feeling Oliver's warmth next to me, I roll over and cuddle against his bare skin, intent on falling back to sleep since sunlight peeks through the blinds.

But even in a drowsy state, I can feel a set of eyes cutting through me.

He's awake.

I stir groggily and shift to see him lying on his back staring at the ceiling. "What time is it?" My voice is gravelly.

His arm brings me in closer to him to mold against his body.

"Go back to sleep."

"No. It's okay. I can't stay in my slumber all day. How long have you been up?" The sheet is a tangled mess around my body, but I don't care.

"Who knows."

I sigh and bring my hand to rest against his chest. "It was wishful thinking, was it? To fuck all night to forget?"

That's what we did. On my belly, back, side. Fast and slow. Dirty talk and silent words. Everything but talking.

"We knew it was coming. I have to dial in for a work call in a bit. Maybe that's luck, as I don't particularly want to face anyone over scrambled eggs."

"Of course not. It has to be sunny side up." I attempt to make him smile, but he doesn't seem in the mood.

"What's on your agenda for the day?"

I grumble. "I'll be brave for us and run into Foxy Rox for coffee to-go. I can bring you one back if you are eager to hide away."

He bites the corner of his mouth. "We have to face the music. It isn't about practicality and ensuring you get the building. That's not what we can yell from the rooftops."

The pit in my stomach returns with dread. "I know."

"We probably need to talk about what it also means for u —" He stalls and doesn't finish the sentence, but I could do it for him, as I know the ending.

My finger jets out to hush his lips. His chin is gruff with short stubble, and it nearly distracts me but not enough. "I think we need caffeine first and to maybe destress once before I go."

At last, his mouth breaks out into a smirk because I've cracked him. I've also prolonged the start of a conversation that has been looming for days. It's scary, maybe messy, and tide-changing. All the more reason I want to hold on to any extra minutes that I can get before we open our mouths on the issue.

"Destress? I could kind of use that right now."

Before I know it, Oliver has flipped me to my back and I have to giggle when he gets frustrated with the sheet, attempting to rip it away. "Remind me to burn these. I don't appreciate obstacles in the bedroom."

I only laugh more until it turns into a whimper because he is touching my pussy with his tip and already pumping inch by inch inside of me.

When our eyes link, we grow quiet but don't look away.

Every minute with him lately binds us closer.

We both know it. We just don't say it.

———

ESME STARES at me blankly as she sits across from me at the table by the window in Foxy Rox. Then takes her straw to sip purposely the last drop of her iced coffee. The noise scratches my ears. It was silly of me to think that I could slip in for coffee unnoticed. It's Everhope.

"I'm sorry I didn't tell you, even if it was obvious."

She huffs a laugh. "I admit that I was blindsided about the marriage part, everything else not." Her shoulders sag and she pushes her drink to the side. "It does sting. I don't know why you didn't share it, but I also respect your decision. Everyone should conduct their relationships in their own way. I'm not going to judge… only wonder."

I gulp because I can predict what's coming. She's going to pick not only for the details but also my mind.

"It seems I got married before you." My effort to bring the focus back to her fails.

"Who cares. Now tell me how it happened? Clearly spur of the moment, right? I mean, you two only hooked up a few weeks ago. Then boom." She snaps her fingers in the air. "He's calling you wifey."

"And he is also doing it to help me get the building for my preschool, so please keep that fact to yourself. I can't have the old lady figure it out until after I've signed everything."

"Ooh, devious." She folds her hands over one another on the table and gets comfortable for the gossip she intends to receive. "Are you staying married? Or, like, I don't know. It's not like you don't have feelings for one another. You've consummated the marriage I'm sure more than once."

"Esme," I warn her, but she just grins cheekily.

"I'm sorry but it is an obvious question. What was the wedding like?"

"Quick. Nothing crazy. The judge and courthouse kind of thing." But it was still somehow oddly special. I don't regret it. Sure, I was missing a lot of elements that I had imagined for my wedding one day, but it was also… perfect.

And that's why I'm on the crazy train.

"Kind of is a bummer we missed that. You're going to have to plan a redo for your anniversary."

I have no clue what life will look like a year from now. Hopefully, I have my new school, and I do picture Oliver in the dream, not entirely sure in what way. We skipped the middle part from dating to official to engaged to married.

"Perhaps," I reply nimbly. "Anyhow, it's Liam or Carter that we probably have the issue with."

Esme begins to howl with laugh and a few others in the coffee shop throw us unusual looks.

"What's so funny?"

She even snorts a little as she tries to control herself. When she finally does gain composure, I swear I see a tear. "You. You're hilarious. Liam will be fine. Carter, on the other hand? He's hurting from unresolved issues. I mean, what is he going to do? Hire his divorce lawyer for you? I mean, using him as an excuse is just obvious. If you think he is the obstacle, then you are hiding under a rock."

"How so?"

"Because your challenge is deciding whether you stay in a marriage that would've come to be one day anyhow, or you scratch that legality into history and begin from square one."

"And? Point being?"

"For a teacher, you have a brain cell missing. You are completely in love with him and have every intention of wearing that ring around your finger for eternity."

My mouth opens and words get blocked in my throat. Instead, I reach protectively for my necklace that I've kept on from habit and acknowledge she is right, but I won't say it out loud.

I am in love with Oliver.

Completely.

We just seem to dance around one another. I'm still not entirely convinced that we balance out, as in he loves me too.

"That is the reality we found ourselves in… yes." I avoid her gaze because I don't want to see her glee.

"You both have the answer. I mean, we all saw something coming. You two have been adorable together for the longest time. It's on Liam for being a jackass and not speaking up that he doesn't care… well, that was until the quickie-marriage part. I just mean that you both would have been together long ago and probably on your first kid by now. Then again, you both could have grown a backbone a long time ago and just gone for it without anyone's permission."

"Oh." It's the only syllable I manage to muster.

She pulls out a tube of lip gloss from her purse to spread a layer on her lips. "It's probably why you guys never told anyone. You think you want to figure it out and it's all on paper, but in reality, it's a front for what you both don't want to admit."

"And this is why we entered our own little world. Our

friends would just give their input as if they are world-renowned psychologists."

She flashes me a stoic smile.

I hear the bell on the door, and over her shoulder, I see my brother enter. He gives me a nod and slowly approaches our table.

Esme notices. "I'll give you two some time." She stands and touches my back in passing for assurance.

"I guessed you would be here."

I attempt a smile. "Fresh muffins tend to lift the day."

Liam sits down across from me, almost deflated, and I watch him, waiting for him to begin.

Liam flicks his eyes up to meet mine. A few times until his shoulders relax. "The thing is, I'm aware that Oliver is husband material."

"He is. Already, he's taken care of me," I say, quick to defend.

Liam holds his finger up. "But it's just... You're my sister."

"Your sister who wants Oliver as her husband. We always thought we shouldn't try to be more than friends for fear it could ruin the harmony of friendship between all of us. "

"I wish this wasn't as fast it is, but I get it. As long as you're happy."

I believe in what I feel. "I am."

"Then... I'll talk with Oliver. Man to man."

I chortle a laugh. "Sorry... are you serious?" One look and I know I shouldn't have laughed.

"I'm not going to brush this all under the rug. I still need to wrap my head around all this and make sure that he will treat you right."

I give him an *oh, really* look. "You already have that answer."

He bobbles his head side to side and rolls his eyes because he knows I'm right.

I reach across the table to hold his hands. "I get it. You're my brother and his best friend, well, now brother-in law." Liam doesn't look impressed by my wit. "Too soon? Fine, but you've said it yourself that you get your best friend and sister together. We're one package."

"Does that come with a fucking bow?" Liam retorts sarcastically.

That's a hint that the conversation is turning and the answer that my brother will be alright.

"It comes with your two favorite people being happy." I smile.

"Love how you leave my own wife off of that favorite list." Liam widens his eyes at me.

I smile awkwardly. "Of course. Her too."

"Mom and Dad need an explanation when they are back from their trip. Heard they booked the next flight back," Liam informs me.

I shrug, not exactly proud. "I'm not getting awards for letting them find out via the Everhope gossip train."

"Ya think?" He's flippant, and I roll my eyes.

"I get the being together part. It's just… fast."

"Liam, he is helping me. Without a husband the lady who owns the building I told you about won't sell."

Lines form on his head. "So like, this all happened for convenience."

I nod. "Something like that."

"But you actually both already had a thing."

I nod again.

"Okay, so you stay married." He is listing questions to try and understand.

I perk my head up gently. "That's still… a conversation." I sound uneven.

He raises his brows. "Might want to figure that one out."

My phone begins to vibrate, and I glance down to see it's Molly. Quickly I hold my finger up to indicate to my brother to wait a second. I hit the green button on my screen.

I don't let her speak. "Hi. Do you have any news?"

She must find my eagerness amusing as she releases a short laugh. "Good day to you too. By chance, Ingrid is actually at my office. We can talk on the phone, but it might be better if you can swing by if possible?"

I'm already standing up, nearly fumbling out of my chair. "Of course. I'm already on Main and can be there in two minutes."

"Great." She hangs up.

I begin to stand with urgency. "Are we okay? I don't want to run, but it's the agent."

"We're okay," he mumbles.

I slide the strap of my purse up my arm and rush to him for a quick hug. "I promise he's only been the best to me," I assure him in a whisper.

As I leave, I hear him call out. "Better be! And congratulations." That wasn't super enthusiastic, but it's good enough for me.

I sprint out of Foxy Rox and gallop down the sidewalk then pause at the corner near the real estate office. Smoothing my hair, I take a deep breath, reminding myself that fate is fate.

You've got this.

I give myself a little pep talk then stand tall when I walk into the office to see that Ingrid is sitting by Molly's desk drinking tea.

"Good morning, Hailey." Molly smiles, but she seems nervous, and that doesn't bode well for me, does it?

"Hi."

Ingrid smiles but it's unreadable. "Have a seat, dear."

Warily, I take a few steps and sit down on the vacant seat next to her while Molly crosses her arms and leans back against the chair.

"I'll get right to it," Ingrid starts.

"Of course." My heart is pounding and my ears feel warm.

"You and your husband remind me of someone."

I gulp some air, unsure of where this is going. "Oh?" My voice is unsteady.

"Yes. Me and my husband. We married after two weeks of knowing one another. We stayed married until his passing recently. I understand from the grapevine that there was a bit of... well, an eventful evening."

My eyes zip to Molly with horror on my face. "Everyone in town already knows about last night?"

She rolls a shoulder back. "I mean, Keats told the Kellys across the street and then they told the new couple with the dog and then someone put a message in the neighborhood chat group which apparently you don't check."

Somehow, I still manage to shake my head ruefully because it is kind of funny... *just*.

Ingrid clears her throat. "I'm not too concerned about all of that, although slightly deceiving, and believe you me that I would no longer consider you if I thought it was all for show. But I met you and your husband and you two are very clearly in love. The kind that reminds me of Fred and me. A long-lasting one. You and Oliver even have more points over us since you've known one another for so long."

We have.

A gift and a curse.

We've both watched the other's life go by, yet we didn't involve ourselves in each other's life. Not in the way that I'd always wanted.

"Point is, dear, you two are good together, and I have no qualms. You could even have told me you weren't married when I met you two and I would have just been convinced otherwise. It's a silly clause. My grandson, he works for one of those tech companies in Chicago, and he was berating me that I need to keep up with the times. I give in. He's right. I can't be a prickly old woman, right?"

My brows rise. "Wait, are you saying in the end we wouldn't have had to marry?"

Oh, fuck me. All of this for nothing. But it's anything but. In fact, it's as though a gust of wind wrapped us together to ensure we confronted our feelings.

"I guess in the end, no. I'm not sure that selling is the right choice anymore, so the clause would be irrelevant. Renting has crossed my mind."

Instantly, I frown. "I see."

Nausea hits, and it's because this dream is wilting away. Renting wouldn't be an option, as I have all of the renovations and changes I would need to make.

She holds her finger up. "It's a good thing, no? You won't have to worry about extra financing."

My face must look sullen as I really was counting on a place to own. "That is true, but unfortunately, you will need to find someone else. I'd really need to make the space my own, and I don't think a landlord would appreciate that."

"I thought so."

The air grows heavy with the mood tampered.

It's more than a few seconds that I sit there, debating if I should be polite and wait for a goodbye or excuse myself already.

"As I mentioned, I have been considering options, *however…*" Hope ticks up inside of me. "Provided all of the paperwork checks out, then it's yours."

My entire body morphs into pure ecstasy. "Really?"

"Yes, really."

I glance at Molly to ensure this isn't a joke, but she has a reassuring look.

My hands find my heart because this is such a milestone. The school is going to happen. It really is.

"Congratulations." Ingrid smiles.

"Thank you."

They give me a minute to let the shock wear off. I knew it was a possibility when I walked in here, but it's different now that it's confirmed.

It's a few minutes of admin and another round of smiles before I'm walking down Main, reflecting on the detail that it's because of Oliver that I was even able to go down this road, at the start at least. It seems to be irrelevant now in buying terms. Now, our marriage takes on a different direction.

It's because I can't shake away that he is my husband, nor do I want to. There are so many things we can be still. And stating the obvious is a start.

I love him.

We've been moving through the actions but not saying the words.

That's not us.

We are two strong-minded people who went off track.

Now, we have to take the step to decide how we want our marriage to be.

Because we are together, and I refuse to break that.

———

Rushing into Oliver's house, I walk on the balls of my feet toward his office down the hall, not wanting to make noise or interrupt in case he's in a meeting.

The tap on my back startles me, and I yelp. Turning, I see Oliver who seems pleased that he caught me off guard.

"Sorry. It was too enticing to do that. I finished my call a while ago."

"We don't need to be married. Not anymore." It bursts out of my mouth without warning, forgetting that I said I would return with coffees after my discreet trip to get them.

His face falls and his eyes widen from the bold words that just flew out of my mouth.

"It was all for nothing. In the end, she didn't seem to mind," I further explain.

A sound cracks and flows through his throat, and his eyes narrow.

Oh… wait.

"That's not how I meant that to come out." The opposite, actually. I'm trying to relay the news that I don't care about any of that because I still want to stand exactly where I am.

I could use some improvement on delivery.

"I just mean, now we need to confront staying married if it's not a necessity, and our pace and future and…" *I love you.*

"Right. Whether we need to stay married or not." The sentence lacks energy. "And the call I had earlier. It was the league again. They offered me the job in New York again. They upped the offer to make it very enticing. It seems the world is trying to tell us something."

"Oh… right. Well, I saw Liam and he's calmed down. But wow, New York."

Everything in that sentence fills me with dread. I don't get a chance to respond with those three little words because we are interrupted by the hammering knock on the door.

Are you kidding me? Who do I need to kill right now?

I can only hope he grasped enough of my last sentence to understand what direction I was leading us in.

But right now, it will need to wait.

24

OLIVER

It was on the tip of her tongue. I know it was. Her wish.

Or I'm simply disillusioned, and it instills a little fear inside of me. Actually, it creates a giant hole that I'm not sure will be patched up.

We are at a crossroads. That I agree with.

All the more reason for why I'm ready to throttle whoever is on the other side of the door. At least use the fucking doorbell.

I hold my palm up to Hailey. "Just wait. I'll get rid of them."

Her face sours. "That ain't happening. Whoever it is won't give up. There are a few people who want discussions."

Like me.

The pounding of the door now fuels a need inside me to rip someone to pieces, and it doesn't even involve a negotiation of a contract.

"Oliver. We know you're there." It's Liam probably.

"Seriously, we're not going away," Keats adds.

Fantastic. Double the fun.

"My brother." Hailey closes her eyes for a second and squinches her face. "Just go, okay? He won't kill you. He was fine when I saw him. I'll head to my house for a bit. Leave through the garage, throw a bone at the neighbor's dog for old times' sake, or even actually go for a power walk to clear my head. So go and deal with them." She sounds sincere and patient. At least she's not showing irritation. Another reason to add to the list of why this woman is only for me.

I release a cleansing breath and walk out of the kitchen to the door. The door isn't even a crack open when both guys stroll on in.

"I'm here because I've slept on it and I want to get this conversation out of the way before the next family dinner. Plus, oh boy, this is a tizzy to be in. Isn't it? So a man-to-man conversation we shall have." Liam is nearly taunting me.

"I'm here to offer an ear and to step in if Liam decides to change his mood or in case your brother shows up. I heard he was working with his boxing trainer this morning." The smug look on Keats's face is actually a welcoming sign of hope.

I feel this is protocol for what you do when friends are in tight spots.

I trail behind them until we're in the kitchen, despite the fact that my living room has a comfortable sofa. Liam peeks at his watch. "Oh goody. It's noon." He opens the fridge door and re-emerges with three bottles of beer, and he struggles to hold the necks between his fingers.

Keats quickly takes one then offers me the other. I'm in no mood for alcohol so set the bottle back on the counter. "Congratulations, by the way," he says.

"For what?"

"The marriage and job offer."

I bite my lip, and Liam swings his gaze to me. "Job offer?"

Rubbing my face with both palms, I wonder why life decided to toss a loose cannon at me this week.

"Yeah, Oliver keeps getting offered a spot on the legal council for the hockey league in New York, and this time, I heard from team sources that they went all out on the benefits package," Keats explains.

A headache is approaching.

"Really? They're still pursuing you? You mentioned before. Are you going to take it?" Liam wonders with concern.

"He would be foolish not to," Keats chirps back.

"Can you two stop?" They both bring their focus to me, eager to listen. "I haven't even thought about it."

Keats whistles in disapproval. "You would be crazy to ignore it."

"Except I can't just pack up a suitcase and leave," I justify why I'm not entertaining the job offer.

"Are you staying married? She told me about the building and what you did for her." Liam sends us straight into the deep end. "I love my sister, and you two are still sinking into my brain. But moving? That… it's not her."

Shaking my head, I shut down that idea right away. "First, I know. Plus, she wouldn't because she has a preschool that she wants to develop. She's not going to give up on that, nor would I ask her to. Secondly, staying married? We kind of need to discuss a few things."

Liam seems awfully quiet—until he opens his mouth, that is. "So you'll give up on your own career for her?"

I roll a shoulder back. "The job offer wasn't interesting last time, and it isn't this time."

"Fair enough. Maybe you were using a marriage to Hailey to ensure you don't make choices that keep you away from

Everhope. Some deep-down psychological stuff," Keats reflects.

"Or I could have just asked her to marry me to ensure she has what she wants," I reply.

"That's the answer I want to hear." Liam begins to smile with affection. "Maybe I came here because this conversation is simple, maybe even a waste of time because we don't need to ask the obvious. We all know you're both crazy about one another. It's not like you were completely reckless and married on a whim without even knowing one another. It's cute. Still, this is all kind of out there. Like you are dating but married or married but dating. Like what comes first on the relationship basis?" Liam remains perched against the edge of the counter.

Aren't they two of the same?

No, actually. I'd rather be married than dating. It hits a little different when I can say she's my wife instead of my girlfriend. To many it shows forever commitment. Romance never dies which means you can still have a hot-as-fuck insatiable dinner together. Always learning new details about each other. Whispering I love you, which I've failed up until now, even though it's not a new sentiment.

"The girlfriend-boyfriend title was never for us," I declare. "We skipped a few steps. Just haven't really clarified that with one another. We still need to hash out those details. Hence, why it would be great if you two could run along now." I fake an overdone smile with my fingers walking in the air.

"Okay, all I wanted to point out is your little secret— helping her my ass—was a secret because you both have completely horrendous avoidance issues when it comes to your feelings, and you both lack solid verbal communication," Liam offers his unsolicited opinion.

I roll my eyes at him. "I really don't think I should be taking relationship advice from you."

Keats chuckles. "Or he is the best person to tell you because he cares more than any of us. Sibling love does that to people. Speaking of siblings…" His face turns pained. "What will you say to Carter? He'll cool off, but you might need to show that there is no confusion amongst your happy marriage, otherwise he might burst again."

Raking a hand through my hair, I try to push the thought away. I was doing a damn good job of doing that today. Also, maybe I assume he would need to cool off. But his mind is still on his ex-wife, and it's affecting him more than I thought.

"It's going to be a tough conversation, and I accept that." Brotherly love means we owe each other nothing and we'll still love one another. But we are closer than that. We can't brush things to the side.

"This is still kind of crazy. It's taking a hot minute to wrap my head around this news," Keats comments.

I drum my fingers on the counter that I'm leaning against. "The last thing we needed was everyone's opinions. We still got that in the end, but c'est la vie."

There is a pause of silence and then Liam slides his drink to the side. "I don't want to keep you long because I think you and my sister have a lot to talk about. But if you hurt her then I'll still kill you then help people look for you." He fakes a smile at me.

My arms begin to flap as if I'm wrangling my friends in, encouraging them to get the hell out of here.

"If you care then you will leave so I can finish any life-altering discussions that I need to have with *my wife*."

They both smirk but get the hint and set their beers on the

counter then follow my indication direction straight the door. "Hustle, boys. No seriously, move a little faster."

"Okay, we get the hint," Keats assures me with Liam by his side.

Walking them to the front, I open the door with gusto and feign a smile at them.

"Call me when we can plan a double date." Keats winks at me.

"And I'll see you at our next family dinner where… Ah, it will be great," Liam boasts with a wide grin.

I grumble a sound, and as soon as they step to the other side, I swing the door shut, causing a loud bang due to the force.

Gathering myself, I return to the kitchen and lean into the counter, rubbing my face due to exhaustion. I hear another door open, and my eyes zip toward the hall to the garage and laundry room.

The sight of Hailey instantly puts my body on full alert and my spine straightens. She's taking her earbuds out and saunters my way.

"You're here?"

She nods. "I was sitting on the step in your garage, unable to leave because my heart didn't want to."

My jaw ticks when she says the word heart. "What did you hear?"

Hailey shakes her head and stops when she stands across from me but keeps her distance. Too much distance. I can't pull her into my arms.

"Nothing. I knew you weren't alone so wanted to tune out. I was listening to a true crime podcast about a woman on trial for murdering her first and second husband."

Stifling a laugh, this is one way to break the ice. "Should I be concerned?"

She slaps her forehead. "Shit. That sounded kind of bad. Not that I'm gathering ideas or anything. Actually, I've been spewing out a lot of gibberish in the last hour."

"How so?" I cross my arms over my chest and tip my chin up as I inspect her body language.

"We don't need to be married."

My eyes pop out because I don't need to hear her say that again or the fact it comes out in monotone from her gorgeous mouth.

She curses the F-bomb under her breath before her tongue dips to the corner of her mouth and slowly slides along her bottom lip. "Not doing great here, Hailey," she berates herself. "I meant that the rules for the building changed and the effort we put in is irrelevant it seems. And now you have that job."

I step forward in a flash, ready to object. "I'm not taking the job."

She seems to be double-checking an answer that she already knows. "Oh, so you're staying here. You don't have to if it's because of me." Her eyes dip down.

My eyes remain set on her with a cold stare. "Not because of you. I don't want the job, as I've said a million times." My words are tart.

Our eyes lock and it's only a second or two before a light smile ghosts her lips. "Okay, one less thing to worry about. Only the staying-married part seems to be the topic on the agenda."

Pursing my lips, a small calming breath leaves my soul. "*Staying* married. We seem to agree on something, so that's a start." My heart is booming in my chest.

"Staying sounds good," she replies shyly.

"Do you know what I think?"

"You're going to tell me, aren't you?"

I press my lips into a faint smile. "The universe was throwing us signs to be together because we were both scared to commit because… we always knew we would be forever."

Now she steps forward, the space between us shrinking. "You're right. You and I skipped quite a few steps, but that's okay. We're not strangers. Most of all, you are the man that I would dream about and the man that I'm in love with. Not just the lust kind of love, but I *really* love you."

"Oh, thank fuck." In a flash, I close our space and my hands weave through her soft long hair, and I hold her in place to punish her mouth with a kiss that will sear her because she's mine.

I moan into her mouth, and she takes my breath away when she sucks on our kiss, making it impossible to break. It's wet, messy, us. Our teeth scrape and our lips seal us together. That tongue of hers tickles mine, and my response is to give her a good thrashing back, exploring her mouth, my hands strengthening around the mold of her face, and the sound of her murmurs only heightening everything inside of me that is about to burst to the other side of the door.

Pulling away, I give a short kiss then another. "I love you." I'm almost panting. "The moment I got stuck with you on a road trip, I knew it was the start of our unraveling. Leading us straight to where we are meant to be but ignoring the obvious. We've been complete fools coming up with ridiculous reasons. All we had to do was grab from the start what we are meant to be."

"We made it even more complicated for ourselves because we had the pressure of a secret somewhat-fake marriage that made us anxious to admit how we really blatantly always felt. Wait, does this mean that neither one of us has any intention of going anywhere?" she asks coyly.

I yank her close with my arm snaking around her middle.

"Not a chance. I would just tie you down anyhow. There was no way I would give you a divorce, even if you told me that's what you wanted. You've made me so fucking insane that it's borderline psychotic, and I'm okay with that."

Hailey howls a tiny laugh. "That's uh… kind of hot?" She's questioning herself. "Or do I need to be concerned?"

I shake my head. "Nah. I now have what I've been waiting for."

She looks down at her fingers now playing with my shirt. "You know, we didn't even have a wedding cake," she laments.

"We had birthday cake."

"Nor a honeymoon," she volleys.

"Later."

Her eyes gleam with a soft innocence when they catch mine. "Our newlywed phase has kind of been unusual."

"Sneaking through yards is a good basis for the adventure that we will have in our marriage. Meh, the living-separately part is going to have to change pronto, though."

Her fingers curl around the fabric on my chest. "I like the sound of that."

"What else? Have we missed something?" My enthusiasm to get us moving on the full-on marriage train is trying to speed us up.

"I guess not. Our families have already met, we both want a dog one day, and I can change my name soon."

"All positives."

We're there. No need to say more. This is us now.

Our mouths crash together at the same time, electrifying every molecule inside of me. I need her naked in *our* bed with that ring perfectly set on her finger and my own, too. Hoisting her up, she squeals delightfully then wraps her legs around my waist, and I begin to tread my steps in the direction that we need to go. Our mouths stay connected, but I feel her smile against my lips.

The doorbell repeatedly getting pushed startles her. We stall and our kiss stops, then both our heads move cheek to cheek to stare at the closed door. Her skin is warm and the corner of her mouth wet and swollen.

"Can the earth stop interrupting us?" Hailey chastises the world.

"Oliver!" Carter's voice is directly recognizable.

"Silly us." Hailey's voice is full of dismay. "We forgot the little detail that your brother had a meltdown."

I loosen my hold on her, and she slides down against my body. Whatever excitement my dick had has vanished due to the doorbell.

"I might as well face him now," I suggest.

"I hear you in there! Open up before I break down the door." Clearly, he hasn't calmed down.

My jaw goes slack, and I take a beat. "Let's get this over with."

HAILEY

arter's stare slices through Oliver and me when he steps through the door and storms right to the living room.

Oliver flashes his eyes at me and tips his head in the direction of the living room, and we walk together toward the dreaded conversation.

Carter is already sitting on the couch rubbing his hands against his thighs as he sits up straight. Oliver and I choose to remain standing, with Oliver leaning against the fireplace that I'm not sure that he ever uses.

My hands are on my hips, and I give him a warning with my eyes. "Are we going to have a conversation like real adults or am I going to be walking right out of here until you finish your timeout and say sorry?"

"Sorry? Are you kidding me? You both decided to uproot your lives due to a little thing that most people call marriage," Carter answers, and we can all see and hear that he is still tense.

I shouldn't be so invested in this conversation. It's

between them, but it's about Oliver and me. I won't abandon my husband.

Oliver rubs his head in aggravation from the direction of this conversation. "You make it sound like a game."

"And? So how is this going to work? Because now that the charade is out in the open then you can get a divorce. Are you going to divorce?" Carter questions.

I try to grasp where he is coming from. We expected Liam to lose it, but in the end, it's Carter. "I think we're going to be fine. We wasted time, and we won't waste any more trying to prove to you that we're not crazy. I mean, we're a little crazy, but that's beside the point." I try to make him smile, but all I get is his face relaxing a smidgen.

I roll my eyes and go to flop on the couch opposite Carter. "If it calms you, I'm moving in here and we are staying married. I love Oliver."

"And I love Hailey."

My gaze lifts to Oliver and a small smile of agreement appears on my lips. I'm his.

Oliver propels himself away from the mantle and comes to sit on the arm of the sofa, placing his hand firmly on my shoulder. "We are clear about what we want. A long-lasting marriage," Oliver reiterates.

"Look at you two forming a united front." I can't assess Carter's level of cynicism.

Carter's nostrils flare, but he says nothing. Carter grows silent and looks forward, and it seems to be in deliberation.

Oliver squeezes my shoulder as he is familiar with my brother's communication style.

"This is promising," Oliver quietly mutters to me.

The long silence that overcomes all of us is unnerving.

"This isn't about us, it's about Rosie." The words fall out

of Oliver's mouth in a string of words as though he was waiting for a balloon to pop.

Yikes. I roll my lips in, recognizing this is confronting.

Carter snaps his sight to Oliver.

"You know he's right," I add, though I'm not sure I should get involved.

"I… I just want my brother to have what I didn't."

Oliver scratches his cheek with the pad of his thumb. "I kind of gathered in your not-so-subtle explanation of marriage that everyone heard."

"Is it so crazy that I don't want my brother to make mistakes or experience misery?" Carter justifies.

Oliver's jaw slides to the right as he forms his words. "It isn't crazy at all. And I'm sorry that this must be… bringing up memories."

"Fuck memories. It's letting something go so easily."

"As in Rosie?" I voice my theory, slightly afraid that I'm saying her name. He's clearly uncomfortable.

Carter doesn't answer, and instead, Oliver takes the lead. "I won't let go of Hailey, I promise."

He huffs a breath and rolls one shoulder back before muttering a sound. "Fine." He's barely audible.

"Fine?" Oliver checks.

Carter cracks his neck in discomfort. "Yes. Fine."

"Is it because you actually want us together and can accept that we're married, or because you just want to end this conversation?" I replay our events and pry into his mind.

Carter stands abruptly with fists hanging at his sides. "Yes. Okay. Fine. This is what it is. My brother can be happy and do things the right way."

Oliver stands to align with his brother. "You've always done what you think is the right way. Sometimes we figure things out differently. And this is Hailey and me and our way."

Carter looks between us both. "I just want you both to be happy."

"We know," I assure him.

I'm beginning to think that I need to find a blind date for him so he can attempt to move on, but I can tell that he is nowhere near ready to let go of his ex-wife.

"We're happy," Oliver affirms.

Carter gives Oliver a look that only they seem to understand, a sort of code. "I expect nothing less than everything from you when it comes to your wife. Just be a good husband."

"You don't need to say it," Oliver firmly agrees.

Carter lets out a deep sigh. "Good."

"Good? Or good you'll be fine at the next family BBQ?"

"Funny. I said good, so good is good."

Oliver tries to suppress his smile.

Carter bows his head slightly in my direction. "Well, welcome to the family."

"Thanks, brother-in-law."

He flutters his eyes as his ears adjust to the title. Carter looks between us. "Now that your little secret is out in the open then put on your damn wedding rings," he reprimands Oliver before he walks on out, bumping Oliver's shoulder in the process before Oliver collapses onto the couch.

I would say the conversation ended on a solid note which is why I beam a smile at Oliver and move to sit on his lap.

"He is right about the rings. I'll be changing that as soon as we're upstairs," he promises.

Giving him a quick kiss, I feel an overpowering urge to lock ourselves upstairs for a while. "That's a start. Can't have anyone thinking you're available."

"Ready to do this long-haul marriage thing with me?"

I bop his nose with my finger. "I am."

My smile dims a little. "I hope Carter can move on."

Oliver licks his lips while he contemplates. "I would love it if he was a little less grumpy. But he hasn't been the same since Rosie left, and that was two years ago."

"He doesn't want us to have the same ending, and we won't."

"Come on, Wifey. We have rings to slide onto fingers right before I slide into you."

He tips his lips up to kiss me. I must still taste of him from earlier when his mouth ravished me. With no protest from me, he stands, and we begin to shuffle our way to the stairs. Circling and stumbling because we are too occupied with our kisses and roaming hands.

Luckily, the map to his bedroom is set in stone in our heads.

———

SITTING on the middle of the bed, already down to my bra and panties since we lost all my other clothes at the top of the stairs—his shirt, too, as we were impatient to reach the bedroom—I watch Oliver dive his hand into his jeans pocket and pull out his ring before discarding his pants.

"You always had it in your pocket?" I wonder.

He tosses himself onto the bed and lies on his side. "Unconsciously, but yeah."

I fumble with the clasp of my necklace but manage and allow the ring to slide off the chain. "It needs a new home." I hold up my fingers, and he smirks with complete gratification.

He steals the ring that I'm holding up in my other hand

and ceremoniously slides it onto my ring finger. "That's better."

Holding my palm out, he places his own ring into my palm. Grabbing his hand, I slip it onto his finger. "That's better," I echo.

His thumb rises and caresses my bottom lip then rides up to my cheek. "I love you."

I take hold of his thumb and kiss it. "I love you, too."

That smug smirk of his appears because he has a hold on me. Not figurately but inside of me.

Slowly, he guides me back until I'm lying flat, and his body encases my own. His warmth showering me and our bodies molding.

"Hmm, what shall we do to celebrate?" His heavy breath cascades down my neck before returning to that spot just below my ear. It tickles but it's sensual and has an effect on my pussy.

The feeling of his cock under his boxer briefs pressing against my thigh naturally causes my body to curve into him.

"I could think of a few things," I rasp when his fingers hunt down my nipple to rub.

"Then come lie on top of me," he directs.

My body is on fire because I always listen when he commands. He leads us, and I don't mind one bit.

We shift and remove all remaining clothing before I straddle him, making a point to rub my slick pussy against his cock in the process. We don't waste a second, and I take hold of him to align him, and I slowly clench down, pulling a moan from both of us.

His hand rests on my hip and his other thumb begins to play with my clit as I find a rhythm on top of him. I drive myself crazy because I can circle around his length to find a rhythm, and occasionally his strong hands lift me slightly, to then plunge me back down on top of him. My entire pussy envelopes him. No matter the position he always fills me up and fits just right.

"That's it, beautiful. Ride me. Take what you want," he whispers.

I slow down for a second, and he brings his elbows to the mattress and holds his forearms up straight to the ceiling, offering me his hands. I interlace our fingers, and I continue on my quest to make us come.

My head falls back and my eyes close of their own accord. Bouncing on top of him, my tits move, and I coo every other breath. My hair is behind my shoulders but feathering my skin with every thrust.

Slowly my head rolls until my sight lands on our hands. Interwoven with rings.

It's all heavenly, overwhelming, and I fall forward, keeping Oliver inside me. Our stomachs press together, and I tuck my head into the crook of his neck as he takes over my body, bucking up into me, letting a grunt release as he speeds up and mercilessly thrusts up into me. But then he slows, and we whisper those three words, over and over as our lips and gazes orbit around a gravitating force that can only be justified by our souls murmuring hello.

I could lie like this forever, and now I get a chance to.

MY ATTEMPT TO cook this vodka pasta sauce I saw on social media is failing. I wince when I hold up the vodka bottle to see I used way more alcohol than I should've, and when I bring the wooden spoon to my tongue darting out for a taste, I gag. Even with the sliding doors open off the kitchen to the beautiful evening, the smell doesn't seem to escape.

Ugh. This isn't cool.

Oliver should be home any moment from work, and I've failed at the housewife thing. It's only been three days since everything unraveled. Still, I'm going to throw myself into the deep end.

Picking up my phone resting on the counter that has a dot of tomato sauce on the screen, I swipe to find what takeout we could do. I'll have to go pick it up unless we order pizza, and because I'm tired from dealing with pre-teen angst today, then pizza it is.

I hear the garage door open, but I focus on the pizza choices on the website.

"What the— It almost smells like a frat party in here." Oliver enters the kitchen carrying a bag, amused but wary as he approaches the stove.

"I was trying to make a sauce with vodka but got a little overzealous, and I know most alcohol burns away when cooking, but I can't get over the smell. Pizza it is."

He chuckles then holds up a bag. "I'm way ahead of you. Got Chinese food on my way back from Lake Spark."

I pout at him, and I dodge his attempt at a kiss. "But you knew I was going to try and cook."

He remains mute, and for a second, I wonder if I should be disappointed for his lack in faith in my cooking abilities, but then… "Thank the heavens because I suck at cooking."

"You always did." He supports my claim.

He sets the bag on the counter, and I feel we can keep it casual and just eat at the island. Oliver sneaks in to kiss my cheek. Virtuous but just as deadly as if he'd twisted my tongue with his.

"One more thing. Check the other bag."

I see that the two bags are different colors. The brown bag doesn't seem familiar or at least not of any place I know. I'm curious, and I get a peek at the contents but my brows furrow in confusion as I pull out a hammer.

"What's this?"

"A hammer." He stands behind me, knitting his arms around me to hold me flush to his body.

"I can see that." My lips thin, but I want to smile.

"When you get the keys for the preschool you need to do a lot of renovations. You should be the one to knock the first brick down. I remember how much you love those home shows."

I'm beaming, as it's sweet. "You are full of surprises."

"I just want to make sure you have everything you dream of."

I turn in his embrace and chain my arms around his neck. "My husband, don't you know?"

"Know what?" He stares at my mouth then travels back to my eyes, and his gaze gleams with desire and strong conviction for the way he feels for me.

"A preschool is nice, but all I need is you to have everything I dreamed come true."

He licks his lips as his cheeks rise from his signature smirk. "We share the same sentiment."

We meet halfway for a kiss that keeps us on earth because we won't let go of one another but has every sensitive spot within me floating.

The sound of a chime draws our attention to the wind chimes from the road trip that Oliver kept. One for him and one for me.

"It seems our dreams arrived with the wind." The back of his knuckles lightly rub against my cheek.

I sputter a laugh. "That was cheesy, but I'll let it go."

"Fine, the chime is sending the message that this time next year, if we feel like it, maybe we should do a vow renewal or something. A real wedding kind of thing." He said it so matter of fact and that makes it better because it's not a big production.

My chin juts out from the unexpected. "Really?"

He shrugs as though it's nothing to do something to make me happy. "Yeah. I believe you probably have a list of *all* the details for a wedding with Oliver since you had a crush on me for so long. Maybe you even doodled little hearts next to my name too."

I playfully shove his shoulder. "Funny. And why do you keep asking me major questions in your kitchen?"

"Because things tumble out of my mouth around you."

"Do I make you nervous?"

"Not at all. It's just your effect on me. But answer before the food gets cold."

I quirk my lips up and pretend to think over his question. "Hmm… yes." My face erupts into absolute elation.

"Oh good, my wife listens to her husband," he deadpans before grinning ear to ear and kissing me.

I wasn't lying when I told him that everything I dreamed is only complete if he is part of it, and I have that all now. But a semi-wedding? Well, that's just the icing on the cake.

EPILOGUE: OLIVER

ONE YEAR LATER

Hailey kneels down with the world's biggest smile as she assists a four-year-old with a flying unicorn backpack far too big for the kid's shoulders, but it's cute. Once the bag is in place, Hailey waves to the little girl running away on little feet to her mother who is waiting with a warm smile of her own.

Every time I see Hailey in her teacher mode, I nearly break our agreement to wait to have kids of our own. She'll be a good mom. But we both agreed that we want to wait and enjoy being husband and wife first.

My wife stands and surveys the area to see that all kids have left. That's my cue that I can leave my car to help her close up her school. Normally, I'm not here. I have a long workday, and a teacher's husband has no place hanging around. Hailey wouldn't give me a tiny dose of attention anyhow, as she is so busy.

But today is different, which is why I walk through the front door with a sign for Early Explorers Preschool. I'm immediately greeted with the latest art project hanging from strings. Huh, clever. They made bumble bees using a toilet paper roll. Following the sound of her voice, I end up in the classroom where Hailey is straightening a few tiny chairs as she agrees with her assistant, a young woman who just graduated, about Monday's activity in the number groups.

"Hi, Oliver." The assistant smiles in passing as she leaves. "Have a good weekend."

My wife peers up at me as she tucks the last chair under the table that only reaches my knee. A wry smile is set on her mouth. "What?"

I throw her a pointed look. "We are already pushing it for time."

She gushes another smile. "We're fine."

My brows rise from her brazen attitude. "We have wedding photos at 3." Because we are actually saying real vows this time, but we don't need to worry about any of that traditional stuff about seeing the bride before yadda-yadda… We're already married. It's just a group of about 50 in my parents' yard, with dinner after sunset.

Hailey walks to her desk, shrugging. "And? It was only a half day of school today which means it's 12 and we have plenty of time."

That's what I love about her. She's laidback. I know she's getting her hair and makeup done but by no means is she stressing.

She pulls out stickers from her drawer and begins to place little stars on a posterboard of names on the wall a few steps away. "That reminds me, we should probably go pick up more bottles of juice for Monday's kids." She quickly glances at her watch. "We have time before we have to pick up Jet from the groomers."

My jaw almost drops, but I keep it together. "Seriously?

Are you trolling me?" Time is tight, and we have to pick up our yellow labrador, Jet. He is our life and is also walking down the aisle with our rings. Because yeah, we became that kind of dog parents.

Her sight whips to me, and for a second, I believe she isn't until a few seconds later a grin crawls on her face. "I would never."

I reach over and grab her arm to yank her to me. "Come on, you."

———

"IT'S A MERMAID BRAID," Hailey corrects me as she giggles in my arms, and we completely ignore the photographer as we stand along the riverbank outside my parents' house. Standing in a tux, I'm distracted.

"You're stunning," I reiterate for the hundredth time. Her dress is Gatsby inspired. Sheer material with little sequins. Absolutely beautiful. But that braid? "It's dying to be yanked later when you're on your knees."

Instantly her lips part, and she glances quickly to her side at the photographer not far away. I clear my throat and force a wide smile. "I mean, you don't wear this style often." I raise my voice a little to correct my public blunder. Luckily, the photographer is busy looking at the screen of her camera. We wanted Esme to enjoy the night as a guest, so she recommended one of her friends.

Hailey playfully pushes my shoulder. "Watch that mouth of yours. I know we're married already, but I think my parents would still like to associate this white wedding dress with their virginal daughter, even if for a minute or two."

I burst out laughing. "I'm not sure this conversation is getting us out of the deep end."

Her eyes dip down at the sight of our fingers intertwined, and her face softens. "You're right. I'll take this opportunity before everyone finds us to say…"

She grows near shy. I bring her hands up to kiss her knuckles, a feathering of lips really. "What is it?"

Her beautiful eyes meet mine. "I'm just going to tell you my vows now before everyone hears them. It's simple, I get to have everything I dreamed because I have you. But the biggest part of that picture? My dream is only complete with you. And I vow to ensure it feels that way every day."

Fuck, hit me in that spot in the corner of my eye that burns with a tear. Framing her face in my hands, I gently force her to look me straight in the eyes. "We'll have to find something new to dream about, and I vow that every single one will be with both you and me… until we die… even if you cut off another finger due to bagels. I'll save you every time."

A blissful smile appears, and I lean down to kiss her, smile to smile, teeth scraping teeth. Parting, I kiss her real quick under her chin on the spot of her neck that makes her shiver every time.

"Oliver," she murmurs.

"You're my wife so I can kiss you the way I like," I remind her.

She swats me again. "And we have a photographer here." Forgot about that.

The woman holds up her camera gleefully. "No problem. The less you realize that I'm here, the better. Plus, I've heard it all from couples."

Hailey wraps her arms around my middle then rests the side of her head against my chest.

"I love you," she sighs, relaxed.

"I love you so much."

We take a few breaths to just be in this moment because we know what awaits. Yes, Hailey has the menu that she picked out, and flowers she approved, the dress she went to Chicago for. But let's make no mistake that the bride and groom will be busy speaking with guests for most of the evening.

Another five minutes of photographs that we intentionally pose for and then excitement bubbles inside of me and it's written all over Hailey's face. "Ready?"

She nods her head enthusiastically. "So much so that I skipped a few steps." She proudly holds up her hand to show the ring on her finger. The one she has worn from the very beginning.

I hold up my own hand to show her. There is a smugness to my smile because of the satisfaction that I made her my wife when it was a crazy thing to do. "Oh, look at that, great minds think alike."

Both grinning, I kiss her forehead, even though I hear my brother in the distance calling my name.

Hailey tips her head to the side. "You told him, right?" Lines form on her face.

I wince and scrub a hand across my face. "Not exactly… yet."

Shock floods her face, and she swats my shoulder. "Are you insane?" Her loud whisper squeaks before she fakes a smile and faces my brother who arrives next to us in a suit.

"Hate to break up the priceless photos between you two well-dressed kids, but I need to steal the groom. Mom and Dad want to have a family moment, and I figured we could have a cigar."

"No problem. Rosi— is here." She realizes her fumble. "I mean, the florist was dropping off more roses, and I need to

check on that. Yep, flower check. I'm just going to do that."
Hailey awkwardly tries to save her blip.

"Sure thing, and Hailey…" my brother says to her.

"Yeah, Sheriff?"

"Thanks for marrying my brother… again. You're good for him and put up with his irrational thoughts."

He gives her a quick hug and my brows knit together, debating if he is joking or insulting me.

"Irrational they are. Must be a family trait." She gawks her eyes at me as a warning until she turns her back and scurries away.

Carter throws a thumb over his shoulder in the direction of Hailey heading to the house. "She isn't nervous, is she? Your dog is actually wearing that bow tie you got him, so no need to stress." He must be sensing her nerves, and it sure as hell isn't for our vow renewal or our badass dog.

"No." I scratch the back of my neck, preparing myself for this firework to explode. "I guess word hasn't gotten to you yet…"

"About what?"

"There is an extra guest. I only found out this morning. Mom and Dad took the liberty of adding someone to the guest list."

Carter's face firms and his nose raises an inch. "Humor me. Who might that be?" His tone is sharp.

"Kind of funny maybe." Nothing I can say will save this.

He gives me a stern look and grows impatient. I remember this version of him when we were kids. "Oliver, say it or I swear I will issue you a parking ticket next time I see your car."

I bite my fist before puffing out a breath. "It's Rosie."

My brother stills and he soaks in the news.

"As in…"

Eeeks. Why am I tasked with delivering the news? "Yep."

His eyes draw a line when we hear an enthusiastic welcome from our mother by the patio where a few guests have arrived. Actually, it's my mother throwing her arms around one particular guest. I can hear the growl my brother is controlling.

Carter's jaw tightens, and his eyes dagger me. "Why is my ex-wife here?

FOUR YEARS LATER

"You're such a good boy, yes you are." I scruff Jet's hair, and he sits patiently on the kitchen floor, waiting for his treat. Jet's tail wagging could perfectly clean my floor, except this big guy is a Labrador that sheds enough to make a blanket… seven days a week.

His doe brown eyes stare up at me and see rights through my soul. Holding out his milk bone, I lean down, and his mouth gobbles the treat at record speed. Who knew drool dripping onto my jeans could be cute? But Oliver and I live for Jet, so he gets away with a lot.

He begins to wiggle, knocking me to the floor before climbing all over me. He gives me his big dog kisses, causing me to squeal and smile as I move to sit cross-legged. "Whoa there. Do you want to play? Where is your rope thingy that your dad insisted you needed?" because Oliver spoils this guy.

Our weekends include heading to the farmer's market, grabbing a coffee, and always stopping at the big pet store near the highway. We're really racking up points on our membership card.

Jet ignores my suggestion and instead lies down and rests his head on my lap while I pet his smooth coat. "You know as much as I love you, and it's great the three of us, I'm kind of thinking…"

Great. My dog is my therapist. But Oliver has been gone for two nights. A stupid defenseman went on waivers and caused paperwork galore that took my husband away from me. He wasn't even a good player.

"We've been married for a few years, but it's not like requesting steak at dinner." His little ears perk up and then fall, but he continues to listen as he is our faithful canine.

"However, I've come to accept that having a human baby is what I want. I don't want to wait anymore. We both wanted to postpone the baby equation because we kind of skipped a lot in the dating/marriage equation. Oliver and I agreed on that. But now, time is ticking. I'm not sure if it's our brothers having their own families, Esme and Keats, too. Or the fact your grandma basically eyes what I'm drinking at every family gathering. It's just little things are adding up. I mean, I think I will rock the pregnancy body."

Jet continues to rest his head on me, but his tail wags. I sigh because I know what Oliver will say, but it still feels like a profound moment. "I'm being silly, right? He will be with me on this. It's not like I need to tie him to the bed and insist." I smile to myself.

"But it could be a lot more fun if you did."

Startled by Oliver, my body reacts instantly. My eyes fly up, and I turn my attention to the kitchen entrance. I thought he was on a call; he had been for the last 45 minutes.

Jet reads the room faster than I do. He rises to his paws

and patters to Oliver for a pet. Standing, I feel slight fear, but Oliver's smirk is soothing.

"I didn't realize you were there." My eyes latch with his. "Our dog failed me on the warning front."

Oliver steps closer while Jet leaves, probably to head to the living room to rest on the couch. "He is the worst guard dog. You know that." The moment Oliver slowly wraps his arms around my middle to embrace me, I feel warmth in my body and soul.

"How much did you hear?" My face skews.

His fingers feather my hair to behind my ear. "Enough." I roll my lips in and can't figure out what to say. "I'm on board."

My eyes grow a smidgen. "As in baby? You, me, a baby? The humankind?"

Oliver snickers, and his eyes remain locked. "Yes. The humankind."

I can't help but chuckle. "So we are doing this?" I need to check once more.

"Yeah, we are doing this." He has a suave grin that always melts me. "Should we start tonight?"

Now, I'm taken aback. "Well, kind of need the birth control to wear off, but no harm in practice."

His sinister laugh comes from deep in his throat. "We don't need to practice, but I'll play along. Besides, my swimmers are strong, and I'll deliver the goods."

I burst out laughing because it's just funny.

His face turns serious. "Now, let's start."

And with that, he hoists me up and plants me on the counter. With speed, he begins to strip me from my pants before he runs his hands up my thighs, straight to my panties. I lean back and rest on my forearms to watch him drag them down my legs, slow enough to be agony. He doesn't need to do much because my clit is throbbing.

His eyes are full of mischief, and he gives me a warning glare. "Let's start with me tasting what is mine."

My eyes close as his breath trails up my thighs, leaving a path of warmth. The moment the tip of his tongue lands on my clit, I gasp. My pussy clenches as I surrender to his touch.

"Mmm, that's perfect." Because he knows what my body needs already from our very first time.

The sight of him peering up while he points his tongue and slowly licks down and up to find my clit again. His hands hold my thighs open, and I need more of him.

"Please put a baby in me," I rasp.

"That's what I intend to do," he murmurs against my pussy lips. Backing away, he unbuckles his belt and unzips. I nibble on the corner of my lip because I always enjoy watching him on a mission. His persistence always drives me insane.

His hand hooks under my knees, and he yanks me to the edge of the counter, spreading me before he begins to pump inside of me. We are not going to be tender in this moment. Instead, we are fueled by a fervent need and our desire for our current moment and hopeful future changes.

***

I stare down at Jet walking by my side down the stairs. "Will you stop following me around," I huff because it's getting to be annoying as fuck, although cute, but I need me time with a little space. He's been extra clingy all week.

The sound of Oliver cursing in frustration in the living room tells me that he is not happy with the way an away game for the Spinners is turning out. When I reach the living room, he is in one of his concentration moods where I could tell him the house is burning down, but he wouldn't hear me. Hockey does that to people.

But I have just the thing to change his current mood. I stop in front of him and idly nudge my leg between his thighs as he sits. He attempts to peek his head around my body to watch the game but my hand push him back and I drop onto his body to straddle him.

Finally, I have his attention.

He looks at me and is amused. "Yes?" His voice trails.

"Oh, goodie, I have your attention." I contritely smile before it softens into a genuine smile. I say nothing, and he waits for me to speak, but I remain quiet.

"Can I help you with something?" His hands rub along my hips and drive slowly to my ass.

My eyes turn to saucers. "Really? You haven't noticed?"

Lines form on his head. "What?"

I gawk at him, but he can't seem to catch on until he does.

His sight climbs down my body until that lands on my hand that's gripping a pregnancy test, and it is obvious.

"Damn." A smirk appears on his face. "I succeeded at getting a baby in your belly, it seems."

"You did."

He pulls my body flush to him, and I loop my arms around his neck. "We're going to be parents." My heart blooms a new feeling.

"Well then, looks like I need to make love to you pregnant and beautiful."

We meet for a kiss, a different kind. One that seals us in a new way.

Jet barks, and we both look down at him in a funny way. "Yeah, you're getting a human brother or sister. Oliver's swimmers were strong, and now we are going to celebrate. So go find a chew bone or something."

Because I have even more than I ever dreamed.

THANK YOU

There is no better place to start than readers. Thank you so much for always reading, whether new to me or someone who has joined my journey long ago.

To Rachel, the wizard that I've been searching for (finding a hat is still a work in progress). Thank you for helping in so many ways.

To Lindsey and Lindsay, thank you always for the editing and cover design. We've been through a lot of books.

Family, pets, coffee, probably a mystical moon somewhere... I'm thankful, as always.